FAE AWAY

BOOK ONE IN THE FAE BLOODLINES SERIES

ROSE GARCIA

For the Queens of the Quill

THE FAE REALM OF
FAEVENLY

TORCH
LAKE

STRONG
HAVEN EAST

MOTHER
OF RIVERS

SUMMIT
RANGE

SAND
BLUFF

GREEN
FALLS

THE
GREAT
COVE

THE MORNING SEA

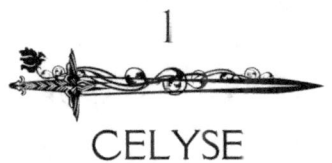

1

CELYSE

Through the thin trees, between the bark and brush, I could see the shimmers hovering over Torch Lake. The mysterious, glowing orbs that provided a gateway from the faerie realm to the human realm were a rare sight. No one was allowed a viewing without permission. Even then, access was rarely granted. Even for me.

"We should not be here, Celyse," Jaid whispered.

He was right. If I were ever found here, I would never be allowed near them again. Yet still, the risk was worth it. It always was.

A palace guard and my best friend since we were young, Jaid reluctantly indulged my foolish pursuits, including my requests to access the area, showing me unguarded paths to the lake. Not that I asked often. But Mother and Father were away on official Strong Haven business as the High King and High Queen of Faevenly, and my twin sister Malena and I were left alone for a few days with our minder, Maid Rell. Which meant no one was watching me as closely as they should.

While Malena pursued royal things in the palace, I

sought adventure. And there was nothing more exciting than the shimmers.

"Oh please, Jaid." I rolled my eyes at the tall, slender, silver-haired, violet-eyed fae. Even though his allegiance to duty was boring, I most certainly did not want him to get in trouble. I lifted my skirt and pulled out the black onyx knife I kept strapped to my thigh. I pressed it to his neck. "If we should be caught out here, you may tell everyone I held you at knife point."

He swatted my hand away. "Come now, Celyse. You know I am rising in the ranks. If discovered out here with you, violating my directives, I could lose my position." His gaze scanned the area. "Besides, you know full well unauthorized lake visits are on the rise. It is not safe." Then he muttered under his breath, "As if anyone would believe you could best me with a knife."

Although I knew Jaid was right, I did not think a quick visit would be dangerous. I could handle myself. Plus, I had him with me. I put the knife back in its place, then lowered myself on the ground and placed my head on my hands, as if settling in to watch a play or performance. "Let me have a few moments, and then we can leave."

After a long pause, he sighed, like I knew he would, then joined me on the lush grass. "What are you even looking for?" He waved his hand about. "There are sentinels posted along the perimeter, as usual. The shimmers are floating along the water, as usual. There is grass, there is sky, there are trees. Everything is the same."

"You see nothing, Jaid," I mumbled, keeping my gaze on the glowing orbs in the distance. "I, on the other hand, see magic and beauty and possibility."

I had always been curious about the human realm, and often dreamed of going there so I could see and experience the things Maid Rell had taught me and Malena in our lessons.

Jaid pulled a blade of grass and tossed it. "You are impossible."

I shrugged as I kept my gaze on the lake. "Perhaps I am. But what is wrong with wanting to see another world where the inhabitants watch moving picture stories on giant white screens? Travel the skies in over-sized jet-propelled airplanes, and the seas on floating ships as big as villages? Villages, Jaid! Do you not wonder about the human realm?"

"I do not. And you would do well to banish those fancies. Humans are our enemy. As a princess of Faevenly, you should not forget it."

I threw him a curious look. "You do not want to know what tacos taste like?"

A clanging rang out. Yelling met my sharp ears. My attention zipped to the lake, where sentinels were fighting three fae with spears and swords.

"Thunderation, not again," Jaid spat out, jumping to his feet. "Get back to the palace," he ordered as he rushed toward the melee.

He did not have to tell me twice. I knew the wrath of my mother, the High Queen. If she found out I had been here, she would not be pleased at all. I had heard tales of how she could kill with her eyes when she dropped her glamour. It was not something I wanted to see.

Lifting my skirt, knowing Jaid and the sentinels could handle themselves, I dashed off. I zigzagged between trees, jumped over rocks, and ducked low-hanging branches. When the palace spires came into view and the grounds began resembling a well-kept garden, I slowed my stride. I thought of the three fae who were skirmishing with the sentinels. No doubt they were dead by now since anyone approaching lake waters without permission was executed on sight. But who would attempt to breach Torch Lake at midday? It was a fool's errand at any time, but doubly so in full daylight. Most breaches occurred at nightfall. I would have to ask Jaid about it later.

As I continued at a normal pace, a lone white feather drifting in the wind caught my eye. It twirled and danced as the breeze directed it to a cluster of nearby bushes. It came to rest on a pile of red and brown leaves, looking angelic and pristine against the earthen backdrop, and I thought I should have it.

Surely such a sighting was not happenstance.

Approaching the quill, I bent down for it when a glint of light caught my eye. My breathing hitched. My hand trembled. And I could hardly believe my eyes. Amid the foliage nestled a small shimmer. But how? Every shimmer had been moved to Torch Lake after the Great Shimmer War several hundred years ago. Was this one overlooked? Had it drifted away from the others while no one noticed? Or maybe it had recently separated from the stratus and floated down from the sky?

Scanning my surroundings, I realized I was alone with a lost shimmer and a chance at a private viewing of the human realm. A chance I might never have again. I crept forward, my mind recalling everything Maid Rell had taught me about the shimmers, like how they could be handled and manipulated at the edges. How you could see through them but not hear anything. How it was dangerous to go through them unless you were trained. How time between the two realms moved at the same speed. How they were either attached to a person or a place. Sometimes both.

I wondered who or what this shimmer was attached to.

With my heart racing, I reached out, grazing the round glow with my fingertips. A warm misty sensation connected with my skin, like vapor from a boiling pot of water. I eyed my surroundings again, then cupped the shimmer with both hands and brought it to my face. Peering through, I saw a bedchamber, but I could not make out much detail. I would need to stretch the shimmer so I could see better.

But not in the open.

With my newfound treasure in my grasp, I increased my distance from the palace, rounding my way out of sight and to an area of tightly packed trees. Crouching low, I shuffled my way through a small opening. Surrounded by the pines and sitting on a bed of leaves, I studied the shimmer in awe, thinking it the most beautiful and spectacular thing I had ever seen.

"Incredible," I murmured, as I pinched the edges with my fingertips. Like the thinnest and most delicate silk, I slowly stretched out the glow. When it was big enough to offer me a proper viewing, I released it and let it float in front of me.

A bedchamber came fully into view. Pulling my legs up to my chin, I studied the room. The walls were painted a dark blue while the ceiling was a crisp white. A small bed took up the middle of one wall, and across from that were bookshelves and a desk. Over the bed hung a painting of a foot clad in a strange shoe with spikes on the bottom kicking a white ball. The bedsheets were crumpled and unmade, and piles of clothing dotted the floor.

Covering my mouth, I chuckled at the mess, thinking it perfectly splendid, and wondered what it would be like to leave my bedchamber like that. I did not think Maid Rell would like it.

Suddenly, a person walked into view. I sucked in my breath and backed up as a gorgeous tall human with dark, disheveled hair, brown eyes, full lips, and sun-kissed skin strolled across the room, eyes down as if looking for something.

"My lady, Celyse!" It was Maid Rell, calling for me. "Where are you?"

With a swipe, I collapsed the shimmer until it formed a small ball, then threw a pile of leaves on it. Calming myself, I peered through the trees. Not seeing

Maid Rell, or anyone else for that matter, I crawled out and dashed away from the spot, not wanting her to see where I had come from. I dusted off my skirt, then patted my long silver hair to make sure it was not a mess.

"I am here!"

Maid Rell hurried over to me. Short and stocky with strong arms and thick legs, she waddled when she walked and moved everyone into action with her booming voice. Yet for a dwarf, she was actually on the taller side.

"My lady," she huffed. "You are late for your archery lesson!"

"My goodness! My apologies, Maid Rell. The time must have gotten away from me."

"Indeed, it has." She clapped two times. "Now come."

For the rest of the day, while I practiced with my bow, my head stayed in the clouds as I thought of the beautiful human I had seen through the shimmer. My mind was already calculating when I could sneak away to see him again.

2

JULIO

A knock pounded on my door. It jarred me from my sleep, forcing my eyes to snap open and my body to jolt upright. I lunged for the baseball bat leaning against my nightstand, then shot out of bed and flung open my door.

"¡*Ay, Mijo*!" She pressed her hand on her chest and blinked. "It's me!"

I exhaled, tension draining from my shoulders. "Jeez, Mom." The bat fell from my hands with a thud. "You can't do that."

The last time she banged on my door, it was the night our house was broken into. That was two years ago. I hadn't slept right since.

She dropped her hand. "I'm sorry. I didn't think I was knocking hard."

I blew out as my nerves settled. "I thought something was wrong."

She patted my shoulder. "Nothing like that, *Mijo*. But I do need your help."

"Yeah, yeah." I rubbed my head. "Okay."

She walked away then added over her shoulder, "Bring me your cleats right away so I can wash them."

Eyeing my mess, wondering where they were, I said, "I will."

While most families went to church early on Sunday and rested the remainder of the day, we didn't. We cleaned all day, rested a little, then went to church at night. It was actually the best thing for Mom's busy schedule with her clients and my soccer practices and games. So I didn't complain much.

After getting dressed, I was back on task, scanning the floor for my cleats, when a round glow appeared before me. Inside was the face of a beautiful girl. My breath caught. But as quick as the vision appeared, it disappeared.

"What the –?" I inched closer to the spot, swiping my hand through the now empty space, wondering what I had seen because it most definitely wasn't a spirit. At least, I didn't think so.

"*¡Mijo! ¡Por favor! Your cleats!*"

"*¡Ya voy!*" I called back.

Scratching my head, I shrugged off the vision, chalking it up to the weirdness that sometimes happened to me and my mom. The weirdness I avoided.

"Just find the cleats," I murmured to myself.

I started rifling through piles of dirty clothes, tossing everything around. Under the last pile, and covered in mud, I finally found what I'd been looking for.

I dangled the shoes by their laces, and met my mom in the laundry room. "Here you go."

She smiled. "*Gracias, Mijo.*"

Mom and I fell into the rhythm of our routine. She cleaned her room, the kitchen, and the bathroom, and I cleaned my room, the living room, and tidied up the front yard and the back. As the day went on, I kept going back to my room, checking to see if the vision of the girl would reappear. But it never did. Which was just as well since I definitely didn't want to add another unwanted family skillset to my supernatural resume.

Finally, at the end of the long day, I was back in bed. Staring at the ceiling, I wondered about the girl I had seen. I had come to terms with the fact that I could see dead people like my mom. But visions? That was new. Though I knew my mom had visions, I never had. Maybe this was the same, or maybe it was only a fluke.

With sleep almost taking me, I turned to my side when a soft glow materialized in my room. I sat up and watched it grow in shape and size, stretching out until it resembled a large mirror. Except, it didn't hold a reflection. Instead, it revealed the same girl, looking ethereal and magical, wearing what looked like a white nightgown and a black cloak with a hood.

Dressed in only pajama bottoms, I got up and slipped on a T-shirt. I sat in front of her on the edge of my bed, completely enthralled by her, as she seemed to be by me. Like I had been waiting for her.

She lowered her hood. Long silver hair with a black streak spilled out onto her shoulders. She studied me with sparkling green eyes. I had never seen anyone like her.

"Who are you?" I asked.

She shook her head, and smiled, her lips moving. I thought maybe she was telling me she couldn't hear me. Which made sense because I couldn't hear her.

"Can you hear me?" I asked.

She shook her head again. I lifted my finger, telling her to hold on as I went to my desk and got a notebook and a pen. I sat back down, showed her what I had, and started writing. I lifted the paper so she could read my note.

My name is Julio. Who are you?

She smiled, and pointed at me as she mouthed, "Julio."

I nodded, then pointed at her. She looked around where she was sitting and shrugged her shoulders, shaking her head while she acted out writing a note. Peering at the space around her, I could see she was sitting in the dark with her back to a tree, with no chance to write her own message.

Are you outside? I wrote.

She nodded then put her finger to her lips, signaling quiet. I glanced at my shut door, thinking I didn't want my mom to know what I was doing either.

This can be our secret.

She pointed from herself and then to me and mouthed, "Secret."

"Yeah," I whispered out loud, rubbing the back of my neck, thinking it unbelievable that I was having a conversation with a gorgeous girl in the middle of the night. A girl coming to me as a vision.

We sat like that for a while, looking at each other, both of us in awe. I thought of asking her where she was from, but if there was one thing sacred in my mother's *curandera* business, it was never asking spirits about their location. You may not like the answer, my mother had warned. I thought that was a pretty good rule, so I accepted at face value that a beautiful girl from a magical place was visiting me.

She pointed to the wall behind me with a questioning look. I glanced over my shoulder at the picture of a foot in cleats kicking a soccer ball, then turned back to her with a raised brow.

I wrote, *You don't know what soccer is?*

She read the note, then shook her head.

Well, that wouldn't do. I got up and lifted my newly washed soccer cleats. I pointed to my foot, then grabbed the soccer ball I kept in the corner of my room. She tilted her head, studying me with a perplexed look on her face. I decided she needed a demonstration.

I slipped on the shoe, then dropped the ball down on my toe and kicked it back up into my hands. Her eyes widened with delight. I did it again, but this time I tapped too hard. The ball ricocheted, soared across the room, and knocked down my small bedside lamp.

She started laughing, then covered her mouth, glancing about as if worried someone would heard her. A chuckle threatened to boom out of me too, but I held it in.

With silence settling back down on my room, I took

off my shoe and put my ball away. I sat on the edge of my bed, taking her in, wondering how in the world she didn't know what soccer was.

I wrote, *Soccer is my favorite sport. What's yours?*

"Me?" she mouthed, indicating at herself.

"Yeah, you," I whispered, nodding and pointing at her.

She turned her eyes up for a second, as if thinking, when a spark lit up her face. She held out one arm and cocked the other, as if shooting a bow and arrow.

Archery?

She nodded, then made the motion again.

Cool. I was talking to a gorgeous girl who knew how to use a bow and arrow. A gorgeous girl who felt impossible.

We spent the next thirty minutes or so nodding, writing, and pointing. After muddling through a few questions about soccer and archery, and finding our method of communication less than ideal, she placed her hands together at the side of her face and leaned her head over, signaling sleep.

Will you come back?

She smiled, and nodded, pointing at where she sat, at herself, and then me.

"Our spot," I whispered, pointing at where I sat, at myself, and then her.

She reached out and the shimmery glow grew smaller and smaller until it and she disappeared.

Dumbfounded, I stayed rooted in the same position, not even believing I'd had a conversation with a girl from...wherever she was from. I thought of texting my best friend Manny to tell him about it, but quickly decided against it. Some things you needed to keep to yourself, and this was definitely one of those things. I climbed back into bed; my thoughts so consumed with the girl with silver hair it took me forever to fall asleep.

But eventually, I did.

CLASSES THE NEXT DAY COULDN'T GO BY FAST ENOUGH. All day long, and even during soccer practice, the mysterious girl stayed on my mind. And true to her word, after midnight, she appeared in my room. This time, she was prepared.

She held up a stack of paper and a long skinny pencil, then showed me a sheet she had already written.

My name is Celyse.

I smiled, then wrote, *That's really pretty.*

A blush spread across her ivory cheeks. *Thank you,* she wrote.

She glanced around my room, studying everything, then pointed to a frame on my dresser. I got up and brought it over to her, showing her the picture of my mom and me with our arms around each other's waists, smiling big after one of my soccer games.

Is that your mother?

Yes. That's us after a soccer game.

She is lovely.

Thank you. She's very important to me.

And your father?

Staring at my paper for a while, wondering how I should explain him disappearing because I hated talking about it, I ended up simply writing, *He's not part of my life.*

She scooted closer to the glow, her face taking on an expression of sorrow. Then she wrote, *I am sorry.*

I shrugged then wrote, *It's okay.*

Truth was, it wasn't okay. Not by a long shot. But there was nothing I could do about it. My dad had abandoned my mother, leaving her alone when I was only an infant. Mom insisted something had happened to him, that he would never have done that to her, but I didn't buy it. After seventeen years, if he wanted to come back, he would have. I vowed that if I ever saw him, I'd make sure he regretted the day he walked out on us.

Celyse held up her paper. *Do you have any brothers or sisters?*

It's just me and my mom. But I do have a lot of cousins. You?

I have a twin sister. She is dutiful, much like our mother. I am more like my father.

Oh, so your dad is cool?

Her brows stitched together as she wrote, *Cool?*

Whoa, what? She didn't know what soccer was and now she didn't know what the word cool meant? Despite my mom's rule of not asking ghosts where they were from, I couldn't help myself. Her cloak and her long silky nightgown looked like something you'd see in a historical movie, the kind where the characters lived in mansions and had butlers. Plus, I didn't exactly know what she was—a ghost? Someone alive but from a different time? Or maybe a different dimension? I'd seen enough sci-fi movies to give me plenty of ideas.

I considered what I should write as I held my pen in my hand, then scribbled. *You know, cool. As in, laid back.* And then I wrote on a new sheet of paper, *Where are you from?*

She read my note and her face took on a worried expression. She set her paper down and started fidgeting with her pencil. I thought of writing to let her know to forget it, when she started with her own message. She held up her paper.

I must retire for the evening.

"Wait!" I blurted, as the glowing orb shrank until it disappeared. "Great," I whispered.

Celyse didn't show up the next night. Or the next. I had no idea why asking her where she was from was such a big deal. To me, it didn't matter. But to her, it did.

I was beginning to think she'd never come back, when a week later she appeared. I didn't ask her about our last conversation, and she didn't mention it either. Instead, we carried on as if nothing had happened, which was fine with me.

We saw each other every night for the next six weeks. In that time, I learned a lot about her. Her favorite color was sky blue, her favorite food was bread made of rosemary and honey, and her favorite drink was mint berry juice. She lived in a big house near a large lake with strict parents and a bossy, know-it-all twin sister.

She loved nature and took long walks outside in her garden. She wished to travel to new places and see new things, but her parents didn't let her. The more we talked, or wrote, the more I thought she wasn't from the US but from England, and that she was most definitely not from my era.

But the most incredible thing about our time together was how I always knew when she'd be coming. It was as if we were linked somehow. And even though I'd had girlfriends before, being with Celyse was different. She was smart and curious and interesting and funny. And by far, the most beautiful girl I'd ever seen. I was beginning to have feelings for her—real and powerful feelings. The kind that made my heart expand at the mere thought of her and my stomach flip every time I saw her.

We sometimes talked about things we had done during the day, like me going to school and soccer practice and she going to her lessons. But mostly, we talked about our dreams and desires. She was afraid of getting stuck in a family role she didn't want. I felt the same way.

I didn't tell anyone about her. Not my mom, and not my friends. I didn't think anyone would understand. And as impossible as it seemed, it was as if she was mine, and I was hers... somehow.

Staring deep into her magnificent green eyes and sitting as close as I could to her shimmery glow, I finally held up a note I'd been working on for days.

If there is a way for us to be together, if only for a little while, do you want to try?

Her lips parted, and I didn't have to hear her to know she had gasped. With all the stuff my mom could do and had passed on to me, I had thought maybe there was something we could do to be in the same space. But clearly, Celyse wasn't ready.

I quickly held up the other note I had prepared.

Never mind. It was dumb to ask.

Our conversation the rest of the night was awkward, and she ended up flashing me her goodnight message earlier than usual. But I couldn't let her go away without saying something.

I scribbled quickly, *Can we forget the question I asked earlier?*

She smiled, nodded, then wrote. *It is forgotten.*

Good. Then I'll see you tomorrow. Goodnight.

Goodnight.

Climbing into bed, I decided to never again ask her where she was from or if we could somehow be together. I mean, those were ridiculous ideas, anyway.

Little did I know, she was making decisions of her own.

3

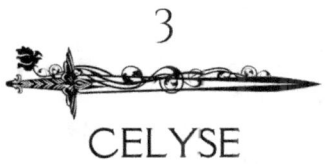

CELYSE

L ove can happen slowly, or all at once. With Julio, it was both. The first time I saw him, a spark blossomed in my heart. Every time I saw him after, it grew even more. But as the months went by and my eighteenth birthday, which signaled my courtship season, approached, I knew my fascination with him could not continue. Plus, our feelings were growing too deep. He had even asked if I wanted to try and be with him if there was a way. And while there was a way, it could never be.

We were mortal enemies. Born of different realms. With duties and obligations.

It crushed me to think of saying goodbye to him forever. How would I do it? What would I say? My heart was crumbling into a thousand little pieces at the mere thought of such a conversation.

"Whatever is the matter with you?" asked Malena. We were strolling in the garden and she had stopped, but I had not noticed. She approached me with her mouth agape. "Is your head in the clouds? You have that look about you."

After six weeks of dashing away in the middle of

the night to see Julio, taking paper and pencil, and then burning my notes after, she had only now noticed my heart soaring.

Before I could answer, she grabbed my hand and asked me eagerly, "Who is it? I must know!"

Gazing at my sister, older by one minute and five seconds, I studied her features—perfectly straight nose, pointed ears, delicately upturned crystal-green eyes, and silver hair. We were nearly identical, except my ears were not as pointed, and my silver hair had a thick black streak, a streak I shared with an uncle on my father's side. Without those differences, it would have been nearly impossible to tell us apart. That, and our desires. She wanted to wed and step into the role of High Queen one day. I did not want either of those things. What I wanted was something I could not have —freedom to make my own choices. And that included the chance to be with a human named Julio Francisco Avila who lived in the forbidden human realm.

I let out a long sigh. "It is no one you know."

She smiled. "I think I do know. It is Jaid."

"Jaid? No!" I shook my head, ridding myself of the thought. "He is like a brother to me. You know that."

"It was a rational assumption. The two of you spend a lot of time together. At least you did before his position on guard detail was elevated." She tapped her slender fingers against her chin. "Well, who then? It is not like we have many visitors. Though whoever it is may not officially pursue your hand until courtship season starts. I hope you remember that Celyse. There are rules."

"Oh, please. As if I do not know the rules. They dictate my life after all." I lowered myself on a concrete bench and Malena sat next to me. I let out a long sigh. "It is not anyone eligible for courtship season."

Her brows stitched together. "It is not?"

"No, it is not." I was bursting with the need to tell someone about Julio. And if there was anyone I could trust, it was Malena. She was not only my sister, but also my best friend. I took her hand. "If I tell you, you have to promise to keep it to yourself. You may never tell anyone. Can you do that?"

Malena pulled her chin in. "That is a serious request." She thought for a few seconds before saying, "I will honor it unless my so honoring puts you in jeopardy."

"I will not be in jeopardy," I said.

After a short pause she said, "If that is so, then I promise."

Gathering my courage, I inched closer and said in a low voice, "Months ago I happened upon a lost shimmer. I know I should not have peeked through it and I know I should have had it returned to Torch Lake, but I could not help myself."

Malena placed her hand on chest, but said nothing, waiting for me to continue.

"Inside the shimmer. I saw a gorgeous human." My voice dropped even lower. "I have been seeing him every night since."

She drew in a sharp gasp. "My sister! How could you?" She shook her head in disbelief, then began listing the things we had been told about humans. "They are our sworn enemy. Their bodies are weak and damage easily. They are barbaric, crude, and ugly. And our taste is deadly to them. Do not forget that, Celyse. If you kiss him, he will die."

I most certainly did not want him to die. Yet I could not let my affection for him go. My head soared in the clouds every time I thought of him because I did not think him ugly at all. He was beautiful. Even though I knew his kind were the sworn enemy of the fae, the war with them had ended over a millennium ago.

Should that not count for something?

To me, humans were amazing, interesting, and harmless. I did not think they needed to be our enemies any longer. Even facing a courtship season and an eventual betrothal, I dreamed of what it would be like to be with Julio, if only for a little while. I imagined holding his hand, his fingers laced between mine. I thought of what his grip might feel like. I dreamed of his lips on mine and our bodies close.

"Celyse," she snapped. "I forbid you from seeing him again!"

My heart caught in my throat because I knew she was right. I swallowed the tears that threatened to gush out of me and nodded. "You do not have to forbid me from seeing him. I know what I must do."

Her face softened and she wrapped her arms around me. "There, there, my dear sister. Everything will be well. Over time you will forget that wretched being. In fact, we will look back at this moment and laugh at the absurdity of it."

I did not think she was right that I would forget about Julio. I also did not think I would ever be able to laugh at this moment. But I did need to stop seeing him and fall in line with my duty. Now, all I needed to do was say goodbye.

Alone in my room, with night falling, I sat at my desk and stared at my papers. I thought of what I would write to Julio. Would I tell him I was a fae living in the faerie realm that overlapped the human realm and that we were mortal enemies? That I was a princess and had a duty to marry? He had asked me once where I was from and then never again. I was grateful for that because it allowed me to be someone else.

If only for a little while.

As the hours ticked by, my mind kept telling me not to say anything to him. That it would be best and easiest to simply stop appearing in his bedchamber. That dealing with me disappearing would be easier than hearing all the truths I had kept from him.

I took my sheets of paper and set them back in my drawer along with my writing device. With so much emotion inside of me, I knew I would not be able to sleep. Instead, I sat on my windowsill and peered out at the brilliant stars dotting the dark sky.

"I hope you will understand," I whispered out loud.

"WAKE UP! OUR DAY HAS COME!" MALENA CALLED OUT as the door to my bedchamber opened. She was the early riser, while I was not.

With my hands tucked under my down-filled pillow, I stayed perfectly still, pretending to be asleep. I was not ready to face the first day of my eighteenth year—a day that would kick off a year of courtships that would culminate in Malena and me becoming betrothed and securing the future of Strong Haven, the ruling house of the five provinces of Faevenly.

My duty weighed heavy on me, so much so I could barely move. There was also my heart. It yearned for Julio. I had seen him almost every evening for six weeks and I now was going on four months of no contact.

Did he miss me like I missed him?

"Celyse, come now." Malena plopped on the edge of my bed and patted my back. "Mother went through this process and came out with Father, and they have been a wonderful match. We will fare just as well. I promise."

I lifted my silk covers over my head, believing if I did that, everything would go away. Though of course, I knew that was impossible.

"Celyse, get up!" Malena urged.

With a groan, I turned over and peeled my eyes open. Soft streams of hazy morning light framed the windows, signaling the start of the day I had dreaded for a long time.

"If I run away, will you tell anyone?" It was a silly question I had asked her when I was little and so mad at Mother and Father I wanted to leave. And whenever I had those same feelings of despondency, I would repeat the question. In fact, I must have repeated it a thousand times over the years.

She smiled and replied like she always did. "Yes, but only because I would miss you."

"My ladies!" Maid Rell bellowed as she practically exploded into my bedchamber, her footsteps heavy on the marble floor. "Why are you both not yet washed?"

"Maid Rell," we said with a start, her presence letting us know how behind schedule we were.

"Do not Maid Rell me." She clapped two times. "Now go."

Malena and I chuckled as Maid Rell flung open the drapes. The soft streams of light that had hugged the windows now swathed the room in brilliance, demanding I get up. Nothing like an order from Maid Rell and a blast of sunshine to get one moving. I forced myself to my feet, telling myself I could handle the day.

No matter what.

Bustling down the corridor to the washroom with my sister at my side, we did our morning washing, then hurried back to our shared dressing room to get ready. Pulling off my white nightdress, I eyed the new gown Maid Rell had draped across the chaise. It was pale blue with a plunging neckline and lace trim. I did not mind wearing gowns on special occasions, but this seemed too much for daytime, even if we did have suitors calling.

"I love the neckline," Malena oozed from the other side of the room, her purple dress with the same plunge as mine already on her tall thin frame as she stood in front of the floor-length mirror. She swayed from side to side, marveling at the way the cut accentuated her ample bosom.

Of course she loved it.

A trio of petite maid servants with an assortment of leaves nestled in their short-cropped dark hair swept into the room—one bearing a tray of mugs and a pitcher of water, another with a tray of freshly scented body oils, and the third with a box of needle and thread. The third one made her way over to Malena and started tending to her dress, fastening the row of pearl buttons that lined the back.

Staring down at my not-so-generous chest, I rolled my eyes because showing my minimal cleavage did not matter. And actually, none of it mattered. I did not want a low neckline, or a dress, or an eighteenth birthday, or a betrothal for that matter. The only thing I longed for was to do what I wanted when I wanted. And that included sneaking away to the shimmer so I could see Julio. Tall, tan, and muscular with the most amazing smile, kind eyes and delightful humor, he was not like anyone else in all of Faevenly.

Doubts over leaving him still plagued me. Had I done the right thing when I decided to walk away and stop seeing him? Was it really for the best? I forced those thoughts aside, telling myself it was most definitely for the best. I was sure Julio had moved on, and I had to move on as well.

A tugging at the back of my head snapped me back to reality as Maid Rell worked on my thick hair. "Ouch!"

"Sorry, my lady," she offered, working on a tangled strand. "But I need to get this out."

With the knot undone, she finished with the brushing and moved on to braiding. "Now, let us discuss the schedule of the day," she announced. "There will be four suitors calling. Two at midday for crudités and tea, and two at nightfall for main course and wine."

"Four today?" Malena squealed with delight. "Please tell me one of them will be Alexander Kane from High Meadow."

"Yes, one of them will be Alexander," she answered. "He will be here at nightfall."

Alexander, the annoying unseelie fae from High Meadow with dark hair, a scowling face, and a know-it-all attitude that grated on my last nerve. How Malena could be interested in someone like him was beyond me. But he did come from a powerful house. They were probably the next most powerful family after ours. It made sense for Malena to target him as her first-choice companion. She thrived on strategy and arrangements.

While Maid Rell rattled off information about the

other suitors, my mind drifted back to the human realm. But this time I halted my thoughts. The idea of being with Julio was just that—an idea, a tarradiddle that could never exist in my reality. It was better for me to forget about him.

But still...

"Celyse, try this," Malena said eagerly, placing a small crystal red jar under my nose.

A delicate floral scent with an undertone of spicy woodland connected with my senses in the most delightful way. "Ooh. It smells wonderful. Like an outdoor garden."

"I know. I thought you would like it." She placed it in my hand, then retrieved another bottle, a pink one. "I picked this one for me."

Taking a whiff, I smelled heavy florals with a hint of powdery musk. "Mmm, perfect for you."

She took a long inhale. "It is so romantic."

I laughed. "Yes, it is."

Finally dressed, with our hair perfectly styled and with the oils strategically applied behind our ears and on our wrists, Maid Rell looked at us admiringly.

She cupped her hands together and held them to her chest. "Lovely, absolutely lovely. Now, your sires, the High King and High Queen await you in the garden. I will leave you to them and shall see you both later."

Maid Rell and the three maid servants shuffled away. Alone with my sister, fear and doubt over my future swept over me, like a hard winter wind. Malena must have seen the dread on my face. I was never good at hiding my feelings.

She stepped forward. This time, she held her head high and her back straight, assuming the role of future High Queen. "You will not ruin this for me. I will not allow it."

Startled at her words and her tone, I stepped back. She often asserted her authority over others but never over me. And I did not like it. "Do not speak to me like that, my sister."

Looking beautifully dangerous, she closed the gap between us. "I have let you have your whimsies over the years. Your distractions. But now is the time for us to fall in line with our duty and leave childish things behind. And when I say *us*, I mean *you*."

I raised my chin. She was right, but I did not appreciate her forcefulness and threatening demeanor. "I know what I must do. You do not have to remind me."

She moved in even closer. A hint of darkness appeared in her green eyes, the kind that preceded a command. Was she about to compel me? As soon as the idea struck me, the dark flicker faded, and her eyes turned back to their usual emerald shade.

"I know you pine for that human." She let her words sink in as she stared me down.

I matched her tone and her posture. "Who I pine for is none of your concern." Suddenly, I regretted sharing my love story with her. If I had known she would hang it over me, I would have never said anything.

"Perhaps." She folded her arms in front of her. "But I need you to know that I will not let anything or anyone, especially a human, ruin your life. Or mine. Understand? I will wed. And I will wed well. And so must you."

I stared at her with unflinching eyes. Ever since we were little, Malena and I knew what our futures would hold. Twins among the fae were rare, and there had never been twin heirs to the throne. But because she was born first, she would assume the throne and have dominion over me. I would be her faithful and trusted second. We spent our lives living out these positions in anything and everything we did. She was always the first sibling introduced whenever we went anywhere. She got her first pick at everything, from clothes to food and even to our lessons and activities. She would also get her first pick at the suitors.

None of her privileges had bothered me until I had stumbled upon that shimmer. There was something about humans and their way of life that had started to change me, softening my heart, and broadening my curiosity. Malena did not and could not comprehend.

"Celyse, do you understand me?" she asked.

Clearing my throat, I lifted my chin. "Yes, I understand."

She narrowed her stare. "And if a time should come for you to end him, the human, I have to know... will you?"

End him? What was she talking about? A few long seconds passed while I processed her question.

She asked me again, this time with more force behind her words. "The safety of our kind will always be paramount to lesser beings. So I ask one more time, if humans become a threat to us, including this human you have become acquainted with, will you end him and any others who cross us?"

At that moment, I had to make a choice. Julio or my family. Even though I hated the ultimatum, I knew what I needed to do. I was fae blood. He was human blood. Our worlds could never mix.

"Yes. If he becomes a threat, I will end him."

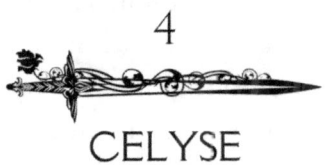

4

CELYSE

Holding my head high, I walked with Malena to the garden to meet Mother and Father. She chatted in her usual way, as if she had not threatened me. As much as I wanted to let it go, I did not know if I could. She had never done something like that before. At least, not to me. I wondered if she had really been about to compel me.

We emerged from the corridor of our second-floor private wing and were almost to the stairwell when she turned to face me. "Oh, come now. You know I love you. Please do not brood like this. Not today."

I sighed, giving in to her like I always did, because I *did* know she loved me. Even when she was over-bearing and demanding and completely irritating, she was my constant companion and my best friend. From playing when we were little, to enduring countless tutorials, and even sharing our secrets and desires, we did everything together. I should not ruin her wedding dreams over my fondness for a human.

I sighed. "I love you too."

She hugged me and kissed my cheek. "Good."

We made our way down the stairs, through the

grand foyer, and to the columned archway that opened to the garden. A glorious day brightened the stone pathway that wove through the hydrangeas, lavender, and jasmine. I breathed in the sweet aromatic fragrance, letting it calm and soothe me, grateful for the work of the gnomes that secretly tended to the gardens at night.

At the end of the path were Mother and Father, sitting at a round wooden table with a spread of jams, breads, fruit, and juices. Mother rose to her feet, every movement purposeful and deliberate—from the elegant way she set her napkin aside with her long, thin fingers to the smooth glide as she scooted her chair back from the table. She wore a long silver dress with a high neckline. Her silver hair was pulled up in a tight bun with strands that spilled out and framed her high cheekbones and refined features. Father's long silver hair was pulled back in a braid that hung thick between his shoulder blades. He wore silver trousers and a loose white silk tunic. His motions were casual and relaxed.

"There are the two most beautiful creatures in all of Faevenly," he declared, beaming with pride. "Happy Day of Birth, my daughters."

"Thank you, Father," Malena and I said together.

Mother approached and gave Malena a long hug, followed by a quick one for me. "A most magnificent day indeed."

"Thank you, Mother," we said.

Father returned to his chair. He stood behind it

while Mother, then Malena, and then I took our seats. I began serving myself a plate of food as Mother started with her usual summary of what the day would hold.

"Before we address the business of the day, you should know that your Father and I have limited your suitors to four. And the four will—"

"What?" Malena's bread tumbled out of her grasp onto the white linen tablecloth. One of the meal servants appeared, taking the fallen bread away with a swipe and scraping up the crumbs. "There will only be four?"

My mind echoed Malena's thoughts. Courtship season often saw suitors in the double digits. Mother and Father limiting the pool was highly unusual. Not that I wanted more suitors, but we were the offspring of the High King and High Queen.

Something was awry.

Mother kept her gaze on Malena. "We are limiting the pool to the ruling families in each of the provinces. No other families will be included."

Now that was a first. Usually, all nobles, even those of lower ranks, were allowed.

"Why only the ruling families?" Malena asked. "Is there unrest in the provinces?"

At one time, Faevenly was divided into the seasonal courts of Winter, Spring, Summer, and Autumn. But at the conclusion of the Great Shimmer War, the elder Strongs—my ancestors—abolished the court system, naming Strong Haven as the high ruling province, with strongholds in the East and the West with our primary homestead in the East. They then designated four allied provinces—High Meadow under the domain of the Kane family, Summit Range under the domain of the Stromm family, Sand Bluff under the domain of the Baffin family, and Cuesta under the domain of the Lind family. The ruling families answered to the Strongs, and the Strongs answered to no one.

"There is no trouble that we cannot handle," Mother declared in her usual aggressive tone.

"Besides, a little trouble now and again keeps everyone in place," Father added. He unstitched his brows and smiled. "Let us not dwell on such things on this day. Faevenly business can wait until another time. Today is all about my daughters."

With a firm nod, Mother went on, explaining that Jorn Lind from Cuesta and Evan Baffin from Sand Bluff would be calling in the afternoon. Alexander Kane from High Meadow and Barent Stromm from Summit Range would be calling in the evening. But I quickly tuned out the discussion. They all probably wanted Malena anyway, so why should I care? And really, why should Malena? She favored Alexander, and everyone knew it. And I favored a human I could never be with.

None of them mattered. My heart was already somewhere it should never be.

A hand touched mine and I looked up to see Father studying me. "All will be well, my love. I promise." Mother and Malena were so busy with their words they did not notice my withdrawal, as usual. But Father did. He always did.

I placed my hand on top of his. "I know. Thank you, Father."

After breakfast, Malena and I had a few hours before our suitors would arrive, which was not enough time to do much of anything except wait. When midday finally rolled around, so did our guests.

Peering from a lookout in the library at the far end of the main wing, Malena and I watched Evan Baffin arrive in a small open carriage. He had two attendants —one who served as whip at the helm and the other who served as valet. He wore fine threads of silver and gray silk with crystal accents that glittered in the daylight. Jorn Lind arrived alone on a brown-and-white steed. He too wore fine threads but his were silver and frost blue with pearlized accents.

Malena's eyes twinkled at the sight. She smoothed out her dress with her hands and stood before me. "How do I look?"

Eyeing my sister, the future High Queen of Faevenly, I thought she looked stunning. But for fun, I frowned and flashed her a worried glance. "Well, I think you need to fix—"

"What?" she asked, staring down at her dress with terror, searching for whatever might be out of place. "What is it?"

I chuckled. "Nothing. Everything is perfect."

"Celyse!"

"Sorry, my sister. I could not help myself."

Maid Rell clapped her hands, signaling her entry into the room. "The suitors are presenting themselves to the High King and High Queen. It is time for your appearance."

Malena squealed with delight and grabbed my hand. "We are ready."

She pulled me with her as we followed Maid Rell to the receiving room. The bulky minder stopped before entering and stepped aside, motioning for us to continue.

The sight before us was as lovely as ever. Shades of blue and silver bathed the grand receiving room. From the light marble floors to the shimmery blue drapes and the silver-hued walls, the space oozed with regal opulence. Orbs of warm light floated along the vine-carved high ceiling. In the corner of the room, a trio of harpists strummed a melodic tune. Mother and Father sat in the middle of the room on oversized white fabric chairs, beaming with pride. Before them sat Jorn and Evan. The pair promptly rose to their feet when they spotted us.

Malena released my hand, raising her chin and pulling her shoulders back. I assumed the same posture, and together we made our way to the chairs to the right of Mother and Father and took our seats.

"Malena and Celyse," Mother said with a grand gesture. "Please welcome Jorn Lind from Cuesta and Evan Baffin from Sand Bluff."

"Lady Malena, Lady Celyse, thank you for honoring me this afternoon," Jorn said with a low bow.

He was tall and lean with long black hair that hung loose at his shoulders.

"I am honored as well, my ladies," Evan added quickly, with an even lower bow of his own. He was similarly built but had silver hair worn in a trio of thick braids.

"We thank you for your travels," Malena replied, answering for the both of us. I nodded in agreement but thought that I did not thank them at all for their travels. In fact, I was already wanting them to leave.

The meal servants, donned in their usual all-white garb, glided in with trays of vegetables and fruit and an assortment of dipping sauces and breads. They arranged the spread on the buffet table along the back wall and retreated to the corner of the room while Mother started a conversation on travel and weather. The boring topics sent my mind wandering to the human realm. If only Julio could be here, in this room, seeking my hand instead of—

"Lady Celyse?" I blinked to see Jorn standing before me with an outstretched hand. "Would you like to go for a stroll?"

Thunderation! My thoughts were so far adrift I had not noticed Mother and Father get up and make their way over to the food. Or Malena and Evan at the far end of the room laughing and chatting.

Jorn let his hand fall. He placed it behind his back. "Or perhaps you would prefer some food first?"

This was my life. A life where my biggest decision would be deciding between eating and strolling, forced to converse with someone who probably only cared about position and stature. If I could choose how to spend my time, it would not be cooped up in a palace entertaining suitors who had no interest in me. It would be exploring and experiencing new things in the human realm with Julio. But that could never be. As much as I hated to admit it, I needed to let those fanciful ideas go like Malena said.

I eyed Jorn. He was not tall, dark, and handsome like Julio. He was tall, fair, and adequate. He was also awaiting my reply.

Rising to my feet, I flashed him my best cordial smile, reminding myself not to ruin things for Malena. Or Mother and Father, for that matter. "A stroll sounds fine. Thank you, Jorn."

Bypassing the food, we meandered to the glass doors that led to the garden. We walked in silence as a soft wind filtered through the trees and shrubs, kicking up the aroma of sweet blooms and earthen cloves.

"The grounds here at Strong Haven Palace are magnificent," Jorn complimented, eyeing the landscape. "Much more so than I had imagined."

I reached out and let my fingertips touch a nearby rose as we strolled by. "Thank you. I love it out here and often spend hours getting lost in the sights and sounds of nature."

He smiled as he continued admiring the scenery. "I can see why. I daresay I might do the same if I lived in a palace surrounded by such beauty."

Interesting. He was a lover of nature. I liked that.

"Pray tell, do you ever get to visit Torch Lake?" he asked. "There is an access point not far from here, correct? Maybe a few miles away?"

Torch Lake—where the shimmers were stored. Fear prickled the back of my neck. Did Jorn somehow know of my found shimmer? Although I had stopped visiting it, I kept it hidden between the trees. Could he have found out I had been using it to see a human? Other than Malena, nobody knew of my misdeed. If I were discovered, I would have to face my mother's wrath and possibly even have to go before the Council of Five. I kept my senses sharp, telling myself I was merely being paranoid. Still, I had to be careful with my response.

"Yes, there is an access point near here," I said casually. "But it is guarded, and visits require strict permission. Even for me."

He slowed his stride and flashed me a look of understanding. "Of course. I never meant to suggest otherwise." He changed the subject. "So, my lady, have you ever visited Cuesta?"

Mother and Father had taken me and Malena on a tour of the provinces once. We were gone for a full season, but that was long ago. I could not remember much of Cuesta other than the views from the Great Peaks as we hiked the mountains.

"I have, but I was merely a child," I admitted. "Unfortunately, I do not remember much of my time there."

"Well, then, I should love for you to visit," he

offered with enthusiasm. "The region boasts the most spectacular mountain views, and no trip to Cuesta is complete without a trip to the Majestic Chasm. The weather is grand with warm days and cool evenings. We even have the annual Lilac Trail approaching."

"Lilac Trail?" I asked.

He smiled, looking pleased to have found a topic to interest me. "The Lilac Trail is a festival of the blooming lilacs. We walk amongst the gardens admiring the florals. There is a grand water fountain at the end of the trail where musicians play tunes for the dancing streams."

"That sounds lovely," I said, imagining rows and rows of lilac bushes, thinking it was a sight I would like to see.

He stopped and drew in a deep breath, admiring the endless blue sky. I did the same, then glanced behind us at the palace in the distance. I had not noticed how far we had walked.

"You are quite close to your sister, Malena, yes?"

"Yes, she is more than a sister to me. She is my best friend."

He continued looking about. "As twins, you two are almost identical. Save for the black streak in your hair. If I may be so bold to say so, it is quite striking."

When I was little, I hated having hair different from the pure silver of my sister, Mother, and Father. But over time I grew to love it. It seemed my suitor liked it as well. I could not help but think maybe he was not so bad after all. "Thank you, Jorn."

He stepped in close and took my hands. "I have actually never met anyone with a streak like that. In fact, I have been waiting a very long time to see it in person and spend time with you. Just the two of us, away from everyone else."

His forward advance surprised me. I moved to step away when his hand clutched my throat in a swift movement. His firm grip choked me, cutting off my windpipe. I could not scream. I could not even breathe. And then his crystal-green eyes darkened. Panic rushed over me like an icy chill. He was about to compel me! And I was defenseless!

"**Hear me.**" The low octave of his voice froze me in place while my body went slack. My will was no longer mine, but his. Nothing else mattered or existed but what he wanted.

"**What is your family doing with the shimmers?**"

My mind jumbled. I had no idea what my family was doing with the shimmers, but I knew what *I* had been doing. I had been seeing a human in secret. I let out a squeak to answer, but his grip was too firm. He loosened it so I could reply when a whooshing wind flew by my face as an arrow ripped through Jorn's head, piercing one ear and sticking out the other. His eyes went wide. His lips parted. He stayed like that a few seconds before his arm dropped and he toppled to the ground.

My mind cleared and I doubled over, clutching my throat and gasping for air while my body quivered with fear and shock.

"My lady!" Jaid rushed over to me, his bow in hand with a fresh arrow at the ready. He glanced at the lifeless form on the ground before focusing on me. "Are you well?"

"I-I-I..." My words were stuck while my brain struggled to make sense of what had happened. I stared at Jorn's lifeless form. Jorn Lind of Cuesta, who had come to pursue my hand, who had compelled me and now lay dead at my feet. I needed my father and fast. "My father," I managed to say while I swallowed, massaging my throat. "Get him."

Jaid nodded. He issued a piercing whistle between his teeth. Three guards showed up at lightning speed. He pointed at one. "Get the High King." He pointed at another. "Alert Maid Rell." Finally, he pointed at the third. "Stay with the body."

He cupped my elbow with his hand. "My lady, allow me to escort you back to the palace."

Dazed and confused, I walked with Jaid back home. My steps slow and deliberate. My mind in a whirl. And when we were almost there, I stopped. Evan Baffin was inside... with Malena. Tears threatened to spill from my eyes, but I held them in. Today was the day of our birth and the first day of our courtship season. And I had ruined everything because I had been spying on the human realm when I was not supposed to and somehow Jorn Lind had found out. Now he was dead. And on our grounds. There would be hell to pay for a son of Lind found dead and murdered at Strong Haven Palace. Maybe even war.

What had I done?

Away from the other guards, Jaid let go of formality and spoke to me as a childhood friend. "Celyse, he had you by the throat and had issued a compel. I had to defend you. I will explain to the High King."

I squeezed his arm, letting him know I was grateful for what he had done. "Thank you, Jaid."

Maid Rell burst onto the scene. "My dear! My sweet girl!" She cupped my face. "Are you all right?" She patted my arms and shoulders, as if searching for a wound. When she was satisfied that I was physically okay, she pulled me in for a hug. Her warm embrace set my tears loose and they spilled out onto my cheeks.

"Yes," I managed to say. "I am all right."

"Come, come." She wrapped her arm around my waist and ushered me inside through the east wing and away from the receiving room.

With each step, the horror of Jorn's death descended on me. The image of the arrow lodged through his head flashed before my eyes. I had never seen a dead person before. My hands trembled. My gut clenched tight. And when I got to my bedchamber, I found my mother waiting. She swept over to me and gripped my shoulders. Her eyes brimmed with fiery anger; her thin lips sealed shut with rage.

She waited a few seconds before speaking. "What did you do?"

Words escaped me as my mind spun. She thought *I* had done something? Without even knowing anything? I knew I was not the favored daughter, but how could she blame me so blindly? Hot tears stung my eyes. I blinked them away while I struggled to hold myself before her.

"I did nothing, Mother," I managed to get out.

Her rage-filled eyes scanned me for a few minutes before she backed down. "Tell me what happened."

My hands fluttered to my neck, to the spot Jorn had held in a vise. If Jaid had not shown up, who knows what would have happened? I forced myself to take a deep breath. "Jorn choked me, and then he compelled me."

Mother's eyes grew wider than I had ever seen. "He compelled you? A daughter of Strong Haven?"

I nodded. "He did. And Jaid saw and he..." The horrid vision of Jorn's lifeless face sprang to mind. "He shot Jorn with an arrow, right through his head."

"Good," she snarled. "Being compelled is a show of force, and to compel a daughter of Strong Haven is an act of treason. Jorn Lind deserved to die."

Mother circled the room, her mind calculating her next move as she often did. "How did he compel you? What did he say?"

I lowered myself onto the edge of my bed and thought of Jorn's exact words. It occurred to me that he did not ask me if *I* had seen a shimmer. He wanted to know about my family. "He asked what my family was doing with the shimmers."

Mother paused. "He used those exact words?"

"Yes. He said, 'What is your family doing with the shimmers?'"

Maid Rell shifted her stance with a raised brow while my mother pursed her lips. Was something amiss with the shimmers? Did it have something to do with the lost one I had stumbled upon? My shimmer with Julio? I kept my thoughts to myself as my heart raced, praying to the Sun, Moon, and Stars that my human was safe.

"Mother, what does that mean?" I wiped my eyes. "What was he talking about?"

She kept her composure stiff. "It means the Linds must be put in their place."

Before I could ask more questions, Father showed up. He crossed the room in a hurry and sat next to me, hugging me tightly. "My dear daughter, you are all right."

I hugged him back and held on tight when I thought of my sister. "What of Malena and Evan? And what will we do about Jorn?" I pulled away, realizing I had done the very thing my sister had asked me not to do.

I had ruined *everything.*

"Your mother and I will see to the matter," he assured. "You need not worry."

I nodded, forcing myself to be calm as I looked down at my blue dress, thinking how dumb I felt playing a role I did not want. Now a death was on my hands.

"My king," Mother prompted. "We must return to Malena and our guest. We will figure out what to do with Jorn and the Linds later."

Father nodded. He hugged me again. "Stay here with Maid Rell until we return."

Alone with my minder, I fell back on my bed and turned to my side. I did not want to talk. Did not even want to think. I only wanted to lay there. Maid Rell draped a soft blanket on me and tucked it around my shoulders.

"There, there, my dear," she soothed. "Just rest."

I closed my eyes tight, trying not to think of Jorn's lifeless body, eager to push the image of the arrow and the blood out of my head, but having very little luck. Why did he ask about the shimmers? And what of my lost shimmer hidden in the woods? While I wrestled with my thoughts, minutes grew into hours until eventually, my door swung open.

"My sister," Malena said with breathless worry. The soft patter of her slippers sounded on the marble floor as she dashed over to me and crouched down on the floor so she could look in my eyes. She brushed a strand of hair from my face.

My vision blurred from a fresh onslaught of tears. "I ruined your day."

"What?" She leaned over to hug me. "Nonsense. The only one who ruined our day was that vile monster Jorn Lind and his treacherous family. They will pay. Every last one of them."

"Oh, they will," Mother replied, coming into the room with Father and standing at the foot of my bed. "And while we handle the matter, we expect the two of you to prepare for the next suitors."

I sat up. "The next suitors?"

"Yes, the next suitors. Alexander Kane from High Meadow and Barent Stromm from Summit Range will be here soon, and my daughters must be ready."

"B-b-but, what about what happened to me? What of Jorn's..." I swallowed. "Body?"

It was Father who answered. "He has been placed on his horse and sent home with Evan Baffin none the wiser. And when Jorn and his steed arrive in Cuesta, the Linds will know their son attempted to defy us and failed. As for our grounds, I have doubled our guards both inside and outside the palace. I have even sent for the wolfbeasts. There is nothing to fear at Strong Haven."

The wolfbeasts? The deadly and vicious animals were bonded to the Strongs and were kept in Quietus Valley. The last time the wolfbeasts had been called was when Malena and I were born. It was customary for them to meet each new Strong after birth.

Mother stood tall. "You and Malena must abide by duty. When the suitors arrive, you will be ready."

Duty. Everything was always about duty, and I hated it.

Before I could lodge another objection, Maid Rell came forward from the edge of the room. "They will be lovely and grand. Do not worry, High Queen."

Do not worry? Lind's death would be considered an act of war. And his death was somehow intertwined with the shimmers. All I could do *was* worry.

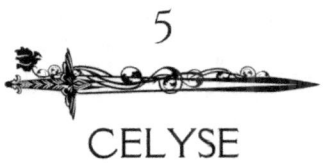

CELYSE

Mother and Father left Malena and me alone with Maid Rell to get ready for our evening suitors. And just like in the morning, we were ushered to our dressing chamber while a trio of maid servants swept in with new dresses and fresh oils. Malena oohed and ahhed over her ruby red, elaborate evening gown, which was puffier and more dramatic than her day dress. Mine was a stunning midnight blue and just as ornate. Even the oils were heavier and more fragrant.

Not surprisingly, Malena prattled on as if nothing had happened while the incident with Jorn plagued my thoughts. Sitting with my silence, my mind stayed in that moment with Jorn while his hand gripped my throat and I lost myself to his command. A command asking about the shimmers. Though no markings stained my skin, the pain from his hold lingered still.

"My dear," Maid Rell called, pulling me from my thoughts and pointing to the center of the room. "Over here, please."

I moved over to her so she could unbutton my day dress. When she finished, she tugged down so I could step out, leaving me standing in my thin satin slip. Moving it out of the way, she returned with the blue dress that had so much lace and tulle I could barely see her.

"Let me help," I offered, taking the hem and parting the fabric until I found the opening and slipped it over my head.

With a shimmy and a few hops, the dress fell into place. Maid Rell heaved a sigh and started fastening the back. Of course, my thoughts stayed on Jorn. With no end in sight to my pondering, I finally had to say something.

"Malena, Maid Rell, are you not curious about what Jorn meant when he asked what our family was doing with the shimmers? Are you not alarmed at his actions?"

Maid Rell harrumphed. "I trust the High King and High Queen to handle such matters while I tend to more important things." She picked up a brush and pointed it at me and Malena. "You two."

"You are so wise, Maid Rell," Malena agreed with an exaggerated nod. "Let Mother and Father handle things while we focus on our suitors."

"You are impossible," I muttered. "Both of you."

My mind remained distracted while I finished getting ready. And when Malena and I were clothed in our gowns, sparkling with jewels, and wearing fresh oils for our evening engagement, we made our way to the receiving room and sat next to Mother and Father where we awaited the arrival of Alexander Kane and Barent Stromm.

We were not sitting very long when the pair arrived wearing their finest threads. Alexander wore black on black, matching his long, loose dark hair. The darkness made his bright blue eyes stand out in a most striking way. He had certainly grown over the years. I guess we all had. I wondered, though, if he was still annoying. Barent wore black trousers with a white top and a pearlized jacket. He had long dark hair too and wore it in a singular, thick braid.

Did either of them have devious designs?

As the evening progressed, I forced myself to smile, nod, and chat. Barent hung on to my every word and was attentive to a fault. Alexander sat close to Malena, the two of them locked in riveting conversation. Mother and Father were near, but not overly so. After a while, I found I needed a reprieve.

I rose to my feet, and so did Barent. "Please excuse me for a moment."

He gave a half bow. "Of course."

As I made my way to exit the room, one of the meal attendants lining the back wall filed in behind me and followed me out. It was a usual and customary gesture, and I thought nothing of it. But when I approached the washroom, the attendant moved in.

"My lady," she whispered urgently.

Her tone stopped me. I turned to face the small-framed maiden. She had short dark hair, delicate features, and a sprinkle of freckles along her nose and cheeks. A worried expression covered her face.

"Yes?" I asked.

She glanced about nervously, wringing her hands together in front of her. With her eyes cast down, she said in a low voice, "I thought you might like to know that I heard the guards will be sweeping the grounds looking for misplaced and lost shimmers." She swallowed hard, then glanced around again. "Any they find will be destroyed."

My gut clenched and my nerves skyrocketed, yet I kept my outward appearance steady and calm. "I do not know what you mean."

She curtsied quickly. "Of course not, my lady. My apologies."

"Apology accepted," I offered as I left her and entered the washroom.

Finding the room empty, I lowered myself onto the chaise as my mind raced. Did she mean the shimmer itself was in danger of being destroyed? Or the subject of the shimmer? And since she told me that, she must have known of my misdeeds. But how? I had been careful every time I went to my shimmer, stealing away at night when everyone was asleep.

The door swung open, and Malena glided in, looking as if her spirit danced on the highest cloud. She leaned against the wall and laid her hand on her forehead in dramatic fashion. "I am in love."

I wanted to be glad for her but was having a hard time. Too many dark thoughts cluttered my mind, but I managed a smile. "I am happy for you, my sister."

Malena inspected her face in the mirror, then checked her hair, yammering about Alexander, while I picked apart what the young maiden had said. If Julio was at risk, then I needed to do something about it. But what? An idea came to me. Perhaps I could go to my shimmer and steal it away and hide it in my room. Surely no one would find it hidden in my things.

It was a ridiculous idea, but the only one I could think of.

When Malena and I returned to the reception, I did my best to engage in the evening. Faking my conversation and counting down to the conclusion of the gathering, I finally found myself in bed for the night, glancing out my window, waiting until every light in the palace dimmed to darkness. And when I thought everyone was asleep, I made my move.

By the light of the bright full moon that filtered through the window, I tiptoed to my black cloak hanging by the door. I lifted it off the hook and slipped it on over my night dress. With an ear to my door, and not hearing anything, I shuffled my feet into my slippers. I cracked open the door and slid out.

"My lady?"

I spun around to see the small-framed attendant from earlier. She wore a simple brown dress with a green belt. A boy with short-cropped hair and brown trousers with a long-sleeved green tunic stood by her side. My mind raced as I scrambled for an explanation as to why I was cloaked and sneaking out of my room in the middle of the night, when the boy spoke.

"If you are going to the shimmer, the grounds are covered with guards." He paused for a moment. "But we can help get you there unnoticed."

The girl chimed in as she glanced about the corridor. "But we must go. Now."

Tingles of fear erupted across my skin. How did they know what I was doing? And why would they want to help me? Going with the boy and girl could cement me in a position I did not want to be in. Yet I needed to make sure Julio was safe.

I nodded. "Lead the way."

The pair glanced at each other, then headed down the corridor, out of the private wing I shared with Malena, and to the adjoining wing that led to the servant's quarters on the third floor.

"We are going up? To your quarters?" I asked, scanning the empty corridor. "Should we not be going down to the grounds?"

"We must first go up," the boy explained. "Then down."

His explanation made no sense, but I was in way too deep to change course now. I gestured them forward with a wave.

I had never been to the third floor, not even to visit Maid Rell, and I surveyed the area with curiosity as we walked up the narrow staircase and down a long stone corridor. Small wooden doors lined each side, unadorned and without doorknobs. Even the ceiling overhead and the floor beneath our feet was plain and undecorated. Moving with haste, we came upon a narrow wooden spiral staircase leading downward.

"These stairs are only for us," the boy said.

"The workers," the girl added.

Stooping down, I followed the pair as we circled our way down to the first floor. "Please explain what this is all about," I said in a hushed whisper, taking care to watch my footing on the narrow steps.

"The shimmers," the girl answered.

"What is being done with them," the boy finished.

I thought of Jorn's command. So something *was* going on with the shimmers. And it wasn't just that I had found one.

We emerged into the dark and empty cookhouse. The aroma of herbs and spices replaced the dusty air from the stairs.

"What is being done with the shimmers?" I asked.

The pair placed their fingers on their lips. Heeding their directive and keeping silent, I followed them to the far end of the room, to a row of shelves lined with pots and pans. The two eyed each other, then me, before placing their hands on one side of the shelves and pushing. With a squeak and a groan, the shelves moved inward, revealing an earthen tunnel.

My lips parted as I beheld the space, imagining a group of workers taking turns with pickaxes and shovels and chipping away at solid ground during the night. "A secret passageway?"

The girl nodded. "Yes. Now come."

Shocked to find a secret way in and out of the palace, I wondered what else was going on under my nose with me, my mother, my father, and my sister unaware. Suddenly, my entire life, my very world, felt built on lies.

What else did I not know?

I followed the pair as we shuffled all the way in. Once we cleared the opening, the pair turned and pushed the shelves shut, enveloping us in darkness. The smell of dirt hung thick in the air.

"I have a torch, my lady. Hold on," the boy assured me.

His footsteps padded away then returned quickly. Moments later, a match struck, and a small flame met the wick of an oil lamp, lighting the tight space with a warm glow. I studied the smooth walls, marveling at the craftsmanship, wondering how long it must have taken to tunnel out the earth so perfectly.

"This way," the girl urged, taking the lead and holding out the lantern.

The narrow space left me hot and sweaty. I desperately wanted to take off my long black cloak but had no place to put it. "One of you had better tell me this instant what is going on," I demanded, assuming full princess mode. "Who built this tunnel? And when? And what in the stars is going on with the shimmers?"

"Yes, of course, my lady," the girl answered. "We will tell you everything. But we must hurry."

They picked up the pace. I stayed close, admiring the intricacies of the tunnel as it grew bigger and wider and included turns and intersecting passages. The boy kept glancing up at the dirt-packed ceiling.

"As you know," the girl said over her shoulder. "No one is allowed visitation to the shimmers without approval, and approval is most difficult to obtain. Yet some are violating this law in the most egregious way."

My brow stitched as I matched her speed. "What do you mean?"

The boy came to a stop. He pressed his hands against the dirt. "Hurry, Adva. I hear them."

"Hear who?" I demanded.

The girl tugged a piece of parchment from her pocket and shoved it into my hand. "Someone with power is using the shimmers to take humans, for what purpose we are not certain. Your human, and all the others, are at risk. And if they are at risk, so is Faevenly."

"We are connected," the boy added.

My blood chilled as my mind spun. "Fae are taking humans?" I uttered.

The girl folded my fingers around the paper. "This note contains the name of a fae living in the human realm. He can help you discover the truth. You must find him at all costs."

My mind reeled as I soaked in their words. And since fae never lied, I knew they spoke the truth. Humans were being taken. But by whom? And how was Faevenly at risk?

"Adva," the boy called out as his eyes roamed the ceiling. "We must hurry."

The girl grabbed my arm and squeezed. "My brother is going to open the hatch. You must go to your human. He can help you find the hidden fae."

The boy reached up and pulled a thick root on the cave wall I had not noticed, cranking it down like a lever. A circular chunk of dirt and clay overhead hinged open.

"When you get through the shimmer, minimize it with your hands so no one slips in after you," he instructed. "Then keep it safe so you can come back."

Terror rippled through me. "Go through? I-I-I have never been trained."

There were two things that had prevented me from jumping through the shimmer so I could be in the same space with Julio like he wanted—not knowing how to cross over, and fear of putting him in jeopardy.

"It is easy, my Lady," Adva encouraged. "All you must do is stretch it wide enough to fit through."

"Like stepping through a doorway," the boy said.

My words were lost while my thoughts raced, my fear taking me from the mechanics of the shimmer to the fact that I could get caught. With the guards doubled, Jaid and his troops were sure to be canvassing the grounds. And even though he was my childhood friend, I felt as if I did not know him at all since his position with the palace had been elevated. If he saw me, what would he do? There was also Mother and Father. If I managed to slip away, they would search for me. What would *they* do if they found me with a human?

And then I wondered how Julio would receive me after I had left him so abruptly. Would he even want to see me?

"My lady," the boy urged. "Do you hear me?"

I found my words. "Yes, I hear you."

"Then please!" the girl begged with a raised voice. "Won't you help us?"

Her desperate eyes locked with mine. Her delicate features were shadowed with fear. I knew many fae still hated the humans, but I thought them kind, funny, intelligent, and curious. The idea of them being at risk turned my stomach because it was wrong. Even when I had studied the Great Shimmer War with Maid Rell, there was much the fae had done to humans that I disagreed with. Helping the humans meant going against my own kind. Was I willing to do that?

An icy chill crept over me, rooting me in place. "I do not know."

The girl took my hand and wrapped it between her small, rough palms. "Just go," she pleaded. "Learn the truth for yourself."

The boy laced his fingers together and crouched low, extending his hands out to give me a boost.

"You can do it, my lady," the boy encouraged.

I approached the boy and locked up at the sky that littered with tiny stars and a bright moon. I thought of the pull I had toward the human realm. If I did not go now, if my shimmer was destroyed, I might never have another chance to see the one who held my heart or discover the truth for myself about the shimmers. And

if Julio and his kind were truly in danger, I had to do
something.

Clutching the parchment in my right hand, I
pulled the hood of my dark cloak over my head and
held the boy's shoulder with my left hand to steady
myself. He hoisted me up and I scrambled out of the
opening, finding myself in the thick of the woods.

"Run," the girl whispered as the earthen hatch
closed.

Even though the cool wind hugged me, heat from
fear and panic crept up my neck and face as I scanned
the woods. I was about to take off when a howl in the
distance pierced the air. The wolfbeasts. They must
have arrived. They were bonded to me as a member of
the Strong family and would give away my position.

I had to run. And fast.

By the soft light of the moon, I scanned the trees,
recognizing my location within seconds. I lifted the
hem of my nightdress and took off. Fully committed to
my actions, I ran with precision and speed while my
cloak flapped behind me. The tall pines and shrubbery
blurred past, and as I dodged a fallen branch, a whistle
sounded and a whir of arrows whizzed past me.

Jaid!

Did he know it was me? I did not know, and it did
not matter. I needed to get to that shimmer.

The familiar sight of my cluster of trees filtered into
view. With a few more strides, I was at the base.
Flinging myself forward, I wedged between the
branches, then crashed to the ground and dug out my

shimmer. The sound of boots and paws crunching against leaves grew louder as I expanded the glow with a whoosh.

Eying the familiar bedchamber, I hesitated. Somewhere beyond the shimmer... he was waiting. And everything in me was pulling toward him.

I said a quick prayer to the sun, moon, and stars before closing my eyes and jumping into the translucent blur, my body tingling as I crossed into the forbidden human realm.

6

JULIO

"*Mijo*, Manuel is outside honking," Mom said, knocking on the door.

Checking my phone, I saw that Manny had texted he was on his way, but I hadn't heard the notification. Now he was here, and I still hadn't found my cleats.

"I'll be right there!" I called out, rifling through piles of dirty clothes on my floor, tossing everything around frantically. My coach had arranged a game with a rival high school, and I didn't want to be late. Especially since it was rumored that a few scouts from local colleges would be showing up. As the captain of my soccer team, I was one of the better players, but still hadn't scored a significant scholarship. I hoped someone would notice me; otherwise, I didn't know what I'd do. We were too poor to pay for college, and loans were out of the question.

So yeah, today was important.

I sat on the edge of my bed and eyed my mess, thinking a visual sweep would help me remember where I had put my cleats, when something else popped into mind—Celyse. She hadn't visited me in four months now, and I knew why. I had asked if she wanted to try and be in the same space together, and her reaction was less than positive.

For nights, I waited for her to show, staying up until morning so I wouldn't miss a visit, but she never came. The girl with the silver hair dominated my thoughts during school, distracted me in soccer practice and kept me awake at night.

Day after day, there was no sign of her. No glow, no feeling that she was coming, nothing. I thought over time I'd get over her, but I still missed her like crazy. I wondered if she missed me too.

I rubbed the back of my neck, then muttered out loud, "Come on dude. Stop it."

"Stop what?" My mom asked, coming into view with a swing of the door, cleats dangling from her fingers.

I ignored her question and smiled. "There they are!" I scooped up the shoes then kissed the top of her head. "Thanks, Mom."

Before bolting, I remembered she was leaving for a weeklong thing with her church group. At least, I thought today was the day. It was also the start of my spring break, and it was easy for me to forget her busy schedule.

"Hey, you're leaving for your church thing today, right? Or is that tomorrow?"

"It's a retreat. Not a thing. And yes, I'm leaving today, but not until after supper. Sister Catherine will be picking me up so I can leave the car for you."

I snatched up my duffel bag. "Sounds good. I'll see you later, then."

I was two steps down the hallway when she called out. "¡*Mijo!*"

I stopped dead in my tracks. Her tone struck a nerve because I recognized the urgency. She'd had a feeling. Or a warning. Maybe even a vision. The last time she'd had one of those with me was when I was a sophomore. I was scheduled to take a flight with my cousin Trent to a soccer camp in California. But she had "felt" something. We skipped the flight and rescheduled for the next day. Sure enough, the plane crashed and everyone on board died.

With a hard swallow, I turned to face her. She stood almost frozen, the color draining from her olive-toned skin. Petite yet strong, she barely reached five feet and seemed way smaller when something covered her with fear. Standing in the hallway with her brow furrowed and her shoulders pulled in as if bracing herself from some threatening force, she looked so tiny.

"What is it?" I asked.

She clutched the small gold cross that hung from her neck and my hand instinctively went to my matching one that hung under my shirt.

"I felt something, *Mijo*. But I can't"—she closed her eyes for a few seconds—"see it."

Closing the gap between us, I placed my hand on her shoulder to ground her like she had taught me so many years ago, when a hurried knock sounded on the front door.

"Julio! It's Manny!"

She released her cross, took a deep breath, and patted my hand. "I'm okay," she said reassuringly, but her words fell far short.

I tilted my head a little and gave her the look. The one that said I knew she was holding back.

"Really, *Mijo. Todo está bien.*"

More knocking came from the door. "Julio! This isn't funny!"

"I'm coming!" I hollered back, as I imagined getting in the car with Manny and crashing on the way to the soccer field. That would suck. "Mom, if you saw something about me, or even Manny, you can tell me."

She smoothed out the lines on her forehead with a rub while the color that had drained from her face slowly trickled back. "It will be okay. You and Manuel will be fine. Now go."

"Well"—I swallowed—"is it you? Will you be okay?"

She laughed, then waved me away. "Oh, yes. I am always okay."

Not giving me a chance to say anything else, she mumbled about needing to tend to her *caldo* that was on the stove, then told me to bring Manny home after the game so he could have some. As if her delicious soup would help me not worry.

Pushing my unease aside, I hurried to the door and jerked it open to find Manny staring at his phone. He shoved it in his pocket. "Dude! We're gonna be late!"

My best friend since forever, Manny was thin and

small at five foot six, while I was tall and muscular at five foot ten. He had skin a few shades darker than mine and thick black hair that grew out instead of down. Kinda like a 'fro. He was wicked fast and never played soccer without his lucky red headband with an embroidered Mexican flag and had it hung around his neck now.

"We're not gonna be late," I said, shaking off my mom's warning as I walked to the car. I needed to play my best and couldn't afford distractions. "Don't worry."

The crisp March day was perfect for a game. The sun shone bright and a cool breeze filled the air. There wasn't even a cloud in the endless blue sky. I hopped into Manny's run-down used car he'd recently bought with his lawn-mowing money and crammed my bag between my feet. Even though I made fun of his ride, it was way better than mine because I didn't have one. I had to share with my mom.

Manny looked both ways as he pulled out of my driveway. "What gives? Did you forget the start time or something?"

"Nah," I said, opening my bag and pulling out my shin guards. "I was talking to my mom."

"Talk talk? Orrrr... witchy talk?"

Whenever we talked about my mom's ability, or mine, Manny referred to it as witchy. Not that we talked about it much, because he knew it was a topic I avoided. He was the only friend who knew my family history, and I wanted to keep it that way.

Shaking my head, I said, "It's nothing."

"Nothing nothing? Orrr... witchy nothing?"

Cleary, he wasn't gonna let it go. I had finished with my shin guards and had moved on to my cleats. "I guess a little witchy."

He slammed on the brakes and screeched to a stop in the middle of the street. "What?" He let out a nervous laugh as he turned to face me. "We're not gonna die on the way to the field or anything, are we?"

"No! Jeez!" A car behind us honked as it zoomed around us. "Now go, or we *will* be late." I rubbed my palms that had slammed against the dash. "And don't do that again."

He started driving, but really slow, like an old lady on a Sunday afternoon. "You'd tell me if I needed to know something, right?"

Manny worried about *everything*. From school to girls to what to order at a restaurant and even which parking spot to park in. He was the most paranoid and superstitious person I knew. I'd never forget the time a black cat dashed across his path when we were little and playing outside. He burst into tears and ran home and then literally didn't leave his house for like two days because he thought something bad was going to happen to him. Which, it didn't.

I started lacing my shoes. "Yes, dude. I'd tell you if you needed to know something. Okay? And can you please drive the speed limit?"

"Yeah, okay," he said. He sped up a little, then added, "Of course you'd tell me. You're my best friend and best friends tell each other stuff."

"Exactly," I said. Right about now I figured we needed a subject change, and I knew just the thing. "Oh, my mom said you can come over after the game for some *caldo*."

He perked up. "Your mom's making *caldo*?"

"Yep, she is." Home cookin' was the way to Manny's heart, or so my mom always said. Especially my mom's delicious *caldo de res*. Manny lived with his dad and their dinners rotated between pizza, hot dogs, tacos, and cereal.

His shoulders relaxed some and his breathing became steadier. "Yeah, okay. *Caldo* after the game sounds good to me!"

We arrived at the field in plenty of time and I ended up having a solid game. So did Manny. We beat the other team by two points, three college scouts were in the crowd, and Manny found himself at the end of the game talking to a girl he'd had his eye on for a while. Giving them some time to be alone, I went back to the car and leaned against the hood. I started checking my messages when a young girl around five or six years old with long blond hair and big green eyes drifted over to me. I sighed, not feeling up for a visit with a ghost, and turned away from her.

"Julio Francisco Avila," she said in a clear voice.

My phone tumbled out of my hand. I managed to catch it with my other one before it hit the ground. I'd never had a ghost call me by my full name before.

"Ummm, yeah?" I glanced about to see if anyone

else was around, but no one was. It was just me and ghost girl. "What do you want?"

She came a little closer to me. "To help you."

Great. I crossed my arms. I had dealt with enough dead people to know how to handle them. Most times, if you ignored them, or told them to leave, they would. "Well, thanks. But I don't need any help. You can get along."

She smiled and laughed. "Yes, you do. That's why I'm here."

I spotted Manny coming my way. "Listen, little girl. I'm fine. And I'm really sorry about whatever happened to you, but my friend is coming, so you need to go. I wish you well."

She eyed Manny, then backed away a little as if to leave. "I'll go, but first I need to tell you to please help the girl."

The girl? One ghost girl was telling me I needed to help another ghost girl? The timing couldn't have been worse as Manny was almost upon us.

"Yeah, sure," I muttered under my breath. "But not now."

"Of course not now, silly. Later. Just be ready."

The girl faded away right before Manny stepped into her space. "I think I'm in love with Addison Clare."

"Yeah, right." I laughed, grabbing my bag. "Now let's get out of here. I'm starving."

Manny tossed his stuff in the car. "She's having a party this weekend and asked me to bring you. Says she has lots of friends who'll be there."

I hadn't been interested in anyone since Celyse because no one could compare to her.

Manny started the car. "Come on. You're the captain of the freakin' soccer team. If you're there, there'll be girls *everywhere*." He motioned wide with his arm.

I shrugged, thinking I didn't want drunk girls hanging all over me, but also feeling like I needed to get myself out there. Maybe it'd help me get over Celyse. Plus, it was senior year after all. "I don't know. I'll have to see."

"Sounds like a yes to me," Manny said, punching my shoulder and then driving off.

Mom's cooking after a game was always a highlight. Her *caldo de res* with beef chunks, cabbage, carrots, celery, potatoes, and squash was my all-time favorite. Manny's too. Together, he and I could easily polish off a giant pot full of the savory soup, along with a few heaping stacks of Mom's sweet and airy flour tortillas. And because she was leaving town for a week, she made extra of everything to load up the fridge.

After stuffing our faces, Manny and I cleaned the kitchen while Mom packed. Not long after, Sister Catherine picked her up.

"Your mom is the best," Manny said, after she'd left. "Now let's have a party! You know, a spring break bash!"

"Dude, you know she'd know," I laughed.

The last time my mom had left for an extended amount of time was two years ago. Like an idiot, I had a small party that turned into a big party. She sensed something was up and called to check on me. When I didn't answer because I couldn't hear the phone over the blaring music, she ended up calling the cops. She forgave me, but man did I feel awful for breaking her trust. I told her I'd never do something like that again, and I meant it.

"Oh, yeah. That's right. The big bust," Manny said. "That was fun, though."

"It was, but I don't need a repeat." I collapsed on the couch; my stomach so full I could barely move. Rubbing my eyes, I added, "Besides, I'm exhausted."

"Me too," Manny said. He got up to leave. "See ya later."

"Yeah, later."

I laid my head back on the couch cushion and closed my eyes. The rhythmic whooshing of the ceiling fan circling overhead relaxed me. The peace and comfort of my simple home soothed me like a soft blanket, and I sighed with contentment. I was looking forward to a quiet week away from mom's clients, and, hopefully, away from ghostly visits.

With sleep threatening to overtake me, I peeled my body off the couch, showered, and got in bed. A few texts later, and after some scrolling on my phone, I turned off my lamp. Laying in the dark, a familiar warm and pleasing feeling struck me. I sat up, peering into the darkness, when a ball of light exploded before me. The force blasted me with a crackling whoosh, enveloping the room from floor to ceiling. I shielded my eyes, squinting at the phenomenon that shone like a small sun, when a person in a black cloak sprinted out of the array and slammed on top of me, our faces inches apart.

Celyse.

Her bright emerald eyes sparkled like freshly polished gems. Silver strands of hair spilled from the hood of her dark cloak. And she smelled like fresh flowers. She was a hundred times more beautiful in person, and she was already beautiful. Her breathing was shallow and rapid, as if she'd been running.

And it was safe to say, she most definitely wasn't a spirit.

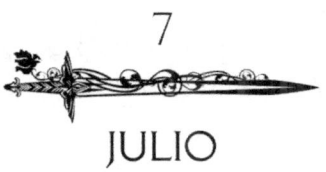

7

JULIO

"Julio," she whispered, wearing a look of surprise mixed with relief and joy.

Before I could respond, her gaze swept over to the blast and her face took on an expression of determined urgency. "I need to close the shimmer before anyone follows me."

She clambered off me and spun around to face the massive orb. She planted her feet wide and spread out her arms, placing her hands not *through* the light but *on* the light. She grabbed the edges, moving her hands together, shrinking it until it formed a small glow that fit on the palm of her hand. And then she stumbled. I sprang out of bed and caught her as she collapsed in my arms. The orb rolled out of her grasp and I scooped her up and laid her on my bed.

The hood from her dark cloak slipped back and I marveled at the sight of her, my heart exploding with emotion. She was in my room, live and in the flesh. My mind raced with a million questions with two overriding all the others. Where had she been? And why was she here now? It took me a few seconds to find my voice.

"You're... here."

She grimaced while she struggled to sit up, holding her left shoulder. "I am here." Her lips tugged into a smile. "I have been waiting for this moment a very long time."

I wanted to hug her, kiss her, feel her against me, but she had left me. I wasn't sure how to act or what to say. I reached out to touch her shoulder. "Are you hurt?"

Before she could answer, my mom's ringtone sounded. The magical-looking girl startled and looked around the room. I lifted my phone off the bedside table and held it up for her as my mom's picture flashed on the screen and her favorite Selena song filled the air. "It's my mom."

She pointed. "Your device."

"Yeah." I glanced at my phone. "My device. I need to answer it."

She tilted her head and studied me while I took the call.

"Hey, Mom."

"*Mijo*, are you okay?"

"Yeah," I said in a low voice. "I'm fine. I was, um, in bed. Why?"

She sighed with relief. "*Gracias a Dios*. I felt something, but I guess it was nothing."

"Really? You felt something?" I glanced at the gorgeous girl sitting next to me, dressed in a long white nightgown and a black cloak. She had scooped up the glowing orb and was holding it close. A nervous laugh escaped my lips. "That's weird."

"I guess, *Mijo*. I guess. Well, we're here at the retreat center. I'll check in with you tomorrow. Call me if you need me, okay? Love you."

"Sounds good. I will. Love you."

Lowering the phone, I kept my eyes on Celyse, not believing she was in my room, on my bed no less.

"You're real," I finally said with a smile, rubbing the back of my neck.

"You did not think I was?"

I'd had a lot of spirits visit me, but a girl crossing over through a portal of some sort? I wasn't sure how to even explain that. "I actually didn't know what to think, other than I looked forward to seeing you." I rubbed my hands on my pajama bottoms. "But then you stopped showing up, so I thought, maybe you weren't real."

Her smile faded and she looked down. "I did not want to stop seeing you, but it was for the best."

I put my phone back on my nightstand and sat next to her. She was still favoring her shoulder. "I should really look at that."

She rubbed it. "It is nothing. But I need your assistance with a most urgent matter."

The ghost girl from earlier had told me to help the girl. She must've been talking about Celyse. And then I wondered if any of the ghosts I had helped in the past were actually alive and from another dimension. At least, I thought Celyse was from another dimension. Was that even a thing?

"If I can help you, I will."

She lifted her hand and unfolded her grip to reveal a crumpled note. She looked at it, then handed it to me. "I need to find this ... person."

I took the thick brown paper. *Traeliorn Letormis.* The name was written in swirly cursive print. "That's, um, quite a name."

When I brought my eyes back up to meet hers, I saw her gaze roaming about my room in wonder, taking in every detail. She had spent a lot of time in here with me, but I was pretty sure seeing it in person was different.

She brought her attention back to me. "You can do it? You can find him?"

"I should be able to. But it would help if I knew more about him. And you. Where are you even from? And what was all that?" I motioned at the spot where the blast had been, then indicated at the orb in her hands.

She smoothed her nightgown and combed her hair with her hands, as if preparing herself for a formal introduction. "I am from faerie, a parallel universe that overlays your human realm. My realm is called Faevenly and my home is in the Strong Haven province." She raised the orb. "This is a shimmer. It allows access between our two lands."

Her words stunned me because I wasn't expecting an explanation like that. But then again, I didn't really know what I was expecting. Just not that. Though with everything I'd seen and done in my mom's *curandera* business, nothing really surprised me.

"The faerie realm," I repeated, clearing my throat. "Like the movies? Lord of the Rings and all that? That's, uh, new to me."

She tilted her head. "Lord who?"

The way she spoke with formality, the shiny silk nightgown, the black cloak with intricate stitching—it made sense for her to be from sort of other-world. She winced and lowered her arm.

"I should really take a look at your shoulder," I said.

She drew in a deep breath, as if to steady herself. "I shall be fine. But please, I need you to help me find Traeliorn Letormis. It is of the utmost importance."

I stared at the paper, thinking there was no way I'd find someone with a name like that, but knew I needed to try. I lifted my phone. "I can search with my phone, um, device."

"Yes, please," she urged. "Thank you."

I ran a quick search for the name. Not surprisingly, the search yielded zero results. "Hmm, I can't find anyone with that name."

Her eyes went wide with alarm. "That cannot be. I was sent to find him, so he must be here!"

"Hey, hey, hey. I'll keep looking." Her eyes glistened with tears while a deep vulnerability shone through and tugged at me. "I got you, Celyse. If he's here, I'll find him."

A spark of hope lit up her beautiful face. "Thank you, Julio. But there is something else you must know."

Something else that was more shocking than what she'd already told me? I braced myself for whatever revelation she was about to lay on me. "What is it?"

She placed her hand on her shoulder. "The guards at Strong Haven use poison-tipped arrows. And when I was running to the shimmer, one of them grazed me."

An icy chill raced down my spine. "You've been poisoned?"

She added quickly, "I need Traeliorn Letormis because he is a fae. He will have fae medicine. He can heal me."

Panic rushed through me. My mind took me to all the injuries my mom had tended in the kitchen. She had a pantry full of herbs and tinctures; maybe there was something in her stash that could help. But first, I needed to look at her wound. I took her hand, finding it cold and clammy.

"Let's go to the kitchen," I said urgently, but also trying to stay calm. Panicking during a crisis only made things worse. "I might have something to help you."

"Very well," she said.

Holding her hand, I helped her to her feet. I held her close to me as we shuffled down the hall and to my living room. We hadn't made it far at all when she passed out mid-stride.

"Celyse!" I scooped her up and placed her on the couch. Kicking into action, I checked her pulse; it was weak but still thumping. I rolled up the sleeve of her gown and saw thick black marks streaking from a small, bloodied nick on her upper arm.

"Holy hell," I muttered.

I needed reinforcements. I needed Manny. I grabbed my phone and texted him.

Emergency. Get over here ASAP. Tell no one. Door open

I unlocked the front door, then dashed to the kitchen. Jerking the cabinets open, I stared at the supplies, racking my brain for what my mom had recently used on a little boy who'd been bitten by a snake. I'd helped calm the kid but hadn't paid close attention to her remedy.

Closing my eyes, I held out my hand, using a trick Mom often used when picking herbs. I pictured Celyse in my mind. "Which one?" I asked out loud.

The front door flung open. "Hey, du—"

Manny's sentence cut short, and he skidded into the kitchen. His eyes practically bulged out of his head. "There's a super hot girl passed out on your couch."

"I know!" I took a deep breath to settle myself. "Listen, there's a name written on a piece of paper on my bed. Search that name on your phone, and fast. That girl has been poisoned and the guy whose name is on the paper is the only one that can help."

Manny's mouth dropped open. "Uh, what?"

"Just do it, Manny!"

He hurried away and I zeroed in on the herbs again, my eyes scanning the jars, my fingertips touching each one. Suddenly, one stood out more than the others—khutora. Snatching it with a swipe, I twisted open the lid, fished out a clump of leaves, dropped them in the mortar my mom kept on the counter, and started grinding.

"I can't find that name!" Manny shouted.

I raced back to the living room and eyed Celyse while I pounded at the leaves. "Keep looking."

The leaves started breaking down, transforming into a chunky green paste.

"I'm freaking out right now," Manny said, his voice in a much higher octave than usual. "Is she, like, dying? We'll get in so much trouble if she dies."

Her breathing was shallow and rapid, her porcelain skin turning ashen. I had no idea if she was dying or not, but said a silent prayer that she wasn't. "She's not dying."

Manny looked from the girl to me and back again. "Are you saying that because of your witchy skills or—"

"Manny! Shut up!"

With the leaves reduced enough, I set the bowl down. I scrunched up the sleeve of her white gown, revealing the thick dark streaks had lengthened, oozing out under her skin in all directions.

"What in the holy hell," Manny uttered. "That's not right, dude!"

Ignoring him, I picked up the bowl, dipped my fingers in, and scooped out a glob of the paste. I pressed the mixture against her cut and held it there.

Heat radiated from the spot, warming my fingertips, which I knew wasn't a good sign. With the paste in place, I applied more on her skin, spreading it so that it covered the black trail traveling down her arm.

I snapped at Manny. "Get me the roll of paper towels."

He dashed over to the kitchen and came back with the roll. Sheet by sheet, I covered the green paste. I sat back, then checked my watch. "I'll give her a minute. If the streaks look better, then I'll know the paste is working. If it looks worse, we'll have to take her to the ER."

Manny sat and chewed his thumb while I paced the living room floor. When the minute passed, I carefully lifted a section of the paper towel and saw that the black streaks hadn't spread any further.

I let out a sigh of relief. "The poison is slowing down."

Manny made the sign of the cross up and down his chest and shoulder to shoulder. "Thank you, Jesus."

With a short reprieve, I grabbed the note with the fae name. "We need to find this person ASAP."

"Well, good luck with that because that name doesn't exist anywhere. I did a regular search then searched the usernames of all the social media sites." He eyed the paper. "He doesn't exist."

I paced the room, trying to come up with other ideas. "I know! Let's look for healers in Austin. What are they called?" I tapped my phone against my forehead. "Naturopaths!" I called out, clicking the letters in the search window.

Manny got busy on his phone too. "I'll look for herbal places!"

After a quick minute searching, we came up empty. With a growl of frustration, I snatched the note from Manny. Staring at the swirly handwriting I said the name out loud slowly and phonetically.

"Trae-li-orn Le-torm-is."

"Hey," Manny offered. "When my dad immigrated to the US, his name was long and weird and hard to pronounce. Hermenegildo Velasquez. No one could spell or pronounce it. Plus, my dad said—"

"Manny! Get to the point!"

"My dad shortened his name to Hermen Vela." Manny pointed at the note. "I bet that guy did the same thing."

Hope sprang inside me. "You're right!"

I grabbed a pen from the basket on the coffee table and stared at the note. "Let's start with the first name. Traeliorn," I said nice and slow.

Focusing on the first four letters, I was about to say Trey when Manny beat me to it.

"Trey!" he shouted.

"Gotta be," I agreed, circling the first part of the name. "It could be spelled T-R-A-E or T-R-E-Y." Staring at the last name, Letormis, I immediately said, "Leto."

"Trey Leto," Manny and I said together.

Manny got busy searching on his phone while I lifted the paper towel to check Celyse's arm. The black streaks were still there, and luckily, they still weren't spreading. They also weren't as dark.

"What is happening?" Celyse asked. Her eyes fluttered open as she looked about.

Manny stared at Celyse with his mouth open but didn't say anything.

"You passed out," I explained. "I applied an herbal paste to your cut, and it seems to have stopped the spreading of the poison."

She sat up, looking in pain, but managed a small smile. "Thank you, Julio."

"I found him!" Manny announced. "I found a T-R-E-Y Leto. He lives on Lake Travis, thirty minutes from here."

Celyse's eyes brightened. "You found him?"

"Maybe," I answered. "If it's him, he's shortened his name to Trey Leto."

She cradled her arm and struggled to get up. "We need to go to him."

"Well, what if this Trey Leto isn't your guy?" I asked.

She stood on wobbly legs, looking as if she was about to collapse. I grabbed her waist to steady her. "He has to be," she said. "And we should go. Now. Before it's too late."

Looking at the sweat beads dotting her forehead and feeling the heat emanating from her body, I cautioned, "I don't think so. You should stay here and keep this paste on. Manny and I will go and get what you need."

"We will?" Manny asked. I shot him a look. "I mean, yeah. We will," he added quickly. "I'm Manny, by the way. Julio's best friend."

Celyse offered him a formal nod. "I am Celyse. I thank you for your assistance. But I must go with you. If you two go without me, Traeliorn Letormis will kill you."

8

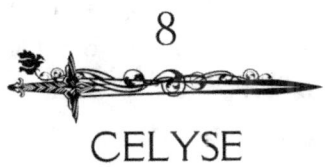

CELYSE

A throbbing pain radiated from my shoulder, extending down into my fingers as I stood before Julio. I had finally crossed over into his realm, but it did not go at all as I had envisioned because now I was dying. If not for the salve on my arm stalling the poisonous spread, I would be dead.

"Did you say he'd kill us?" Manny asked. "This person you've been sent here to find?"

Julio's best friend had dark tan skin, big brown eyes, and wore his hair in a wild and unkempt fashion. And in that moment, he looked terrified.

"He will unless I am with you. Fae are dangerous," I explained.

"Fae?" Manny muttered. "As in, faeries? Are we talking Lord of the Rings? This can't be real."

"Is this Lord of the Rings an important person here?" I asked, curious to hear the name again.

He turned to face Julio. "Is this real? I mean, this is way beyond witchy. Way beyond."

"You're right," Julio answered. "It is real, and it's way beyond witchy. But we're in it, and we're helping."

I had no idea what they meant by "witchy," but it

was not important. My legs shivered. My head pounded. We needed to go before I got worse. Julio eyed me with concern, and I could tell he felt the same way. Time was not on our side.

"Let's get going," he urged. "But let me change my clothes real fast and bandage that arm with the rest of the paste. You also need a drink and some pain relievers."

Julio helped me sit back down, took off to his room for a change of clothes, then darted to another room for a bag of medical supplies. He quickly applied fresh paste onto my cut and the streaks, then wrapped a thin mesh linen around my arm, followed by a stretchy tan fabric.

"Are you a healer?" I asked, marveling at what he could do.

He shrugged. "I can do a few things."

He finished with my arm, then handed me a clear bottle with blue liquid and two small red pills. "That drink will hydrate you, and those pills will help with the pain. You ready?"

I nodded. "Yes, I'm ready." I looked down at my clothes, realizing how inappropriately I was dressed for an outing. "I am still clad in my nightdress and my cloak."

"We can get you some new clothes once we get you fixed up. Don't worry." He helped me to my feet, nodding at the shimmer in my hands. "I guess you need to take that, right?"

"Yes, I do."

"You can put it in this." He snatched a bag from the floor and shook everything out of it. I placed my shimmer inside and then he slipped his arms through the straps and secured it to his back.

"You ready?" he asked.

Fighting the pain, I said, "I am."

Part of my lessons with Maid Rell included human studies, so I knew much about the human realm, including all about automobiles. Normally, the idea of getting in one would have excited me. But I was not feeling well at all, and I worried the apparatus would make me sick. Strapped into the backseat with Julio while Manny drove, I braced myself for the motion, but surprisingly found the ride steady and smooth. This was not at all bad. Nothing at all like a carriage. Now we just needed to hurry.

Forcing myself to stay alert and ignore the pain, I watched the steel buildings and the twinkle of city lights pass by as I sipped on the fruity drink, thinking the human realm more magnificent than I had ever imagined.

"Are you doing okay?" Julio asked in a low voice.

I offered him a half-hearted smile, trying not to show my distress. "I am... okay."

Julio tapped his fingers on his leg, then cleared his throat. "You know, once when I was little, I cut my finger so bad I could see bone. Manny was there. He kept me calm while my mom drove me to the ER by making me tell him a story."

"It helped," Manny said over his shoulder.

"Yeah, it totally helped," Julio said. He inched closer to me. "Maybe that'll help you? To tell me a story?"

"A story?" I tilted my head at him, marveling at his wisdom.

"Yeah, you know. Tell me something funny that happened to you. Maybe a childhood memory or something you love to do."

With my head feeling warm and my fears soaring, I thought his idea a good one. But I could not think of anything funny. There were many lessons with Maid Rell and several formal gatherings at Strong Haven, but I could not think of anything that had made me laugh. Except for the times I had watched Julio through the shimmer. Watching him always made me smile. But I did not want to say that. Instead, I thought of something else.

"Well, it is not a story, but I can tell you something about my sister, Malena."

Julio nodded with interest. "That's right. You told me a little about her. That's really cool to have a twin. Do you two have that connection where you can sense each other's thoughts and things?"

I thought of how Malena knew me so well and I knew her. "Yes, we most certainly have a strong connection."

"Are y'all identical?" he asked.

"We look a lot alike, but we are not identical. Malena has full silver hair, while mine has a black streak. Her ears are also more strongly pointed than mine. We both have pure green eyes, though."

There was much more I could say on the topic of Malena, but my throat started burning. I took a sip of my drink, hoping it would help, though I knew it would not. The poison was taking a hold on me as a sharp pain stabbed my shoulder and penetrated down to my fingers. Stifling a moan, I turned my attention to the window. The lights were soon behind us as the large road turned smaller, weaving in and out of a hilly landscape. Finally, a lake appeared.

"Almost there," Julio whispered. "Hold on, Celyse."

My heart rate had accelerated. My hands grew clammy. I needed to pull it together until we got to Traeliorn's home. He was my only hope for survival.

Manny directed the automobile down a road that looked much different than the others. There were no lights and no homes. I wondered if we had taken a wrong turn until a small solitary cottage came into view. It was nestled back into the trees, as if it belonged to the woods. A stone path circled the perimeter, and vibrant floral shrubs surrounded the facade. Soft yellow light shone through the small windows, and a thin trail of nearly colorless smoke came from the tall, skinny stone chimney.

A fae definitely lived there.

Manny coasted to a stop. He turned to face us. "Now what?" he asked in a whisper. "Do we go in stealth mode, or storm the cottage?"

"Manny, this is not a joke," Julio snapped.

A weak laugh escaped Manny's lips. "I know, I'm sorry. I'm freaking out, and joking is my go-to in these situations."

While Julio calmed his friend, I came up with a plan. Even though I was a high princess of Faevenly, I did not know how I would be received by a fae who had left and was living in secret in the human realm. But then I reminded myself that even though I was out of my element, I needed to not forget my status. I was Celyse Strong, of House Strong, a high princess with great stature no matter what realm.

"I will announce myself," I declared with determined purpose. "And request assistance." I drew in a deep breath, head held high, and shoulders pulled back. "I will not be denied."

I got out of the automobile and headed for the front door. Julio stayed close by my side and Manny flanked me on the other. I was grateful for their protective positioning because I had no idea what kind of fae Traeliorn was or if he would even help me. Fae could switch from seelie to unseelie in a blink. I hoped he would be more inclined toward seelie.

The closer we got to the thick arch-shaped wooden door, the easier it was to see the magnificent detail. Intricate vine carvings with flowers and birds lined the edges. A huge stone knocker with flecks of gold and silver filled the middle of the door.

"Now that's a door," Julio muttered.

I reached for the knocker but stopped short when a searing pain shot through me, filling every inch of my body. My vision blurred. My knees buckled. Julio grabbed me as I crumpled to the ground.

"Celyse!"

His yell fell on me, and I could not respond. My throat was closing, my vision reducing to tiny splotches. I gasped for air, struggling to fill my lungs, but nothing was getting through.

The poison was killing me.

9

JULIO

Celyse's arm fell. Her legs buckled. I caught her before she hit the ground and was shocked to see her face had gone stark white, her mouth wide as she gasped for air.

Manny pounded on the door. "Help!"

The door jerked open revealing a tall thin man with long white hair and a full long beard clad in khaki pants and a long-sleeved white T-shirt. His mouth fell open when he saw Celyse.

"A daughter of Strong Haven?" His gaze swept over to me. "Bring her in!"

I carried Celyse over the threshold, following the man to the couch. He motioned for me to put her down, then shoved me out of his way.

"Get back," he ordered. He hovered over Celyse, peeling open one eyelid, then the other. "What happened to her?"

"She was poisoned," I rushed out. "By an arrow when she crossed over."

"Thunderation," he muttered. "Poisoned by a fae arrow?" He zeroed in on me. "Where?"

I pointed at the spot. "There, on her upper arm by her shoulder. I treated it with a paste of khotura."

The man raised her sleeve and quickly unraveled the dressings. The small cut had grown into a long and deep gooey gash and the black streaks that had looked faint at my house had now taken over her skin so completely, her arm looked charred.

Manny sucked in a deep breath. "Jesus," he whispered.

The man hurried from the room. He came back a few seconds later with a syringe filled with a green liquid. "Hold up her sleeve," he ordered.

I did as he asked and watched him slip the needle with a squelch into the middle of her wound. He emptied the contents slowly and carefully. When he finished, he set the syringe on the table, then whipped his attention to me and Manny. He didn't say anything for a while as he studied us with a keen stare.

Breaking the tense silence, I asked, "Is she going to be okay?"

He rubbed his long beard, eyeing us, then said abruptly, "Yes, now be gone. You two are not welcomed here." He grabbed our arms and started pushing us toward the door.

"Hey!" I called out, digging in my heels.

"What the hell, man?" Manny yelled.

"Matters of Faevenly do not concern humans," he said, his grip firm for an old guy.

Having been in plenty of soccer skirmishes, I knew exactly what to do. I kicked my right foot out, hooked it around the fae's ankle, then shoved his upper body while sweeping his leg out from under him. He tumbled to the ground.

I shuffled back, feet wide, hands fisted, ready to kick his ass if I had to. "I'm not leaving Celyse," I gritted between clenched teeth. "Got it?"

"Me neither," Manny tacked on, joining my fighting posture.

The man hopped to his feet quickly. He considered me and Manny. "How are you two even acquainted with the daughter of Strong Haven?"

I had no idea what it meant to be a daughter of Strong Haven, but I did know how I felt about Celyse. There was no way I was losing her again. Especially not to a crazy old man. "She's my friend," I answered.

"Yeah," Manny added. "She's our friend, you psycho."

The guy backed away. He stroked his beard for a few long seconds, watching us suspiciously. He moved to an oversized brown leather chair and sat. He motioned to two chairs across from the couch where Celyse lay. "You may stay until she wakes. Then you two, and she, must go."

"Fine," I said. I slipped off my backpack and Manny and I took a seat. "As soon as she wakes up, we're outta here."

Trey Leto sat back and folded his hands together. He reminded me of the old hippie dudes you see around the most eclectic parts of Austin. The kind of dudes who recycled everything, smoked homegrown weed, never wore deodorant, and jammed to Willie Nelson. Except he didn't look like a happy hippie dude, but more like a pissed off hippie dude. With purple-colored eyes.

"How long?" I asked, worried that whatever he gave her wouldn't work. "How long will it take for that green stuff to work?"

He kept his stare on me. "I am not sure. But seeing as we have the time, answer me this." He leaned forward. "How is a daughter of Strong Haven in the human realm?"

I let out an incredulous laugh. "You're being a total asshole but now you want answers? She said you were a fae and you could help her. So what gives?"

After a short stare-off, he finally said, "You may call me Leto."

"Okay." I rubbed my hands on my jeans. "That's a start. I'm Julio and this is Manny."

Manny raised his hand in greeting but kept quiet. Which was a good idea. Old Leto didn't look like he was in the mood for games. I decided to give him only bare minimum information. Celyse could fill him in on whatever she wanted when she woke up.

"Well, to answer your question about how Celyse got here, I was home when a shimmery blast filled my room. She ran through it and right into me. She had a note with your name on it and told me I needed to help her find you. That she needed you for something." I stopped and stared at Celyse, noticing her breathing had steadied. "Not just with her wound, but with something else."

"Do you know what the 'something else' is?" he asked.

"No," I shook my head. "I don't."

"Hmm," he muttered. With his hands still folded, he raised his index fingers and started tapping them together. "Do the two of you have the slightest idea who this young lady is?"

"Well," I offered, "like you keep saying, I guess she is the daughter of Strong Haven."

"She is indeed, young man. And if you knew what that meant, you would be shaking in your shoes right now. You both would."

An audible swallow came from Manny as he looked from Leto to Celyse and then to me. Before I could say anything else, a howling from outside pierced the silence.

Leto's brows shot up. "Wolfbeasts."

"Wolf what?" Manny asked, clutching his armrests and looking terrified.

"Beasts," Leto answered in a low voice. He rose to his feet and walked to the nearest wall. He placed his hands flat on the surface. "Wolfbeasts are killer wolves that are bound to the Strongs. If such a beast is in the human realm, it is most certainly searching for this daughter. To what end, I do not know. But I would rather not find out. At least not whilst the princess is in this state. Now, nobody speak while we hide."

Hide? And did he say *princess*? My gaze drifted over

to Celyse. She had told me a lot about herself, but nothing about being a princess.

Manny sat rigid while I held my breath, watching as Leto kept his hands pressed against the wall and started whispering in a strange language. One that sounded a lot like Gaelic.

Gandalf, Manny mouthed to me with wide eyes.

I shushed him with a glare when another round of howling came from outside. This time, the wailing was so close I thought the wolfbeasts were right outside the front door. Manny looked ready to jump right out of his skin, and I couldn't blame him. The idea of a pack of killer wolves bursting through the door and mauling us to death had me freaked. And I didn't freak easily.

Another howl sounded, but this time it was farther in the distance. Finally, there was silence. Leto kept his palms on the wall a few seconds more before dropping his hands. "They are gone, for now."

"For now?" I asked.

"Yes, for now." He narrowed his stare on Celyse. "If they want their daughter, they will be back. The Strongs always finish their jobs."

Manny let out a nervous laugh. "That sounds, um, terrifying."

"It should, because it is," Leto warned.

Leto returned to his seat and an awkward silence smothered us. I rubbed the back of my neck, wondering what the old guy had done that sent the wolfbeasts away. As the minutes ticked by, my curiosity grew.

"So, um, what exactly did you do with your hands, and what was that chanting?" I asked.

He hesitated before saying, "Something your feeble mind could not even begin to understand."

Feeble mind? What an asshole. I had seen my mom chant and use her hands on people and even on things dozens of times. I thought for sure he was doing something similar, channeling his aura energy or something, but how did that hide us?

A soft moaning came from Celyse. She sat up slowly and brought her hand to her arm, patted it, and then moved it around. She looked from me to Manny to Leto. She smiled. "Traeliorn Letornis."

"You may address me as Leto. And you are Celyse, daughter of Strong Haven." He bowed his head in reverence. "Your visit is most unexpected."

My mind kept replaying Leto's words about Celyse's family being ruthless and cunning, and maybe *they* were, but she wasn't. There was no way. I had spent a lot of time with her and was a pretty good judge of character. Plus, her aura didn't give off that vibe at all, and I was never wrong about someone's aura. At least, I'd never been wrong before.

Celyse kept her chin slightly raised. "My visit here is as unexpected to me as it is to you."

Leto raised a brow. "How so?"

"It was not my plan," she explained.

"Whose plan was it then?" Leto asked, leaning forward a bit.

"A young girl and boy pleaded for my help, telling

me the human realm and the faerie realm were at risk, and that it had something to do with the shimmers. They told me you could help me discover the truth."

"The shimmers?" he asked.

"Yes," she answered. "The shimmers."

Leto stroked his beard, then said, "Fae can never lie, so I believe what you say is true." He leaned forward and narrowed his eyes a bit. "But you have now entangled me in your muddle, and I do not take that exposure lightly. The wolfbeasts were practically at my door this night looking for you."

Celyse considered him for a moment, as if unsure how to respond. "My apologies. I assure you, that was not my intent. But I was told you could help. Was that incorrect information?"

He drew in a deep breath. "It was not incorrect. But there is much here that needs my consideration, and it is late in the evening. I must retire for the night with my thoughts." He arose from his chair. "I advise the three of you to stay until morning, seeing as the wolf-beasts are roaming the area. My home is triple warded and safe. The sofa is comfortable and there are linens in the closet at the end of the hallway. Next to the linen closet you will find the washroom. I shall see you three in the morning. Please make yourselves comfortable."

The tall and mysterious fae left the room and I found myself relieved he was gone. I got up and sat next to Celyse. "Do you know that guy? Because he's a real jerk."

"No, I do not know him. But I did warn you about

fae. We are lucky he has agreed to let us stay here." She moved her arm around, testing its mobility.

"Can I look at that?" I asked, curious to see what had happened to her wound.

She stilled her arm. "You may."

I rolled up her sleeve. The black on her arm was gone. Only a thin cut remained. "That's remarkable," I said, lowering her sleeve.

"Um, Julio?" Manny cut in. "I, uh, need to talk to you."

"I'll be right back," I said to Celyse.

"Of course," she said.

Manny and I ducked away to a nook off the side of the living room that had a rocking chair and a wall filled with shelves of antique looking books. Manny huddled in close.

"Dude, what is happening right now?" He asked in a whisper. "These people are fae, something called a wolfbeast is out to get us, and our realm is in danger? And this house is triple warded? This is way beyond any witchyness I'm used to. Way beyond."

Manny was right. Even by my standards, this was a lot. "I know. I feel the same way. I'm sorry I got you messed up in all this."

Manny started chewing his thumb. "I say we bail. When everyone is asleep, we get the hell out of here."

Rubbing the back of my neck, I snuck a glance at Celyse. She was sitting on the couch, her hands wrapped together on her lap, and she looked lost—

scared even. She needed my help. And my mom had always said helping people was our duty.

Nuestro deber.

"I'm serious," Manny urged. "We are out of here when everyone falls asleep. I mean it. Okay?"

I had no intention of leaving Celyse but didn't want to break it to Manny right then and there. I needed him to stay calm. I figured I'd let him know after a night's rest. "Fine, okay. But let's at least stay here tonight. We can leave in the morning. Sound good?"

He went back to chewing his thumb as he considered my suggestion. "Fine," he said, giving in. I could tell he wasn't thrilled at all to be staying the night at a fae's house. And I couldn't blame him. I didn't want to be here either.

"Let's get the blankets and pillows," I said.

We grabbed three blankets and three pillows from the linen closet, then returned to Celyse.

She took what she needed and set her things on the couch. She eyed the hallway. "Excuse me while I visit the washroom."

When she left for the bathroom, I surveyed the space. "Celyse gets the couch," I said to Manny. "I can move the coffee table and bunk here on the rug. You can take the floor over by the reading nook."

Manny nodded. "And tomorrow we're gone. I don't care how hot she is or how much you're into her."

"Hey, come on now," I said.

Manny yanked a pillow and blanket from my hand.

"I'm serious. Don't think I haven't noticed the way you look at her. Or the way she looks at you."

I hadn't told him about how she used to appear in my room at night, and I didn't think it was smart to do so now. It might send him over the edge. But then the last part of what he said registered. "How does she look at me?"

Manny raised his pillow like he wanted to throttle me, but lowered it when Celyse came back. She made her way to the couch and spread out her blanket. She leaned the backpack against the sofa, wrapped her cloak around her nightgown, then her blanket around her cloak, and settled in for the night facing into the couch and away from us.

"See you in the morning," I said to Manny.

"Goodnight," he said, mumbling about how he didn't think he'd get any sleep as he made his way to his corner.

I turned off the lights except for a small lamp on the far side of the room, then slid the coffee table over so I could lie on the floor. Crackling from the dying embers in the fireplace drifted in the air while an awkward silence settled over the room.

Celyse turned and looked down at me. "Before I fall asleep, I want you to know that I appreciate every-thing you have done for me. I would not be alive right now if not for you."

"You're welcome, but it wasn't me. It was Leto. He gave you a shot of some green medicine."

"I know. I saw it." Her gaze drifted to the remnants

of the liquid in the syringe on the coffee table. "There are healing waters in Faevenly called the Green Falls. The water falls clear into a pool where the algae and other vegetation are so green, it turns the water green. The healing properties from the undergrowth are so powerful, it is said that a cup of the liquid can bring a person back to life. But the falls are hidden. Only those deemed worthy by the spirits can find it, and it only heals physical injuries."

"That's amazing," I said, imagining the magical falls.

"It is." She hesitated before adding, "I am alive because you stopped the spread of the poison and got me here quickly. I am forever grateful."

Her long hair spilled down over the couch. I found my eyes drifting from her incredible green eyes across her perfect pink lips, and before I knew it, my gaze moved down her neck to her cleavage. When I realized what I was doing, I snapped my attention back to her face. The last thing I wanted was for her to think I was some sort of creep.

"You're welcome," I whispered. "I'm glad I was there for you."

"I am glad too."

I thought of asking her why she had stopped visiting me, but before I could say anything, she added, "Goodnight, Julio."

"Goodnight, Celyse."

She turned to face the back of the couch and pulled the blanket up over her shoulders. I stayed on my back and watched the shadow from the lamp spread across the ceiling. There was so much I wanted to ask her and say to her, but she clearly didn't want to talk. Maybe she was still not feeling well and didn't want to tell me. Maybe she needed to rest. Or maybe she just wasn't into me anymore.

While the night crawled by, my every thought was consumed with her. No matter what she was going to face, I was going to stay by her side.

No matter what.

10

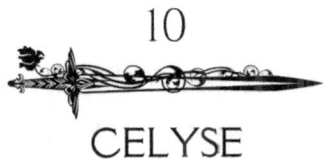

CELYSE

Lying on the couch, I thought of the conversation I had heard between Julio and Manny in the far corner of the room. Unbeknownst to them, fae have heightened senses and superior abilities in comparison to humans. We could run at high speed, see with precision and clarity, and we also had the ability to hear the slightest sound and the most faraway conversation.

Manny wanted to leave. Julio agreed. And they planned to leave in the morning. I could not blame them. I had put them in grave danger. Plus, I had stopped seeing Julio without saying a farewell. Clearly, he had moved on like I hoped, but secretly feared.

A sharp pang filled my heart as sorrow fell down on me. My affection for a human had been nothing more than a fanciful whimsy, just as Malena had said, and I felt foolish. Yet I was here. And this world, as well as mine, was in some sort of jeopardy. I needed to stay and see what I could find out so I could relay the information to Mother and Father. Strong Haven would need to know of any impending danger so that it could prepare. It was the least I could do for my wrongdoings. I hoped Mother would go easy on me when I returned home.

With everyone settled in for sleep, I told myself it did not matter that Julio was leaving. He was a human and his kind have long been enemies to the fae anyway. It was foolish for me to think anything else could come of us. Especially since nothing could ever come of us. And yet, my thoughts filled with him as I slowly drifted to sleep.

———

THE SOUND OF STRUMMING HARPS TUGGED ME AWAKE. The crackling and popping from the fireplace beckoned me to open my eyes. When I did, I found myself snuggled into the couch while music played in the room. I laid there for a while, wondering how long I had slept. Lifting my head, I noticed sunlight from a late sun streaming through the windows. Had I slept all day? I reached for my shoulder, rubbing the spot where I had been injured. A slight throbbing remained, which was strange since fae healed quickly. I wondered if perhaps I needed more water from the Green Falls.

Then I remembered Julio and Manny saying they would be leaving in the morning. I sat up and eyed the spot where Julio had been, but he was gone. Glancing over at where Manny had slept, I saw his place empty as well. I blinked away a sting of tears, telling myself it was for the best, when Julio walked into the room.

"Good morning," he said. "Or I guess I should say, good afternoon."

My heart leapt as a smile tugged at my lips. He had stayed. "Good afternoon."

He pointed at the spot where I had been injured, his face taking on an expression of concern. "How's your arm?"

Trying to hide my relief at seeing him, I said, "It is fine. Thank you. What is the hour?" I glanced at the windows. "Is the sun setting?"

"It's about five, and yes, the sun is setting."

I stood and drew my cloak around my nightdress, nearly forgetting it was what I had been wearing this whole time. Earlier, I had been so weak from being poisoned that traipsing about in my nightclothes had been the least of my concerns. But now, feeling back to my normal self, a blush of embarrassment overcame me.

"I must use the washroom. Please excuse me," I said.

Taking my leave, I quickly made my way to clean up. There, on a counter next to the water basin, sat a pile of clothes. On top was a note written in swirly letters.

Trousers and a tunic for the Daughter of Strong Haven. I hope they fit. TL

"Thank you, Leto," I whispered, grateful for his sensitivity to my attire.

Picking through the two-piece outfit, I found a pair of thick, dark blue trousers and a white long-sleeved tunic with a V-neck collar. I rubbed my hands over the scratchy blue fabric, not believing I was in the human realm about to don the customary attire. It was not the refined threads I was used to, but it was marvelous nonetheless.

Setting the outfit back on the counter, I stripped out of my nightdress. I had familiarized myself with the washroom the night before, so knew where everything was. As I finished washing up, I noticed a long thin scar across my shoulder. I moved closer to the mirror, rubbing the raised flesh with my thumb, surprised it hadn't gone away yet.

"Strange," I mumbled.

Dismissing my shoulder, I took a closer look at the clothes. Eager to try them out, I slipped on the tunic. The fabric was cool and light and mostly soft. Then I examined the trousers. I had never worn trousers before, and I could not help but chuckle to myself as I thought of what Malena would say about wearing something so crude. I did not think she would like it at all.

I slipped one leg through the opening, then the other, then lifted them up to my waist. After pulling up the bulky zipper and fastening the clunky button, I walked around for a bit. The trousers were stiff and cumbersome, squeezing my body tightly. The sensation was horrible and magnificent all at the same time.

I turned around and looked at my backside in the mirror. "Oh my," I muttered. The fabric left little to the imagination as it hugged my curves tightly. I thought of

Julio, wondering if he would like what he saw. My cheeks flushed at the thought, and I forced myself to focus.

With everything donned, I went back to the living room and saw Leto, Julio, and Manny sitting around a tray of fruit and pastries.

So Manny had stayed too. I had no idea what had caused the pair to have a change of heart, but I was glad for it.

"Good afternoon," Leto said. He offered me a glass of orange juice. "Please help yourself to the food."

"Good afternoon," I replied, taking the juice and a piece of bread and sitting in a chair. "Thank you very much for the clothing and the food and drink."

"You are most welcome. I hope my selections are to your liking and fit well," Leto said.

"They are more than suitable," I said, noticing Julio and Manny had on the same type of trousers as the ones I wore.

Leto steepled his hands together and studied me. "There is much to discuss. And now is as good a time as any to expand on what you told me last night, if that is okay with you."

"It is okay with me," I nodded.

"Your appearance in the human realm is most unexpected," he said. "Do tell, what is happening in Faevenly that has brought you here? I have not been there in some time."

This was it. My chance to tell him, and even Julio

and Manny, what was going on so I could get help. I set my things on the table.

"Something is amiss with the shimmers," I began.

Leto raised his hand to silence me. "Is it permissible for you to speak openly before these two humans?"

Fae were not only dangerous, but private. Our secrets ran deep, our very existence hidden, but I knew in my heart that I could trust Julio. He had helped save me. And if he trusted Manny, a lifelong friend, then that was good enough for me. Besides, I was breaking every rule in Faevenly by being here anyway.

"Yes," I nodded. "It is permissible."

"Very well," Leto said. "Explain then what you mean by something being amiss with the shimmers."

I cleared my throat. "The son of Lind compelled me and almost killed me because he wanted to know what my family was doing with the shimmers."

"Someone tried to kill you?" Julio asked, cutting in with anger brewing in his brown eyes.

Leto joined the sentiment, scooting to the edge of his chair. "The son of Lind? But the Linds are your ally."

"Yes. They are. Or they were." I could have said more about where Jorn Lind and I were and what we were doing when he attacked me, but did not want Julio to know it was courting season and I would be betrothed in twelve moon cycles. Not that it mattered —he and I could never be—but some things I wanted to keep to myself.

"Um," Manny cleared his throat. "I get the whole thing about some guy trying to kill you. But what is a compel and what is a shimmer?"

"Good questions," Julio said. "We should probably start from the beginning so he and I can understand everything." He kept his gaze on me as if we were the only ones in the room and asked, "You're a princess?"

His tone was laced with emotion—hurt, betrayal, and surprise because I had not told him that about myself. After all our visits, and sharing a great deal, there was much he did not know about me.

Luckily, Leto cut in. "Perhaps, my lady, I should provide these humans with some background information before we proceed further."

"Of course." I nodded, grateful for Leto's offer because I felt horrible for keeping things from Julio. "Some background information would do well right about now."

Leto gave Julio and Manny his full attention. "Faevenly is the fae realm that overlays the human realm." He placed one hand on top of the other but kept them slightly separated. "In between our realms is the stratus, sort of like a thin connective tissue between our worlds. Shimmers are portals. They allow passage between the two realms."

"Like an Oreo," Manny said. "The realms are the cookies; the stratus is the white stuff."

"Really, dude," Julio said. "Food?"

Leto considered the analogy with a smile. "Actually, that is not bad, Manny." He placed his hands on his lap and sat back, as if settling in for a long tale. "Thousands of years ago, fae and humans interacted peacefully and regularly, traveling freely through the "white stuff." We would come here, and your kind would go there. But then, as all civilizations do, one wanted to dominate the other. In this case, it was the humans."

"The humans?" Julio asked.

"Yes," Leto answered. "Humans coveted what the fae had— our resources, our land, our entire way of life. Thus, a war ensued. As you can imagine, the fae, far superior to humans, were the victors. To prevent anything like that from ever happening again, the fae gathered all the shimmers and stored them in a location in Faevenly. Torch Lake, specifically. When the task was completed, the fae wiped the human realm of all memory of the war and of the fae by using a glamour."

"A glamour?" Julio asked.

"A glamour is the fae magic that alters what a person can see and even remember," Leto explained. "Used on a large scale and distilled into a liquid, a glamour can even alter an entire population. That is what the fae did, and continue to do, to the human realm."

"All of humanity was and is...mind-wiped?" Julio asked, his brow stitched together as if trying to understand everything. "But how did y'all do that? How is something like that even possible?"

"The kelpie were used," I answered. "They projected their glamour into the human waterways.

Every human is touched by water every single day. So the glamour holds."

"A kelpie?" Manny asked.

"A kelpie is a shape-shifter that lives in our waters," I answered. "They are part fae and part water horse."

An audible gulp came from Manny. "Okkay."

"What does it mean to compel?" Julio asked.

"Like the word itself suggests," Leto explained, "to compel someone is to force someone to do something with a verbal command that renders the person powerless to disobey."

"Wow. That's, uh, pretty intense," Julio replied, rubbing his hands on his legs.

"Indeed, it is. And it is not done lightly," Leto said, pausing for a few seconds while everything sank in. "Now, back to the shimmers. The Great Shimmer War brought about significant change in Faevenly. The seasonal courts were abolished as the seelie and unseelie fae came together against the humans in ways never imagined."

"Uh...what and what?" Manny asked.

Giving Leto a break, I took over the explanation. "In the most basic of terms, seelie fae are considered kindly; unseelie are, shall we say, not as kindly. As fae, we can shift between the two."

"What are y'all?" Manny asked.

"My family is mostly unseelie," I answered.

"I am seelie," Leto answered.

Julio glanced at me. "Oh."

Seeing Julio's changed expression, I felt like I need

to expand on what I had said. "It is not that unseelie are unkind. We are simply stricter and more formal. But the Great Shimmer War brought seelie and unseelie together, as Leto explained. And we still are. We live harmoniously divided into provinces, and each province has a ruling house. My family name is Strong, and my province is Strong Haven. We are the ruling province above all others."

Manny shifted to Julio and said, "Above all."

"Yeah, I heard that," Julio uttered.

I waited for Julio and Manny to ask further questions, but they had none. In fact, they rather looked shocked. "Is that enough background information? Does it all make sense?"

"Yes," Manny squeaked out. He cleared his throat, returning his voice to its normal octave. "I mean, yes."

With that part out of the way, I continued with my explanation for why I had crossed over. "After Jorn Lind threatened my life, a young boy and girl came to me and told me the shimmers were at risk, as well as the human and fae realms." I motioned to Leto. "They gave me a piece of parchment with your name on it and said you could help me. Now I am here."

Leto stroked his white beard for several long seconds while the harp music continued playing in the house. I wondered where it was coming from. Finally, Leto spoke. "Did you tell the High King or High Queen about the note?"

"I did not."

"Did you tell anyone?"

"No."

"Did you tell anyone you were coming here? Other than the boy and girl?"

"No."

"Good." He rose from his seat and circled the room, stroking his beard. "My lady, there are goings-on in Faevenly you are not aware of."

Goings-on? I did not know what he meant, but from his tone and the serious expression on his face, whatever was "going on" was not good. "What do you mean?"

Leto returned to his seat. With his long silver hair and long silver beard, clad in human attire, only the pointed ears poking through his silver strands gave away his identity. And his violet eyes.

"I know what is happening with the shimmers," he half-whispered.

Julio and Manny shifted in their seats to give Leto their full attention. I did too. Even the music paused, as if giving Leto proper deference.

The tall fae drew in a breath. "There is a province using the shimmers to cross over and take humans, unbeknownst to the other provinces, and forcing said humans into slave labor, mining a rare and precious stone that is said to be all-powerful."

He let his words sink in, giving me time to react, but I had nothing to say. I was stunned.

"What?" Julio asked, ending the silence. "Someone is taking humans and making us slaves so we can mine stones?"

"Yes," Leto said, his face turning into a scowl. "But these are not ordinary stones. The stones, in powder form, give a rush of super strength. Nothing can hurt the user after ingesting the powder. The effects wear off after a few days, depending on the person, but last long enough for a battle or two."

Tingles dashed across my skin as I thought of another province invading Strong Haven. "Is this province planning an uprising?"

Leto nodded. "You could call it that."

Fear and anger surged inside of me. "If someone is planning an uprising against my family, I need to know. Which province is responsible? Who is to blame? Tell me at once who these vile monsters are!"

Leto kept a steady gaze on me. He lowered his hands from his beard, placing them on his lap. He leaned forward. "Strong Haven is the vile monster."

I froze as his words worked their way through me, chilling me to my core. "What?" I paused, grappling with accusation. "What do you mean? My mother and father are the ruling house. How can—" I let my words trail off. "Are you saying that is *why* they are the ruling house?" I stood. "Impossible!"

"My lady, I beg your pardon, but it is indeed most possible. It is also true."

"My mother and father rule with strength, but also with honor and fairness! What you claim is nothing short of treason!"

Leto raised his hands up a little. "I am making no claim. I am simply stating what I know to be true." And then he added. "Have you ever considered the possibility that your family is...the villain?"

"Absurd!" My blood boiled and my body shook with anger. As much as I wanted to argue with this treacherous fae, I did not think it would get me anywhere. I was surrounded by strangers, in a realm not my own. I needed to pull myself together.

"Please excuse me," I said abruptly.

As calmly as possible, I made my way to the front door and outside. The last remnants of sunshine were peeking through the tall oak trees, and between the branches I caught the glint of the waning light reflecting off the lake. I drew in a deep breath, letting the smell of dirt and leaves fill my lungs and erase the sinking feeling in my gut as I took off toward the water. I refused to believe my parents were involved in something so heinous. They were strict rulers, but they were honorable. There had to be something else I did not know.

"Celyse!" I turned to see Julio coming my way, hands shoved in his pockets. "Can I walk with you?"

I wanted nothing more than to be with him and spend time with him, but now I was the unkindly unseelie girl with a ruthless mother and father who were kidnapping humans to stay in power. Even though I refused to believe any of it, a cloud of doubt had been cast on me. He probably feared me now. Or even hated me.

"You may join me if you wish."

We walked through the trees and to the grassy

downslope that led to a wooden dock. The magnificent view reminded me of Torch Lake… and the shimmers. Were my mother and father truly involved in such deception? And if so, is that what Jorn Lind was asking me about? Was Jorn Lind the good, while we were the bad?

We stood at the end of the wooden walkway, and I stared out at the calm waters, thinking there was nothing calm about what I was feeling inside.

"That was quite a lot of information back there," Julio said.

"It was."

"Are you, you know, handling it okay?"

Doubt and skepticism along with hurt and betrayal coursed through me. Along with anger. I let out a sigh. "My feelings are all over the place," I admitted.

He turned to face me. He had the most perfect full lips, high chiseled cheekbones, and a strong jaw. The setting sun cast a ray of light across his face, showcasing the most magnificent mahogany eyes with flecks of gold and amber. They reminded me of the richness of the earth. And with the sun shining down on his tan skin, he looked like an earthly god.

He held out his hand. "Since you're a princess and all, I'm thinking I should ask your permission to hold your hand. In my family, human touch helps when people need grounding. And right now, after that conversation, I feel like you could use some grounding."

I studied the strong hand he offered me, longing to take it. "You are not afraid of me?"

He shrugged. "Afraid? Nah. I know a lot of people with messed up families."

"Messed up?"

"You know. Families that aren't perfect."

I had thought my family was perfect, but now I did not know. I placed my hand in his. He held it in a firm yet gentle grip, then he placed his other hand on top. With my heightened fae senses, I detected a warm and strong yet peaceful vibration coming from him. It set my heart pounding and my stomach tumbling.

"You didn't tell me you were a princess," he said.

I looked away for a few seconds, searching for what to say, thinking whatever I offered would not be adequate. "I wanted to tell you but believed it best that I did not."

He kept my hand between his. "I'm sorry you felt that way."

"Me too," I whispered.

Standing before him, hardly believing we were together, I took all of him in—the smell of fresh soap laced with spice, the different colors of golden brown in each strand of hair, the perfect peaks of his full lips.

He undid me in ways I did not understand. A deep longing pulled me toward him, and he to me. I wanted more than ever to give him my first kiss, to wrap my arms around his neck and feel his lips on mine, but being together would mean certain death for him.

I pulled my hand out from his and moved back. "I cannot."

"Oh," he said. "Yeah, of course. I'm sorry. I didn't mean to, uh—"

"Julio! Celyse!" Leto shouted, breaking the awkwardness of the moment. "Come back!"

"What now?" I muttered.

We hurried back to the house and found Leto and Manny standing around the backpack. Manny pointed. "It's alive."

The black fabric was glowing, and a low hum was coming from within. I studied it curiously. "I have never seen anything like that, but I also do not have a lot of experience with shimmers," I said, wondering what was happening to it.

Leto grabbed a blanket and draped it over the pack. "The shimmer is here, but a trace of it must still be in Faevenly. Whoever is looking for you is near the spot where you crossed over. In theory, that is."

"That's, uh, bad, right?" Manny asked.

"Very bad," Leto answered.

"We should get the pack out of the house," Julio suggested.

"Good idea." Leto retrieved the pack, went outside with it, and came back a few minutes later empty-handed. "It is safe and secure."

"Thank you," I said. "But now what do we do?"

Leto stayed locked in his thoughts for a bit before he spoke again. "I have to confer with my sources. But to do that, I will need to leave for a bit."

"Fine. We will all go," I said with a nod. "I seek the truth and I want answers."

He let out a laugh. "Oh no, my lady. If my sources see you, they will shoot arrows first, then ask questions later."

"Is that so?" I asked, not sure if I should be flattered or highly insulted that I was so ill-revered.

"Yes, that is so."

I crossed my arms, considering the situation. "Well, if I am at risk here, and at risk there, then it does not matter then, does it?"

Julio shifted as he glanced at me with a look that was equal parts worried and impressed. "Celyse has a point. Danger is danger. And I always say, there's safety in numbers. So I'm with Celyse. We should all go."

"Whoa, what?" Manny asked. He looked at Julio with his mouth hung open a little. "He just said they'd shoot arrows, dude."

"I heard him," Julio said. "But it's Celyse's call. If she wants to go, then we're going. All of us."

I flashed Julio a look of appreciation before pressing Leto. "Well?" I asked, waiting for his response."What say you?"

"I say, fine. I will grab you a cap. Maybe no one will recognize you."

"A cap?"

"A cap is a certain style of hat," Leto explained. "You will understand when I get it."

Leto's automobile was much bigger than Manny's. The tires were bigger, the length was longer, and there was much more room in the back where I sat with Julio. It also smelled better. We drove out of the wooded lakeside area and onto the roads as darkness took over the sky. Fidgeting with the head covering called a cap that hugged my head tightly, I wondered how such a thing could hide my identity.

"Here," Julio said, reaching out to me. "Wear it a little lower in the front. Like this." He gripped the extended portion of the cap and nestled it down a bit. "Does that feel okay?"

His fingertips brushed against my cheek and ear, and tingles of desire rushed over me. "Yes," I whispered. "It feels fine."

His eyes lingered on mine, and I do not even think he realized he licked his lips. "It's a good look on you," he said.

My heart skipped a beat as my entire body grew warm. "Thank you."

Leto cleared his throat from the driver's seat. "We are headed to a late-night bakery that some of my friends from Faevenly own. They keep tabs on the motherland way more than I do."

"Where are your friends from? What province?" I asked.

"I have no idea. The fae who live in the human realm rarely speak of such things. Here, we are not from provinces."

"Then how do you know we can trust them?"

Leto glanced over his shoulder at me. "I can trust

them. Whether or not they can trust you remains to be seen."

11

JULIO

When I was little, my mom always said that if I was ever in danger, I had to trust myself, that I had what it took to get out of whatever situation I was in.

"You have a powerful mind, *Mijo*. So powerful, that if you call upon it to help you, it will."

"Really?" I remembered asking, excited to use my mind to help me do things like jump over fences, fly off roofs, and lift cars with my bare hands.

"Yes, really," she had replied, touching the cross she had given me for my church confirmation. "You also have the power of God and his angels. Never forget that."

I was never able to jump over fences or fly off roofs, or any of that stuff, and I had the broken bones to prove it. But as I grew older, her words took on a different meaning and were less about physical things and more about trusting that no matter what, I'd be okay. That if I was ever in trouble, things would somehow work out for me.

Sitting next to Celyse as we drove to a bakery to

meet some fae who could help her had me tingling all over...and thinking of trouble.

Something wasn't right.

I rubbed my shirt where my cross hung and stared ahead at the road, telling myself that going to a bakery was harmless. That a bakery was probably the safest place to meet someone.

"What is it?" Celyse asked in a low voice, catching on to my worried mood.

"Nothing, I'm only... thinking."

Manny turned to me from the front passenger seat with a look of terror on his face. "Thinking thinking? Orrr... witchy thinking?"

Celyse tilted her head at me. "Manny has used the word witchy now twice when referring to you. Are you one?"

Leto angled his rearview mirror down so he could see me. "You are a witch?"

"No, I'm not a—"

My mom's Selena ring tone cut my sentence short. I pulled the phone out of my back pocket, declined the call, then texted that I was in the middle of something and would have to call her back.

"*Bidi Bidi Bom Bom,*" Manny said. "That was your mom calling."

I rubbed the back of my neck. "Yeah."

Leto kept peering at me. "What is happening?"

"I get these bad feelings sometimes," I said.

Manny's words spilled out in a panic. "So does his

mom. And every time, something awful happens. Like, people die. I think we should pull over."

"Manny's right," I agreed. "We should pull over so I can check in with her and see what's up."

Leto considered the situation. "I will stop the car." He put his blinker on, slowing down to turn off the dark two-lane street.

Celyse angled toward me. "What does that mean? To get these bad feelings?"

Before I could answer, a car slammed into us, the force so powerful we flipped into the air and started rolling. My seatbelt tightened around me as metal creaked and glass shattered. My arms and legs flailed before we rocked to a stop right side up.

I sat stunned, as if I'd been pummeled by a wrecking ball, my ears buzzing with a high pitch. I glanced at Celyse, unable to say anything for a few long seconds.

"Hey," I finally managed. "You okay?"

She nodded slowly. "I think so."

Her eyes met mine and she gasped. "Your head is bleeding."

My hand shook as I brought it up to my forehead, swiping away at thick wetness, but not feeling any pain. "I'm fine." I glanced up at the front seat and saw Manny holding his face.

"Oh my God," Manny groaned.

"Is everyone all right?" Leto asked.

My mom's ring tone sounded again and my tingling

amped up. We were in danger. "Everyone out of the car! Now!"

Celyse fumbled with her door, then slammed her shoulder into it with a grunt. "I cannot!"

Mine opened with a hard push and a metallic screech. I clambered out then reached back in for her, unbuckling her seatbelt. "Slide over here."

She scooted over to me and reached for my hand. She took it with a firm grip, and I steadied her while she scrambled out and into my arms. I held her tight while intense emotions filled me— longing, affection, and the fiercest need to protect her. We separated slowly, eyes locked, before Leto and Manny joined us.

"There's the car that hit us," Leto said, indicating at a black truck stopped maybe twenty yards away. The headlights were off, but the engine rumbled low.

Blood dripped from Manny's mouth. "Hey! You hit us, you asshole!"

The small two-lane street was empty, yet my senses kept nagging at me, telling me to get out of the area. "We really need to get out of here."

"There's nowhere to go," Leto said. He hurried to his trunk, yanked it open, and took out a bow and a quiver filled with arrows.

"Um, y'all," Manny uttered. "Someone is getting out of the truck."

A man dressed in all black with a black hood stepped out of the truck. He moved into the middle of the street. He raised a bow at us, aimed, and released.

All at once, everything my mother ever said about

my abilities rushed to the forefront of my mind as my instincts took over.

I needed to protect Celyse.

I pulled her behind me with one arm and raised the other. With my fingers outstretched, an explosion of blue light unleashed from my palm. The arrow collided with the radiant haze, then clanked to the ground.

Leto discharged a barrage of his own arrows at the figure, but our attacker dodged each one in a blur, then hopped back into the truck and sped off.

The light coming from me had dissipated, but I kept my arm up as I studied my hand in disbelief.

Celyse came around to face me, her eyes wide with wonder. She touched my hand. "How did you do that?"

"I... have no idea."

Manny gawked at me with an open mouth. "Your mom always said your aura was blue, and the light that came out of your hand was blue, dude!"

Mom had always talked of power and auras and energy, but she had never said anything about an actual light force blasting out of me.

A white van with the name *Wonder Waffles* painted on the side screeched onto the scene, then skidded to a halt beside us. A man and a woman jumped out and rushed over to us. They wore their long black hair in braids and were dressed in jeans and white T-shirts with the same logo as the van.

"What in the thunderation happened?" the man

asked, scanning our faces before zeroing in on Celyse with shocked glare.

"I will fill you in later. But we need to get out of here quicker than yesterday," Leto urged.

The woman sprang into action. She looked at the guy she was with and said, "I will take them to the bakery. You stay here and handle the car."

"Got it," he said. He dug his phone out of his back pocket and started clicking away.

"Come on," the woman urged, ushering us to her van.

We piled in, bruised and bleeding, and I couldn't believe what I had done. Neither could anyone else. With startled eyes, open mouths, and stitched brows, they were as shocked as me.

Leto broke the tension. "Everyone, this is Ferna. Ferna, may I introduce Manny with the busted lip, Julio with the cut forehead, and I am sure you know Celyse, the daughter of Strong Haven."

"Yes, I know the daughter of Strong Haven," she said over her shoulder as she drove.

Wonder Waffles ended up being only a few streets away from where we crashed. The one-story white building resembled a diner. Floor to ceiling windows lined the front, and inside stretched a long counter with stools and a few tables.

Ferna parked in the parking lot at the rear of the building, then let us in through a back door. With one step inside, we were plunged into the delicious smell of sweet bread, cinnamon, and vanilla. Baking dishes stacked the shelves on one side. On the other were large clear canisters of ingredients like flour, sugar, chocolate, and sprinkles. There were two industrial-sized ovens and several waffle makers. Off to the side was a door marked *Office* and we filed in one by one.

The plain white space had a table, two desks, a sink, a refrigerator, and a row of cabinets. Leto had said that the fae here would shoot arrows first and ask questions later if they saw Celyse, but other than Ferna and the guy who stayed at the crash site, and the two guys manning the front of the bakery, no one was around. Not wanting to leave anything to chance, though, I stayed close to Celyse, and she stayed close to me.

Ferna opened the cabinet and drew out a first-aid kit. She handed it to Leto and Leto handed it to me. Then, with a flick, she whipped out a large black knife and pressed the tip to Celyse's throat.

"When you told me you were coming to discuss a matter regarding the daughter of Strong Haven, I did not know you actually had her with you, Leto," Ferna hissed between clenched teeth.

I glared at the black-haired woman, thinking there was no way in hell I was going to let her hurt Celyse. I raised my hand. "You don't want to do that."

"Neither of you want to do that," Leto added. He placed his hand on Ferna's arm. "You know me better than that, Ferna. I would only bring someone here whom I trusted. And right now, I trust this daughter. So please, let me explain."

"I mean no ill will," Celyse assured calmly, keeping as still as possible as she stared down the woman without showing the slightest sign of fear.

Ferna lowered her weapon and stepped away from Celyse. "Explain," she commanded Leto.

Leto rubbed his beard and took a seat. While he began telling Ferna everything, I moved to the side and went to work on Manny's busted lip but kept an eye on Celyse. Rifling through the first-aid kit, I found anti-septic wipes and a couple of butterfly stitches.

"Dude," Manny whispered to me excitedly as I worked on his lip. "You've got, like, superpowers."

"Shh," I whispered, flicking my eyes in the direction of Ferna. "We don't know if we can trust her." I had no idea what I had done with my hand, but I most definitely didn't want to broadcast it to someone who'd held a knife at Celyse's throat. "Besides, I don't even know what I did back there."

Manny whispered back. "You should tell your mom. She can probably explain what you did."

My mom! I texted I'd call her back and hadn't yet. She was probably going out of her mind. I pulled out my phone and started clicking.

Mom, sorry. Manny and I were...

I paused, not knowing what to say, when my phone rang. I answered it quickly, then ducked out of the office.

"Hey, Mom."

"*Mijo!* What is going on over there!?" she practically screamed.

"Going on? Nothing's going on. Manny and I are at this new bakery, trying out their famous waffles, and I had my hands full when you called earlier."

She cut me off. "If there is something happening, you need to tell me!"

"Mom," I said in a soothing voice. "I'm fine. I promise. I'm at a waffle place right now with Manny and some friends. We're... hanging out."

After a long pause, she asked in a somewhat calmer voice, "Are you sure? I felt like something was wrong."

"Wrong? No, nothing's wrong." I touch the gash on my forehead. "Oh! Maybe you felt something when I accidentally walked into an opened cabinet and cut my forehead." I let out a nervous laugh. "It really hurt."

Another long pause. "Well, I suppose that's it."

Guilt wrestled my gut. "Sorry, mom."

"No need to apologize. But please, make sure you take care of your forehead."

"I will."

"I'm going into a late-night adoration, now. I'll call you tomorrow."

"Sounds good. Have a good adoration."

"Okay, *Mijo*. Love you."

"Love you."

As I turned to go back into the office, an opaque haze entered the room. It was not something from Celyse's world, but something from mine. A haze I knew all too well.

"Go ahead, show yourself," I said.

The haze took on a more definite shape until it

formed into the little girl I had seen at the soccer field. Long pale hair, big green eyes, lace-trimmed white dress.

"Julio," the ghost girl said, gliding over to me.

"You."

"Yes, me," she said in her clear voice. "Abigail."

My mom always said ghosts came for two reasons. One was to ask for help; the other was to give messages. I guess this little girl's message was for me to help Celyse, which she had already told me. I wondered why she was back.

"I'm helping the girl you told me about," I said.

She smiled and drifted closer. "I know. I am so glad."

And then I wondered what connection the little dead girl had to Celyse. "Why are you helping her, anyway?"

"I'm helping you, silly. I know your family. Your cousin Trent, and your grandfather, and great-grandfather even."

I tilted my head. "What?"

The two guys working the front of the bakery came to the back of the store and Abigail vanished. They flashed me curious stares as they started cleaning up, and I couldn't blame them. My forehead was bloodied as was my shirt. I'm sure the rest of me looked like hell. I nodded at them, then went back inside the office. Ferna was shaking Leto's hand, and Celyse appeared satisfied with whatever they had discussed.

"What did I miss?" I asked.

"Ferna says she and her partner, Parlan, will help us," Leto explained. "But as the hour is late, we are adjourning this discussion until tomorrow. We are banged up and need rest."

"I agree we need rest, but what about the guy that attacked us? Who was he?" I asked.

Ferna shook her head. "We have no idea."

"We do not," Leto confirmed. "But Ferna and Parlan will be checking around for us. The fae community in Austin is small."

"And that's okay with you?" I asked Celyse.

She nodded. "I trust Leto. If he trusts his allies, then I must too."

"That sounds fair, I guess," I finally said, not really liking the situation, but ready to get out of there.

"Now what?" Manny asked.

"Now we head back to my place," Leto answered.

We piled back into the van and Ferna drove us to Leto's in silence. After she dropped us off and we all went inside, the quiet remained.

I tended to Manny's lip with fresh antiseptic and bandages. Then I took care of the gash on my forehead. Leto and Celyse only had a few cuts on their arms, but insisted they were fine, explaining how fae healed quickly.

With my first aid duties finished, I eyed the group. "I suppose we need to figure out our next move."

"We rest," Leto answered. "And wait for word from Ferna and Parlan. That is our next move."

"But shouldn't we talk about everything?" Manny asked.

"No," Leto said. "Not tonight."

With a raised brow, I glanced at Celyse and Manny as Leto retired to his room.

"He must have a reason," Celyse offered, settling on the couch.

"Which is fine with me," Manny said with an exhale, shuffling to his nook. "I'm beat."

With exhaustion trickling over me, I took to the floor and lay on my back. With the silence deepening and my thoughts drifting, I stopped thinking about everything that had happened and found my thoughts filled with Celyse. I didn't care if she was an unseelie fae, whatever that was exactly, and I didn't care if her parents were evil. I was drawn to her in every way imaginable and vowed to help her however I could. Even if she had stopped seeing me and had pulled away from me back on the dock, I wouldn't abandon her.

"Julio," she whispered.

I shifted to my side and looked up at her on the couch. "Yeah?"

"What you did back there outside the van was incredible," she said in a low voice. "And it makes the second time you have saved me."

I sat up. "I'll save you a million more times if you need me to."

A surge of affection filled me, as did the overwhelming need to be close to her, when something else occurred to me. I hadn't told her how I could see dead people, and that I initially thought she was dead when I saw her. I also wanted to know why she stopped appearing in my room.

"I need to tell you something," I said.

She propped herself up on her arm. "What is it?" Her green eyes studied me intently while her shiny silver hair draped over her shoulders.

"When I first saw you in my room, I thought you were a ghost because I have this thing where I can see dead people." I paused for a few seconds, waiting for her reaction, but she didn't say anything. "And when you kept appearing, and we started spending time together, I didn't care if you were a ghost. Or even if you were a vision of someone from a different time. I just wanted to be with you in whatever way we could be together. And then..."

She moved from the couch to the floor and sat next to me. "And then what?"

I rubbed the back of my neck. "And then you left me."

The glow from the lamp in the corner of the room showcased the tears welling up in her eyes. "As badly as I wanted to see you, and as much as you had my heart, I had to stop because I am fae; you are human. Our kind are enemies."

A tear slid out onto her cheek and I wiped it away. "I don't care if we are enemies," I whispered, tracing her perfect face with my fingertips. And in that moment, I wanted nothing more than to feel her lips against mine.

She took my hand and placed it on her cheek. "I do not care if we are enemies either, but there are certain things that cannot be between our kind."

I inched closer to her. "Why not?"

Closing her eyes, she moved my hand down her neck. "I want to be with you," she whispered. "In every way. But it is not possible."

I traced her collarbone with my fingertips, caressing her soft skin, wanting desperately to press my lips against hers. "You haven't told me why."

Her beautiful face took on a look of sorrow. "There is something you must know."

My stomach dropped because I had no idea what she wanted to say. But from the sad look on her face, I could tell it wasn't good.

I pulled my hand away and placed it on my lap. She scooped it up and held it between her own. "Julio, I—"

Leto broke into our moment, rushing into the room with a dire expression on his face. "There are fae outside, and they mean us ill."

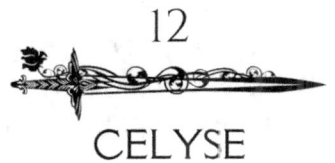

12

CELYSE

My heart was breaking at the thought of telling Julio my kiss was deadly and I was to wed somebody else, but Leto spared me from my task with a dire warning.

Fae were outside.

And I knew they were there for me.

Julio and I joined Leto by the window. Manny came over too. His breathing was rapid and his eyes filled with fear.

"There are fae where?" Manny asked.

"Outside," Leto whispered. "My glamour on the house is holding, but I fear it may drop soon."

"How did they find us?" Julio asked. "I thought this place was protected?"

"They must have found the shimmer's trace, then used another shimmer to get here," Leto suggested, his focus on the sliver of window he was peering through. "And somehow they have penetrated my wards."

Julio's fingertips found mine as my mind churned. His touch was everything.

If Leto was right and I had been tracked, then it

was Jaid outside. He was the best tracker in Faevenly and I was pretty sure Mother and Father had sent him after me. If he thought Julio, Manny, and Leto meant me harm, he would kill them like he had Jorn. I could not let that happen.

"They want me," I said. "And if I do not go with them, they will kill you all."

Julio's eyes widened. "No way," he said. "I'm tingling all over. It's not safe for you to go out there."

"If Julio knows," Manny added, "then he knows."

A crash reverberated against the house, like a massive wind, followed by another. The force was so loud I thought the cottage would split in two. And it was all because of me.

I squeezed Julio's hand. "I am not letting them hurt you."

Before Julio could form an objection, I hollered. "This is Celyse! I am coming out!"

Julio stared at me with a stunned expression. "What are you doing?"

"You have saved me. Now I am saving you." I glanced at the others. "All of you."

The front door slammed open with a kick, and in strode Jaid, arrow at the ready. "My lady," he said with formality. He scanned the room. "Are you harmed?"

Head up and shoulders back, I released Julio's grip and walked toward my childhood friend. "I am not."

He nocked his arrow, pointing it at Leto. "A renegade fae?"

"Yes, a fae, but not a renegade. You will do him no harm. I command it."

Jaid peered at me with a questioning look, then lowered his bow. "As you wish."

I walked outside and Jaid followed. The brilliant moon overhead revealed his troop of guards. Roaming at their heels were two silver-haired wolfbeasts. The waist-high guardians trotted over to me and licked my hands. I patted their heads in return.

"Celyse! Wait!" Julio yelled.

I turned to see him standing outside the cottage, looking heartbroken and shattered.

"There is no other way," I called out. *Not if I wanted him to live.* I forced myself to turn away from him, my own heart echoing his.

Jaid gripped my arm and started issuing commands. He pointed at one of the guards. "Cover the rear." He pointed at two others. "Flank the sides." He pointed at the remaining two. "Lead the way to the shimmer."

Surrounded by the guards, Jaid stayed in the middle with me while we made our way into the trees. I thought of my mother. What she would do when she saw me?

"Is the High Queen furious?" I asked.

Jaid hesitated, as if he did not know how to answer. "The High Queen is as you would expect, my lady."

I shuddered on the inside, scared to death to see my mother, knowing exactly what I could expect and dreading it. After a short distance, we came upon a large shimmer. Through it I could see my woods, and in the distance, Strong Haven. Before stepping through the glow, I hesitated. So much sorrow gathered inside of me because I did not know if I would ever see Julio again. I also did not know what I would do with the knowledge of the horrid things I had learned about my mother and father and what they were doing with the shimmers.

"My lady," Jaid said, motioning for me to go through.

I drew in a deep breath, steadied my emotions, and considered Jaid. Once, he was as close to me as if he were my own flesh and blood. I had shared my desires and fears with him, my foolish pursuits, and my ridiculous notions, and he had always supported me. Always. Now, he was my captor, leading me to certain punishment.

"I do not even know you," I said to him.

He kept his unfeeling violet eyes on me. "One day you will."

He nudged me forward. When I passed through the translucent glow, Mother sprang into view. She stomped over to me, slammed her hand across my face, and shoved me to the ground. My knees pounded against the dirt while I sprawled before her.

"Mother!"

She glowered at me. "Look at you, dressed in the attire of lesser beings. How fitting," she hissed, her eyes so full of hatred they bored right through me. "Do not move from your place."

Stunned, I did as she asked, keeping close to the dirt and grass as if the ground could somehow protect me from her. I knew I would draw her wrath but did not expect her to lay hands on me. What else was she going to do? And where was Father?

Jaid and his group stepped through the shimmer after me. They dispersed, except for Jaid. Mother pulled him to the side and started drilling him with questions.

"Where did you find her?"

"At the home of a renegade fae."

"Was anyone else with her?"

"Only the fae and two human males."

"And they are there still?"

"Yes, they are."

"Very well. Step aside as I deal with this traitorous princess."

He bowed low. "Yes, my Queen."

Mother pressed her lips together in a thin line as she came back to me and circled me like a wild animal hunting its prey. "How dare you think you can go against me." She fisted her hands at her side. "Sneaking away through a shimmer. And to be gone for two full days. Did you not think Jaid would find you? You insolent fool. And to take refuge with two human males and a rene-gade fae. Humans are our sworn enemy. How dare you!"

Fear and panic shivered through me, rooting me in

place as my head hung low. I dared not mention Leto's accusations of Strong Haven wrongdoing, lest I would be ended on the spot.

Speaking in a low menacing tone, she sneered, "I know all, Celyse. Do you understand me? All."

"Yes, Mother," I answered in a low voice. "I understand."

"Now stand!"

Drawing in a deep breath, I rose to my feet. Under the moonlight and surrounded by the forest, she unleashed her unseelie self. Her glamour lowered as her body stretched out and towered over me, looking down on me with red eyes, pointed teeth, and a hideous, green-tinted face with an elongated nose and chin. I felt as small as a child and wished to disappear but held my feeble position.

She raised a shimmer. It was the one Jaid had used. She held it before my face.

"Look," she ordered with a click of her tongue.

Staring into the ball, I saw sparks from a roaring fire. It took me a few seconds to recognize the flames were engulfing Leto's home. I gasped. She had ordered the deaths of Julio, Leto, and Manny? Tears choked my throat as my vision blurred over.

"No, Mother," I choked out. "Please. They did nothing wrong."

"This is your doing," she growled in a deep, cold voice. "You have killed them. You are a murderer." She squeezed the shimmer between her hands with a grunt until it burst, obliterating into tiny bits of vapor floating in the air.

It felt like she was crushing my heart along with the shimmer, taking life from my very soul. And I could hardly believe the depths of her cruelty. But then I remembered Leto's words. He knew what she was capable of.

Now I did too.

13

JULIO

Leto and Manny gathered close to me and together under the night sky we watched as Celyse and the guards disappeared into the forest, all except for one. He hung back, staying close to the house.

"What is he doing?" I asked.

Leto narrowed his eyes at the figure. "They have other plans for us. I must grab my things." He dashed inside the house and Manny and I followed.

Manny panicked. "Other plans? Wh-wh-what does that mean?"

My mom's ringtone sounded, sending Selena's salsa beat cutting through the air in a surreal and terrifying way. If my mom was calling at three in the morning, then something serious was about to go down. I snatched my phone out of my back pocket and silenced the music.

"Oh, no," Manny muttered. He pointed at the phone. "Bad. Very bad."

"I know." I turned my ringer off, then slipped the phone back in my rear pocket, my heart racing on overdrive.

Manny stood in front of me, chewing at his thumb. "Are you getting a witchy vibe?"

I was, all over, and it was intense.

He cut me off before I could answer. "You know what, don't answer that. I already know."

We turned our attention to the guy outside and watched as a tall and ominous figure cloaked in black emerged from the woods. I wondered if he was the same arrow-flinging guy from the car crash but couldn't tell. He faced the house and held up his arms.

"What the holy hell," Manny uttered.

The man looked like a freakin' sorcerer or wizard, intent on killing his target. Namely us. Manny and I backed away from the window.

"Uh, Leto!" I shouted. "Better get over here!"

Leto dashed over with two duffel bags. He peered at the menacing figure standing outside in the moonlight. "Never thought I would see him again."

"You know that guy?" Manny asked.

"I do." Leto spun around. "Follow me, quickly."

Manny and I raced behind Leto through the living room to the kitchen. The house shook. The windows shattered. Leto glanced at the ceiling, muttered under his breath, then reached for the back door. He twisted the knob, but the door didn't budge. He set his bags down, then slammed his shoulder into the frame. It wouldn't give.

He turned to me and Manny. "We are in a dire predicament."

"No, shit, Gandalf!" Manny exclaimed.

Angling in, I tried the knob to see if I could open it. It wouldn't turn. "Now what?"

The house shook again. This time, wisps of dark smoke trickled into the kitchen from the front of the house and the stench of wood burning flooded the air.

"The house is on fire!" Manny yelled.

"Calm yourself, Manny," Leto ordered.

Manny clamped his mouth shut, then nodded.

"You," Leto barked at me. "I need you to place your palms on the door and summon whatever power you have within you."

He pressed his hands against the wall like he did when we heard the wolfbeasts our first night in the house. I joined him, pressing mine against the door.

He brought his face close and said in an eerily calm voice. "Concentrate on this door, Julio. Visualize it opening. I will channel my glamour to match. Do you understand?"

I understood visualizing because my mom had often talked about seeing things in her mind. It was something she'd taught me too. And I thought I knew what he meant by glamour since we had kinda talked about it, but I wasn't exactly sure.

"I-I-I don't really get what that means," I stammered.

"I think you do," Leto said. "Do not dwell on details. Concentrate on what you feel in your gut. Your innate gifts."

The room grew warmer, the smoke overhead thicker. In a flash, a whoosh of air blew into the kitchen, followed by tongues of fire crawling across the ceiling.

"Julio, now," Leto commanded.

"Do it!" Manny pleaded.

My gut twisted tight, but I forced the panic away. I had to get us out of here. Pushing all other thoughts aside, I closed my eyes and pictured the wooden door. Leto murmured in his strange language, while behind me Manny started coughing. I directed my thoughts to the door, saying the word *open* over and over in my head. The insides of my nasal passages started burning, and my throat started clogging with smoke. A hacking cough escaped my lips as I struggled to keep my mind on the door.

Leto's chanting grew louder and more hurried. Matching his urgency, I gritted my teeth, pushing all my thoughts to the door.

"Opennnn," I grunted.

An electrified hum rang in my ears, followed by a surge at my fingertips as the door wrenched, then hurtled outward with a blast. Leto, Manny, and I spilled out into the night, hacking out our lungs. We looked back at the cottage in disbelief.

Flames erupted from the roof, crackling and spraying heat and embers in all directions.

"We should not be so close," Leto cautioned.

We backed away from the structure, dumbfounded at the spectacle. Leto circled around to the front of the house as sirens blared in the distance. My phone vibrated in my pocket and I knew it was my mom. I pulled it out and stared at it, wondering if I should answer.

"You'd better get it before she calls the cops," Manny warned.

He was right. I needed to answer before she flipped out. I cleared my throat as best as I could. "Hey, Mom."

"*Mijo*! I've been calling!"

"I know, I know. I'm sorry. I was, uh, sleeping. And then well, uh..." My mind blanked, and I had no idea what to say. Manny swiped the phone from my grasp.

"Hey, Mama A. It's me, Manny. I'm with Julio. I forced him to go with me to a friend's house, and we fell asleep."

Manny stayed silent and I could hear my mom 's screeching voice laying into him.

"Oh, yeah. That's um, a fire. The house next to my friend's house caught on fire and Julio and I came outside to check it out." Manny's eyes widened as he shrugged his shoulders at me. Then he added quickly, "I promise we're okay. It's only a small kitchen fire, I think. Um, you know, popcorn in the microwave or something like that."

The flames roared as they danced against the sky. The sirens in the distance grew closer. I grabbed the phone from him. "Mom, Manny's right, we're okay. We didn't mean to fall asleep at his friend's house. I'm so sorry. It just happened. And now there's a small fire next door."

Her voice shook with fear. "Go home! Right now, *Mijo*! Something is not right and I'm worried sick!"

Of course she knew something wasn't right. How could she not? "I will, I promise."

"Call me when you get there."

"Okay," I said. "I'm really sorry, Mom."

I slid my phone back in my pocket and watched as flames engulfed the cottage. Manny and I backed up into the trees and watched the inferno take over, lighting up the area in a sea of heat and smoke.

Leto walked over to us. "I have scanned the area. The Strong Haven guards are gone. As is their witch."

"That dude was their witch? Do they have"—Manny swallowed, looking up at the sky—"anything else? That flies maybe? Like a dragon?"

"There are things that fly, but no dragons." Then he murmured. "Not here, anyway."

"Things?" Manny asked, watching the skies with terror. "What things?"

A firetruck screamed onto the scene and a flurry of activity ensued as the crew got to work setting up to douse the house.

I rubbed the back of my neck. "I don't understand what is happening."

Leto dumped his bags at my feet. "I know you do not. And mostly I do not either. Before I can even entertain your inquiries, I must have my own addressed. Take these to your home. I will meet you there later."

"Whoa, what? You're leaving us?" Manny asked.

"We are in grave danger. Once the Strongs figure out we have escaped the fire, they will be back. Strongs always finish their jobs, remember? If we are to survive this, then I need my own answers. When I get them, I will join you."

Survive this? I thought of Celyse. If a team of guys with pointy ears and bows and arrows came for her, along with their own witch, then whatever was happening to her had to be bad. So bad they wanted us dead.

"What about Celyse?" I asked.

"I hope to gain information on her as well. Now go." He pushed our shoulders. "You two should not be standing around a house fire."

Manny and I stared at each other as Leto nodded, then walked into the woods and disappeared from view.

"Come on," I urged, picking up the bags. "Leto is right. We're two Mexicans standing outside a house fire in the middle of the night. I'd say we need to get out of here."

Manny froze with fresh fright. "You're right."

With Leto's things in tow, we walked as inconspicuously as possible along the edge of the trees to Manny's car and drove off without the busy firefighters noticing us and before the cops arrived. Neither one of us spoke as the horror of everything that had happened sunk in.

"We're messed up in something serious, aren't we?" Manny asked.

"Yeah, we are."

When we got to my house, we dropped Leto's stuff on the ground and sank into the couch. I ran my fingers through my hair. "I can't believe what's happened. I mean, I'm kinda in shock right now."

"Me too," Manny said, rubbing his face but being careful not to touch his lip.

"I need to call my mom," I said, taking my phone out of my back pocket.

After a short conversation, calming her as best I could and promising her everything was okay, she finally settled down. And with my eyelids growing heavy, I decided I needed some sleep. After all, I figured I should be ready for whatever was coming next.

Because without a doubt, more was coming.

14

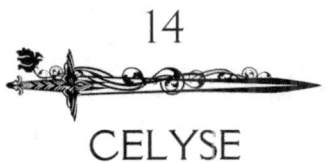

CELYSE

Mother had always favored Malena. She smiled at her differently, spoke to her in a softer tone, and even made more eye contact with her. I did not notice any of this until Maid Rell pointed it out to me one day.

I was ten years old, and Mother had spent a full afternoon with Malena, teaching her the finer points of proper posture and how to greet royal visitors. When they were finished, I excitedly got up from where I was sitting so I could have my turn, but Mother promptly left the room with a whoosh of her dress and a flick of her hair. Malena seated herself at the table and carried on with her regular lessons, oblivious, while I stood there for a bit, fully expecting Mother to return.

She never did.

"I am sorry, my dear," Maid Rell had said, taking me to the table where Malena sat busily writing her letters. The minder set pieces of parchment before me and gave me a quill. And then she muttered, "I wish the High Queen would not do such things to you."

That was when I knew how Mother felt about me.

Really and truly knew, though something inside of me had suspected it all along.

Over the years, I settled into Mother doing more for Malena and less for me. It drove me to seek solace outside with nature, away from Mother and all the things I was not. And while I wanted to blame Malena for having Mother's favor, I did not because it was not Malena's fault. The fault was solely Mother's, and there was nothing I could do about that.

I distanced my emotions from Mother, guarding my heart from hurt and disappointment. And when I found my shimmer and met Julio, he filled a hole within me. He exuded love with his mother and she with him like I had never seen before. And he had so much joy with his life and his friends—things I desperately yearned for. Now he was dead because of me. So were his best friend and a fae who was trying to help me. Killed in a house fire because I had gone to the human realm.

I felt ill.

Alone in the woods with my mother in the middle of the night, it was clear she hated me more than I even fathomed. Despair and heartache worked its way through me, filling every inch of my being.

"Why, Mother?" I gathered the courage to ask. "Why do you despise me so?"

She narrowed her cruel eyes at me as she restored her glamour, her face morphing from deadly and monstrous back to cold and beautiful.

"You cannot begin to understand things, Celyse.

But you will understand this. You will tell your father and Malena, and anyone else who asks, that you wanted to do some exploring on your own before you became betrothed. You will say you returned in the middle of the night and asked me to relieve your burden and choose your mate. You will use whatever trickery you must to not divulge that you had gone to the human realm or that I had anything to do with your return or your decision." She glared at me with narrowed eyes. "Now, repeat after me, 'I wish for you to pick my mate.'"

I worked my jaw a few seconds before I muttered, "I wish for you to pick my mate."

Her nostrils flared with satisfaction. "Once you are wed, you will leave Strong Haven forever, and I shall never have to see you again."

I bit the inside of my cheek to steady my trembling lip. I did not want her to know how badly she was hurting me. Swallowing the tang of blood in my mouth, I asked, "What if I refuse to wed?"

She stepped so close to me I could see darkness seeping into her pure green eyes. She was about to compel me, but stopped. "Refuse and you will not even know your name."

A hard shudder passed through me. A fae's name held ultimate power. To not know your name was worse than giving your name away because it was a death sentence. I trembled at the thought of being nameless, mindless, powerless.

Her lip snarled. "One final thing. Your wedding will

be three days hence. Arrangements will be made quickly."

She glowered at me with sick satisfaction because she had me right where she wanted me. But I could not let her have the last word. I would not. "What if Father and Malena do not believe me?"

"You are the inferior daughter. They will most assuredly believe you."

Inferior daughter?

If a heart could shatter more than once, mine certainly had. I had lost Julio, and now I was losing my identity, reduced to an insignificant daughter to be married off and sent away.

She snapped her fingers and Jaid came forward. "Fetch a nightdress from Lady Celyse's bedchamber." With a nod, he took off.

Mother glared at me. "Remove those wretched clothes."

With a swallow, I took off my tunic, trousers, and my underthings, leaving them crumpled on the ground. Standing there naked, I felt utterly humiliated. But I would not let Mother know. I kept my posture straight, refusing to give her the satisfaction she sought by stripping me down to nothing, exposed and vulnerable before her in the cool night.

Mother circled around me but kept quiet. I kept quiet too. Thankfully, Jaid returned quickly with a folded nightdress. He handed it to me, and I thought I detected a hint of sympathy in his downcast eyes.

"Thank you, Jaid," I said, taking the garment and slipping it on.

I stood there, waiting for whatever was next, when Mother finally said to Jaid, "Take her to her room."

"Yes, High Queen."

With my heart in my throat and my vision threatening to blur over, I held my head as high as I could and walked with Jaid to Strong Haven Palace. Sorrow and dread over my lot in life overwhelmed me with each step closer to home.

And there was nothing I could do about it.

When we were far enough away, Jaid whispered under his breath. "I am sorry, Celyse."

I did not acknowledge his sympathy, because if I did, I would lose it. Instead, I kept a steady pace. When we got to the palace, I expected to find Maid Rell ready to greet me, but she was nowhere to be seen. I thought of asking Jaid her whereabouts but decided against it. I did not need to involve him in my affairs, lest Mother's wrath fall on him too. I would not do that to him even if he had done it to me.

Not giving Jaid a glance or sparing him a word, I followed him upstairs in silence. And when I got to my bedchamber, I gave him a nod, then slipped inside. I stood in the darkness, looking at my things all in their places as if nothing had happened.

Yet everything had happened.

My heart sank to the furthest depths of me as I crawled under my covers and let the tears stream down my face.

Maid Rell usually greeted me at daybreak with a vigorous good morning, a pull of the drapes, and an announcement of what my day would hold, followed by the sweeping entrance of maid servants to bring me water, fruit, and oils.

This morning, it was eerily quiet.

I got up and looked around to see a note on the table by my bed.

There will be no attendants today.

High Queen of Strong Haven

Fresh tears sprang to my eyes as the note fell out of my hand. I had been reduced to a lesser fae. Disfavored and discarded. And even though I wanted to hide away in my room forever, I needed to wash up and face my day. I would not let my mother get the best of me. I would investigate Trey Leto's allegations regarding Mother and Father and the shimmers and see if they were indeed taking humans in secret for a mining operation. Though I did not know what I would do with the information, if any, it was the least I could do for Julio and Manny, and Leto too.

I pulled open my drapes and sat on the window seat, assessing my predicament. I leaned my forehead against the glass and looked out at the grounds of Strong Haven. I sighed at the beauty of the flowering shrubs all around the palace and the magnificence of the elm, maple, and oak trees beyond. If forced to wed the suitor of my mother's choosing, would I end up in a place like this? Surrounded by beauty? I thought of the suitors scheduled for Malena and me. With Malena more than likely choosing Alexander Kane and with Jorn Lind dead, that left Barent Stromm of Summit Range and Evan Baffin of Sand Bluff.

Then I wondered whatever happened with the Linds. Jorn was sent home dead on his steed. By now he had been found. I wondered how the Linds responded.

A clinking interrupted my thoughts. I sat rigid, waiting for the sound to return. It did, and was coming from my window. I peered through the glass, searching for the source, when I spotted one of the garden gnomes below. I sucked in my breath. The gnomes stayed hidden and never revealed themselves, choosing to tend to the grounds at night only, but there one stood—small, dark green, blending in almost entirely with the grass and shrubbery. In fact, I only spotted it because of its arm movement. It was waving me to come down. I waved back, letting it know I had seen it.

I scurried down the corridor to do my washing, then quickly returned to my room to get dressed. Stripping off my nightdress, I rifled through my dresses and settled on the most beautiful one in the lot. Pale green with a low neckline. I was a daughter of Strong Haven, after all. I would look and act the part. All the stars in the sky could not take my birthright away from me.

Mother be damned.

With my dress on, I went to work on my hair, then

applied the perfect amount of face paints. Looking at myself in the mirror, I thought I had hidden away all signs of despair.

As if nothing had happened.

My first order of business would be to find the gnome. After that, I had no idea what I would do, but I was sure something would come to me. I wondered if Father or Malena would seek me out to discuss my disappearance. But I thought not. No one was cleverer with words than Mother.

Stepping out into the corridor, I nearly collided with Jaid. I stumbled back. "Jaid. I did not know you were here."

"I have only arrived. The High Queen has asked me to accompany you," he answered with a half bow.

Now I was being watched? I glared at him, knowing it was his position and his duty to follow orders, but sad for our lost friendship. Now that he was keeping an eye on me for my mother, the trust we once had was long gone. "Follow me if you must."

Making my way down the corridor, I took the stairs to the first floor and went out into the garden. Instead of taking the path to the left where the morning meals took place, I swerved to the right, to the area where I had seen the gnome.

"My lady, the breakfast table is not this way," Jaid said.

I flicked my fingers at him, brushing him off as I continued, knowing the less he knew the better. "I know where I am going. And if you are to be serving me as a minder, you may do so at a close distance or fall back. It makes no difference to me."

Of course, I issued the insult because I knew Jaid would not appreciate being referred to as a minder, and hopefully it would encourage him to fall back. I could not risk him knowing a gnome was trying to contact me. From the pause in his step, I could tell my words were successful.

"I will fall back," he announced.

"Fine," I said with a shrug.

With his footsteps fading, I slowed my own pace, my eyes flicking about as I searched for the gnome. Since he was small and green, I did not think it would be easy to spot him, especially with Jaid trailing me, so I took my time. I meandered close to the bushes. I bent down and picked flowers. I even lowered myself to the ground pretending to pick a rock out of my slipper. Finally, I locked stares with a pair of small, beady, black eyes.

The gnome was nestled in the middle of a bramble. As I neared, it blended back into the thick. I moved closer to the spot where it had stood and inspected the nearby vines. There on the ground, tucked beside a rock, was a small rolled-up piece of parchment. Clever. Leaning in as if to admire the blackberries, I bent down to adjust the hem of my dress and scooped the note into my hand.

"Celyse."

I turned to see Maid Rell. With the note secured in

my palm, I dashed over to her. "Oh, Maid Rell, where have you been?"

"I have been with Malena." She smiled and hugged me, patting my back as if to tell me everything would be okay. I wondered what she knew.

I released her and flashed her a smile of gratitude. "Where is my sister now?"

"She has finished her morning meal and is practicing her flute in the music room."

"Oh, I see."

Maid Rell peered at me with questioning eyes, then turned to face Jaid who was standing nearby. "I require privacy with Lady Celyse," she bellowed at him.

Jaid hesitated a few seconds, then bowed. "I will increase my distance."

She harrumphed and watched him walk away and then nudged me to go with her in the opposite direction. She kept her voice low. "I was not surprised to hear that you had wanted to explore before a betrothal, but I *was* surprised to hear that you had returned with a desire to wed in haste, with the mate of your mother's choosing."

"Oh, yes," I swallowed, thinking of a way to twist my words. "It was not anything I had planned. It happened rather suddenly. For some, it is for the best."

Maid Rell tilted her head a bit. "Is that so?"

I offered her the slightest head shake. "It is so."

Passing through the garden, as if everything was normal, she said in an even lower voice. "There are workings here neither of us can control."

Relief washed over me at knowing I was seen and had someone on my side. With my note still hidden in my grasp, I said, "You know me so well, Maid Rell. Better than my own mother, I think."

Maid Rell slipped her arm through mine. "You and your sister are like my own. So yes, I know you like I know the sunrise." She stopped, then turned to face me with sad eyes. "I also know your mother."

I drew in a deep breath. "Then you do not have to ask me if something I am claiming is true, for you already know."

She patted my hand, then cast her eyes down. "Yes, you are right. I already know."

We continued with our walk, passing perfectly lined and manicured hedges, both of us lost in thought. I wanted to tell her so much more but dared not. I could not risk Maid Rell falling into some sort of peril because of me.

"I will support you in any way I can, my lady," she said in a hushed voice. "Though, my ways are limited."

Hiding my sorrow, I said, "Thank you, Maid Rell. Your ways are comforting, and I am grateful for that."

We strolled in silence for a bit more. After a while, she said, "I wonder if you should speak with your father. Perhaps, using the correct phrasing, he can assist you."

I did not think my father would or could do anything, but thought her idea worth trying. "Do you know where he is right now?"

"Last I saw him, he was in the study, alone."

With Mother away from Father, I could prod him for information. He was my only hope of escaping Mother's plan. "Thank you so much, Maid Rell."

"You are most welcome, my lady."

With Maid Rell taking her leave, I slipped the gnome's note in my bodice, then headed back to the palace. When I neared the entrance to the main wing, I was met by Jaid. He fell in step behind me and followed as I briskly entered the palace and walked to the study. I wanted to get there before Mother or Malena showed up. Jaid stayed outside by the door as I went in.

Father was standing at the desk, studying a map of Faevenly with a frown on his face. It erased when he spotted me. "There is my lovely girl."

I offered him a small smile. "I am here."

He came over to me and kissed my forehead, then cupped my face with his strong hands. "Are you better now? Mother told me she spent some time with you last night after you returned."

Hiding my despair, I said, "I am well."

"Good. I was worried about you, my daughter. But I am glad to hear everything has worked out and that your mother was there for you when you needed her."

Hatred boiled inside of me at the thought of Mother slapping my face, shoving me to the ground, threatening me with her glamour lowered, and stripping me naked. "Oh, she was certainly there for me."

I sat on a vine-patterned green fabric couch and Father sat across from me on a brown leather chair. He smiled the kind of smile that made me feel safe and loved. If I could, I would collapse into his arms, let my tears run, tell him what Mother had done, and ask him to help me. But I could not. She would make good on her promise to take my name and figure out a way to dispose of me. I wondered if he noticed how she had treated me differently for so many years.

"Celyse, is something the matter?" he asked.

A rush of tears threatened to gush forth. I blinked them away and swallowed the lump in my throat as I struggled to hold it together "Father," I said cautiously, trying to formulate my words. "I—"

"There you are," Mother exclaimed, sweeping into the study. "When I did not find you in your bedchamber, I came looking for you. There are many decisions to be made for your special day."

Disgust for her and her devious ways raged inside of me, but I kept my outward appearance calm. "Of course."

"And speaking of your wedding," she added, "your chosen mate will be arriving this evening for supper and wine. Is that not grand?"

My stomach turned at the idea of marrying someone else when my heart belonged to Julio. Even if he had gone to the Passing Place, I did not think I could ever get over him.

"Who will it be, Mother? Barent or Evan?"

"Neither," she announced. "I have chosen your mate from a region eager to join the Council of Five as a new province. With your father's approval, of course."

My heart stopped and my gut clenched. I looked from Mother to Father. "You approved, Father?"

"Indeed, I did," he answered.

I tried to hide my gulp as I turned my attention back to Mother. "Who is it?"

The corner of her mouth lifted in a sick satisfying grin. "Rook Cailean of the Sublands."

The Sublands? My face grew hot as my mind reeled. The Sublands was a region of dry terrain, steep slopes, and minimal vegetation. They did not belong to the Council of Five because the inhabitants were rebellious fae who had been banished from their own provinces. They were wild, untamed, and deadly.

I glanced at Father for his reaction, but if he had one, he kept it hidden. "Will the Council be renamed to the Council of Six?" I asked.

Mother glanced at her silver-painted fingernails. "If all goes well, yes. It is a strategic move and the best thing for Strong Haven."

"It will be well, my daughter," Father soothed. "The region has seen significant growth over the last few years, and they are eager to please your mother and me."

Mother wrapped her hands together in front of her and flashed me a forced smile. "What you are doing for our house is commendable, Celyse."

Father nodded in agreement. "I am most proud of you, my daughter."

At a complete loss as to what to say, I smiled back. "Thank you, Father."

I thought of all the times I had told Malena I wanted to run away. Those same feelings rushed back, but this time they were accompanied by resolve. I was finally going to do it. I was going to leave. I had no intention of being my mother's plaything and marrying a vile creature from the Sublands.

My mind churned with ideas of where I could go, when the shimmers came to mind. Even if I had lost my Julio, leaving the realm was my only hope. I would need to brave Torch Lake and get one.

And not get caught.

Pulling my emotions in check, I left the study, eager to retreat to my bedchamber so I could strategize and read my note. With Jaid on my heels, I walked with speed through the palace and back to the privacy of my room. I hurried over to my desk and took the parchment out from my bodice. I unfolded it and brought it close to my face so I could read the small writing.

We are alive. Stand by for more.

TL

The note fell from my grasp as a surge of relief soared through me and my heart rejoiced.

Julio was alive.

15

JULIO

When I finally fell asleep, it was one of those shallow sleeps that was more like being awake. The kind that leaves you tossing and turning and hearing every little noise—wind against the windows, creaking from the house settling, tires screeching from a car driving down the street. But the loudest thing in my head was my worry for Celyse.

Was she okay?

"Hey, are you awake?" Manny asked. He was in my room on the floor because he didn't want to be alone on the couch. Which was fine with me because I didn't exactly want to be alone either. Not after that witch attack and the fire.

"Yeah." I touched the bandage on my head, making sure it was still in place, every bone in my body aching.

"Me too." Manny shuffled his pillow around while grunting and moaning. "Where do you think old Leto went? And when do you think he'll be back?"

I blew out and rubbed my eyes. "He's probably with Ferna and Parlan. Hopefully, he'll be here soon. And hopefully he'll have news about Celyse."

"Dude, you've got it bad for her. I've never seen you

so crazy about a girl, and so fast." Manny paused. "Actually, I've never seen you like this with anyone. Are you in love? Like a love at first sight kinda thing?"

I turned to my side, deciding to tell him everything. "Well, it's kinda like love at first sight, I guess. But my first sight wasn't when she appeared in my room with the cut on her arm. I've seen her before, tons of times, in a vision."

He sat up with a bolt, the streetlight filtering through my window blinds outlining his fro. "What?"

With a sigh I explained. "She visited me here in my room for months. And then, out of blue, she stopped showing up until she reappeared in the flesh two nights ago."

"Are you serious?"

"Yes, I'm serious." I rolled to my back and stared at the ceiling.

"Why didn't you tell me?"

"Because I didn't even know if she was real. Besides, you know how you are with witchy stuff."

"That's fair," he said, laying back down on his makeshift bed. He continued with his fidgeting, every groan and mumble louder than the one before, until finally he said. "I can't sleep."

"Me neither."

"Hey, I've got an idea. You hungry?"

I leaned over my bed to look down at him. "Your idea is to eat? You're not seriously hungry right now. Are you?"

He thought about his answer for a few seconds. "I

mean, maybe a little. Stress makes me hungry. Plus, I can't sleep, and neither can you. So..."

With sleep eluding me, I thought a bite couldn't hurt. I tossed off my covers. "Fine. Come on."

Mom had left the fridge stocked for the week while she was away, so I had plenty of food to offer. Sorting through the prepared meals, I rattled off the choices. "I've got cheese enchiladas, beef quesadillas, and some *caldo*."

Manny rubbed his hands together. "Ooch, enchiladas."

I took out two plastic containers and popped them in the microwave, then got two bottles of orange Jarritos, my favorite flavored soda from Mexico.

When the microwave dinged, I took out the meals and set them in front of us. We were digging into the scrumptious cheese and corn tortilla goodness when a knock sounded on the front door.

"Leto," we said.

With a clink, we dropped our forks and hurried over to the door. We opened it to find Leto had... changed.

His long hippie hair that had hung to his elbows had been cut several inches so that it now stopped just past his shoulders. Pointy ears poked through his shiny silver strands that were braided in the front and tied together at the back. His thick facial hair and long beard had been shaved away, revealing a smooth young face. He had ditched the grandpa khaki pants and white shirt and wore dark green pants with a black shirt. He even had a quiver and bow slung across his back.

Old man Trey Leto was a total bad ass, and he wasn't old at all.

"Holy Legolas," Manny muttered. "You're not an old hippie anymore."

Leto bent down a little as he stepped into my small home. "You don't even know what old is."

Shutting the door and following Leto to the living room, I said, "Maybe we don't because you're a fae and all, but you definitely don't look like you used to. What happened?"

"I was in hiding, and now I am not, thanks to you two and Celyse. Now that I am back in the fray, I may as well look the part. And before you ask"—he zeroed in on me—"I do not know what has become of Celyse. But I have sent a note to her letting her know we survived the fire. Assuming she is alive, she will get it."

I glanced at Manny, then back at Leto, my stomach twisting tight. I thought she was in trouble, but I didn't think her life was at risk. "You think she might be dead?"

"If you knew her mother, the High Queen, you would think the same. She is pure evil. All we can do is assume Celyse is alive and proceed with the plan my allies and I have devised."

"A plan." Manny nudged me with a hopeful look. "That's good, right?"

I shrugged, peering at Leto for an explanation. "Depends on the plan."

Leto circled the small living room. He took note of his two duffel bags in the corner, then positioned himself near the fireplace. "There has been unrest amongst the Faevenly provinces for a while now. There are those who support the Strongs and those that oppose them. I know because I was part of it. We knew what the Strongs and their band of loyalists were doing to the humans, and we were planning to stop it by cutting off access to the shimmers between our worlds forever. Close the door, if you will. But the plan got derailed. Now, considering recent events, the plan has been reactivated."

"Whoa, hold up," I said. "Celyse is over there. We can't obliterate any door without getting her."

"Correct. She is over there. And in fact, there are many there who would like to come here, including the humans who have been taken. Hence, the first order of business will be to get Celyse and get out those who want out and those who were taken."

"Okay, how?" I asked.

"The same way Celyse came here. Stepping through the shimmer. I still have hers, and others that I have accumulated over the years."

Manny raised his eyebrows, looking from me to Leto. He shrugged his shoulders. "Sounds easy enough."

Manny was right, it did sound easy. Which meant there had to be a catch. "If it's easy, then why hasn't it been done? Why was the plan deactivated?"

"Because," Leto said. "None of it will be easy."

"Of course not." I flopped on the couch, the exhaustion of everything finally catching up to me. "Well, let's hear it, I guess."

"We will have to slip over there—undetected, get out as many fae and humans as we can—undetected, and then destroy the shimmers—undetected."

"Uh, forget what I said about it sounding easy," Manny said.

"Exactly," Leto agreed. "Every part of the plan will be dangerous. Our lives will be at risk, and the likelihood of failure is high."

I studied the fae for a minute, thinking there was something he wasn't telling me. "You're holding something back though, aren't you?"

Leto slipped off his bow and quiver and set them aside. He moved over to the chair and sat across from me. "Assuming we get to the third step of the plan, we will need a powerful witch to face off against theirs and obliterate the shimmers."

"Like that dude in all black?" Manny asked.

"Yes, like him," Leto answered. "That has been our biggest problem and why our plan got derailed. We did not have one. But now, we do."

I sat forward, placing my elbows on my knees, feeling a little optimistic. "Great! Now we're getting somewhere! Who's your witch?"

Leto tilted his head and stared at me with intense violet eyes. "You."

"Uh, what?" I sat back. "Are you out of your mind?"

Leto kept his stare on me. "I saw what you did with

that energy blast both at the car crash and again at my back door. You have immense power inside of you, Julio, and we need it."

"Yeah, I don't know about that. Whatever I did was completely unintentional. It's also not anything I've ever done before. I don't even know how I did those things."

"I am aware. That is why I am going to train you," he said. "We start at dawn."

16

JULIO

The idea of Leto training me on something I had no idea I could do filled me with so much anxiety I couldn't finish the enchiladas I had warmed up. And I loved enchiladas. Luckily, Manny was more than willing and able to finish his serving along with mine. Leto wasn't hungry and ended up retiring to my room, leaving me and Manny alone in the kitchen.

"You can do it, Julio," Manny said. "I have total faith in you."

My knee bounced underneath the table. "You would not be saying that if you were in my shoes."

He finished his last bite, and I marveled at his appetite, wondering where he put all the calories because he had zero body fat. He wiped his mouth, then scooted his chair back. "You need a good night's sleep. You're always grumpy when you're tired."

"I suppose," I said.

After we cleaned up the kitchen, we went to my mom's room since Leto was in mine. Manny sprawled on the floor with a blanket while I took the bed. And when my head hit the pillow, I was out. But not for long. True to his word, Leto woke us up bright and early with a hard knock on the door.

"Day is breaking. Time to get up," Leto called out.

A long moan trickled out of Manny. "I'm a wreck, dude."

Pulling my covers over my head, I groaned. "My entire body is throbbing with pain."

Another knock sounded on the door, followed by a creak as it swung open. "Your heightened adrenaline from last night has faded, and now your human flesh feels all the aches and pains from the car accident. This will help you both."

I peeled my eyes open to see Leto handing me a small glass of yellow liquid. "What the hell is that?"

Manny sat up and eyed his glass with a frown. "Looks like piss."

"I saw your rather impressive assortment of herbs and spices in the kitchen and whipped this up," Leto explained. "Human soft tissue can hold on to an injury for days. Months even. This will help."

"Human soft tissue? So fae don't have that problem?" I asked.

"No. We do not."

"Lucky us," I muttered. I brought the glass to my nose and took a whiff. The concoction reeked like the bathrooms at the soccer field. A surge of saliva filled my mouth and I thought I might barf.

"Come on, now," Leto encouraged me. "Take it in one gulp."

Manny pinched his nose and held the glass up to

his mouth. "I'm desperate to feel better, so I'm in." He tossed his head back and downed the drink in one gulp, then let out a hacking cough. After a few more hacks, he found his voice. "That was awful."

Leto laughed, then motioned at me. "Your turn, Julio."

"Great," I muttered. Before I could second-guess myself, I tossed the liquid down with a chug. The concoction hit my stomach hard, and I shuddered. "That was vile."

"Good work. Now get ready," Leto said. "We have lots to do today."

While I showered, Manny went home to do the same. About an hour later, we were freshly dressed and feeling pretty good, sitting in the living room with Leto. The tonic had definitely done its job.

"Before we start your training, I would like for you to tell me about what you can do," Leto said, eyeing me with keen curiosity. "Spare no detail."

I glanced at Manny. We had been friends for a long time, and he knew I could see ghosts, but we had never gone into any detail about it. His brows were raised and he looked excited to hear more about my "witchyness".

"Well," I began, clearing my throat. "For starters, I can see ghosts."

Leto's hand went to his face, as if to stroke his beard, but he must have remembered he didn't have one anymore and dropped it to his lap. "You can see spirits?" he asked.

"Yes."

"Explain."

"It all started when I was little. According to my mom, I used to see a man in the house all the time. As I got older, I'd see people everywhere. It took me a while, though, to figure out they were dead."

"That must have been frightening," Leto said.

"Well, not really. My mom is a *curandera*, so weird stuff like that has always been a part of my life."

"A *curandera*?" Leto asked.

"That's a Mexican witch," Manny explained.

I raised my hand to silence Manny. "I don't know if I'd say that. A *curandera* or *curandero*, depending on if it's a man or woman, is a healer who uses natural remedies to help people. Sometimes that includes using"—my words drifted as I thought of how to explain everything my mom could do— "psychic or supernatural abilities."

Leto's brows stitched together. "I would say that is a witch. Now, please expand on what you mean by psychic or supernatural abilities."

I rubbed my hands on my jeans cause now we were getting to the nitty gritty. "By psychic or supernatural, I mean reading tarot cards, palms, crystals, and even auras. That kind of thing. My mom also has premonitions, or feelings about things that are going to happen."

"Bad things," Manny added. "Like people dying."

"You can do all these things too?" Leto asked, leaning forward. "Including getting premonitions?"

"In a way," I said. "I get vibes from people and feel things, but I've never really explored it. I guess you could say I'm not exactly sure what I can do because I've always ignored my abilities so that I could be normal."

"Really?" Manny asked. "You can do more than see ghosts? Why would you ignore your superpowers? With great power comes great—"

I raised my hand at him. "Don't even start with me, Manny. Life is not a superhero movie."

"But you can do things!"

For all of elementary school, I was the weird kid who talked to imaginary friends. I was bullied and ridiculed by everyone. I worked hard through middle school to shake that reputation. Things finally got better for me when I went to high school, had a huge growth spurt, and made the varsity soccer team my freshman year. It also didn't hurt that, as mom would say, I was *muy guapo*.

"Trust me," I blew out. "It's not all it's cracked up to be."

"I can understand that," Leto said. "But you should embrace who you are, Julio. By turning your back on yourself, you are turning your back on your destiny."

Manny motioned to Leto and nodded. "That's exactly what I'm saying."

"I guess," I muttered.

The fae got up and moved about the room. "Is there a spirit in here?"

Glancing about I said, "No, it's just us."

Leto paced a little, as if thinking of his next line of questioning. "I think we should talk about your gift with auras."

"Okay."

"Can you see auras readily? Or do you have to do something to see them?"

I took a deep breath while I thought of what I could see. "Well, some people's auras are boom, in your face. Like really bright. But with most people, I have to concentrate to see them if I want to."

"Really?" Manny asked excitedly. "What color is mine?"

"Mostly orange, with yellow and some white."

"Whoa! Is that good?" He smiled. "It sounds good."

"They're all good," I answered. "At least, that's what my mom has taught me."

Leto studied me intently. With his piercing violet eyes, his pointed ears, and his braided silver hair, he looked mysterious and deadly. "Have you been able to see your blue aura before?"

A memory came to me, almost out of nowhere, a memory I must have buried. "Well, now that you ask that, there was this one time when I was little I got real sick. My entire body burned with fever. It got so bad that my mom filled the tub with icy cold water and put me in. While I was laying there, I saw a blue haze come out of me and hover over the water, like a fog. Later, when I got better, I asked my mom about it. She said it was nothing, and for me not to worry about it. I think she didn't want to tell me what it was because I was too young to understand."

Leto kept his hand on chin, nodding as he took everything in. "Very well. I think that is all I need for now. Let us begin."

"Right here?" I asked.

"Outside," Leto directed with a wave to the backyard.

My house was small and understated, but my backyard stretched out like a soccer field, which is exactly what I used the space for. Beyond the back patio and past my mom's garden, sprawled a grassy area big enough for soccer goals on each end. The few oak trees that dotted the middle served as defenders. I spent countless hours out there alone or with Manny dribbling the soccer ball back and forth.

"Nice space," Leto said. "I hope you do not mind, but while you were sleeping, I got acquainted with the area and practiced some archery out here."

"Yeah, sure. No problem," I said.

I glanced around the patio looking for his stuff and saw his quiver and bow on the patio table. He walked over to it, took out a fresh arrow, and lined it up for a shot. He drew the bow string back, aiming at a tree.

"When facing a foe," he instructed as he kept the arrow taut, "it is of the utmost importance to be ready for anything." He swung his weapon around, aiming at my head. "Like this."

"Whoa!" Manny called out. "Leto!"

I swallowed hard, my nerves skyrocketing, but kept still. "Uh, Leto, this isn't cool."

He kept his stance and held his aim. "Fae are ruthless, vengeful, and manipulative. We cannot lie, but we do not need to because we are cunning and devious. We are immortal, but not impervious to being killed. We are incredibly strong, but fall down to iron."

I held up my hands in a defensive posture. "Why are you telling me this?"

"It is easier to defeat your enemy when you know your enemy."

"Okay, I get it. I know the fae. Now freakin' lower your arrow!"

Leto held his position. "If you give a fae your name, you give away your power. If a fae causes you to not know your name, you lose all sense of yourself. If a fae's name is hidden and you know what it is, you can use it against the fae."

If Leto wanted to give me a fae lesson while pointing an arrow at my head, then the lesson sucked. And I wanted it to end. "Cut your crap, Leto."

"What I am going to cut is your head...in two." He pulled back the arrow even more. "Right between your eyes."

Keeping my focus on Leto, I detected movement from Manny in my peripheral vision. He was advancing ever so slowly toward Leto, looking ready to pounce.

"One more step, Manny, and you'll be the first one to meet my arrow. This is between Julio and me."

Manny froze in place, not daring to move another muscle, his eyes flicking around like he didn't know what to do.

"Good man," Leto said. He continued staring me down. "Now, Julio, on the count of three, this arrow is coming for you, and you need to stop it."

An icy chill worked its way from my scalp all the way to my toes while my heart slammed against my chest.

"One."

I raised my hand like I did at the car and extended my fingers, pushing my thoughts to my blue aura.

"Two."

I focused on the palm of my hand, telling myself to stop the arrow. Willing my power and everything I was as an Avila from my dad's side and a Rodriguez from my mom's side to come forth.

"Three."

My jaw clenched. My muscles tensed. My mind screamed *stop* as Leto released his arrow. It whizzed at me with lightning speed, grazing my hair as it flew past and lodged into the wooden fence.

Manny let out a relieved gasp, doubling over and resting his hands on his knees. "Thank God, you missed."

Leto lowered his weapon. "I did not miss. I changed my aim at the last second."

Staring at my hand, I wondered why I wasn't able to bring out my aura. If I couldn't make this work, then we'd never be able to save Celyse. I picked up a rock near my shoes and tossed it with a grunt.

"Good," Leto said. "Get mad. Maybe it will help you."

He whipped out another arrow from his quiver and aimed it at me again. "Shall we try again?"

Leto fired off dozens of arrows. Still, I couldn't get my aura to activate. And I was pissed.

After a while, Leto put his things away. "We should probably try a new approach."

I flashed him an exasperated look. "Ya think?"

"Yes. I think. But let us take a break first."

The warm March sun had crawled overhead, beating down on us with its golden rays. Sweat beads trickled down my neck and back, and my gashed forehead was killing me. I most definitely needed a break.

We went inside and sat around the kitchen table, the three of us drinking water in silence. My hopes of being the one to save the day and get the girl had long been dashed. I felt awful. I wondered what we would do now.

Stuck in my thoughts, it took me a while to notice Leto studying my mom's wall of crosses. In the middle hung a portrait of Jesus. All my cousins had the same sort of set up in the kitchen. As a Catholic, religion was important to us. I wondered if the fae knew who Jesus was, or if they had a religion of their own. Leto's attention moved away from the display.

"Julio, there are a few things you need to know about Celyse," he began.

His statement surprised me, and I tensed, waiting for a punch to the gut. "Like what?"

Leto wrapped his hands around his glass of water. "Her family, the Strong family, is the purest, most evil fae bloodline in all of Faevenly."

I gulped but kept silent, letting him continue.

"Her mother and father, the High King and High Queen, are responsible for much death and suffering. If they could kill the entirety of the human realm, they would."

Manny flashed me a worried look but followed my lead and didn't say anything.

"There are two Strong daughters. They are twins. Malena was born first, and Celyse came after. Of the daughters, the High Queen favors Malena and seems to tolerate Celyse. Some say it is because Malena was the first one out of the womb and shares the full silver hair of her sires, but no one really knows for sure. But the High King, he favors them equally."

While I knew some of this, I didn't know the full extent of it all. I looked down, feeling horrible for Celyse, not even knowing how I would feel if I had a parent who treated me like that.

"That really sucks," I said.

Leto agreed. "It does. My allies and I do not really know what the implications are that Celyse is treated so, or how it factors into our plan, but it is knowledge."

"Know your enemy," I half whispered.

"Exactly," Leto said, then went on. "There are two

more things that are important, especially as they relate to you. Things you should know."

"Why is there always something worse?" I said, lifting my shoulders, tired of all the surprises. "Can't anything ever be easy?"

"Right?" Manny said with a laugh that trickled away because no one else laughed.

Leto's tone was even more serious than before. "Humans are the sworn enemy of the fae, like I told you. But there is more to it. Fae are deadly to humans. If a fae should ever kiss a human, the human will die."

Die? I felt like someone had punched me in the gut. My chair scraped across the tile floor as I got up from my seat. Now I knew why Celyse pulled away on the dock before we kissed. She didn't want to kill me.

"One more thing," Leto said.

I rubbed the back of my neck. "Really? Only one more?"

"Celyse recently turned eighteen, the age of courtship. She is scheduled to be married at the end of the year. If she is alive, that is."

Manny sucked in a breath. He looked at me with shock and pity because he knew how I felt about Celyse. She had worked her way into my heart, and I had worked my way into hers. But for what? If she was alive, which everything inside of me said she was, we could never be together.

Enraged at all the unknowns and obstacles before me, I formed a fist and pounded the kitchen cabinet, splintering the wood as my knuckles crashed through.

The tension in the air hung thick, and I couldn't bring myself to look at Leto or Manny. With my eyes cast down, my mind scrambled. No way was she being forced into marriage. There had to be a way out. There had to be something we could do.

"Can you send Celyse another note?" I asked Leto.

"I can."

"Tell her I said we are coming and to not get married."

"I will."

I brushed off my hand and headed back outside. "Let's get back to work."

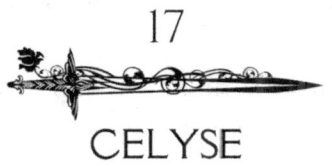

17

CELYSE

My feelings were all over the place. I was relieved that Julio and the others were alive but devastated that Mother had arranged for me to wed a monster from the Sublands. It might as well have been a death sentence. But I was not going to do it. I was either going to run away and find a way back to the human realm, or Julio and the others would show up and help me escape.

Question was, which one would happen first?

Peeking at the note from Leto, I thought I should burn it. I dropped it in a glass bowl, then retrieved a candle. I lit the paper and watched it catch fire. It crinkled into ash, sending wisps of smoke into the air. I pushed the bowl away, wondering how long it would take for me to hear from Julio, thinking I could not and would not wait.

I needed to act. But what to do?

"Celyse!" Malena dashed into the room and hurried over to me. She grabbed my hands. "I have learned that you will be wedded to someone from the Sublands! I am horrified! And I am sorry!" Her look of concern gave way to a scowl. "But you should not have run away!"

It was just like her to be sad and concerned for me in one breath, and disappointed and critical in the next. Gazing upon her innocent green eyes, realizing she knew nothing of Mother's plan, I cautioned myself to be careful with my words.

"I should not have done a lot of things. But it is true. According to mother, the Sublander is coming tonight." My voice trailed off a bit. "We wed in three days."

Her hand went to her chest while her lips parted in surprise. "He is coming tonight? And the wedding will be in three days? Mother did not tell me."

Interesting that Mother had not informed Malena of my hasty marriage. For a second there, I almost felt sorry for my sister. Almost.

"I fear Mother does not tell a lot of things," I cautioned.

Malena pursed her lips and crossed her arms. "Do not speak ill of Mother; she does everything for us."

I wanted to say something about how Mother did everything for *her*, but kept my words to myself. It would do no good. Malena must have thought the same because she continued on.

"Do you know anything about the Sublander?" she asked. "What did Mother say?"

I shook my head. "She did not say much. Only that his name is Rook Cailean."

"Rook," she said, accentuating the K as if the name

were a bad word. "Sounds absolutely horrid." Then she lifted her chin and took on an expression of determination. "But you will make the best of this! And I will help you!" She glanced about the room. "Hmm, where is a maid servant when you need one?"

I wanted to say the maid servants were forbidden by mother, but held my tongue. Instead, I said, "I do not know where they are."

"Do not fear, my sister. I will see to it. I shall be right back." She got up and dashed away. When she returned, she brought with her our trio of maid servants.

Malena started issuing orders. "You will prepare the dressing chamber at once. Fetch Lady Celyse and myself the finest gowns for tonight's guest." She glanced over at me. "Do you have any special requests?"

"To not get married," I answered.

Malena raised her brow at me, then said to the them, "No special requests. But we require four dresses to choose from. Now go, and hurry. And make sure to bring water and fresh fruit. Lady Celyse and I will meet you there."

Malena sat on the edge of my bed as the crew scurried away. She folded her hands on her lap, waiting for the room to empty. "Before we head to the dressing chamber, I want to talk to you about why you went off like you did."

My back straightened as I waited to see where she was going with this.

"After all these years of you saying you wanted to run away, I never thought you would. I can only assume it had something to do with the shimmer you had found and used to visit that dreadful human you told me about."

My stomach dropped. I had no idea where she was going with her words, but knew I needed to do whatever I could to protect Julio and the others. I kept silent so she could finish.

"I am in agreement with Mother that it is best for the sentinels around Torch Lake to be doubled. And for all the lost and misplaced shimmers to be destroyed. No one should be using the shimmers without permission or manipulating them in any way. Least of all you, a daughter of Strong Haven."

Unable to bite my tongue any further, I asked, "And what if Mother and Father are the ones committing misdeeds with the shimmers? What then?"

Even though I had no proof that Mother and Father were involved in any such actions, I firmly believed Leto's assertions that they were. Especially Mother. I had seen her darkest side.

Malena's nostrils flared. "Mother and Father are the High King and High Queen. They will only act in a way that supports this house, their rule, and us. As the future High Queen, I understand this burden. As a princess of Strong Haven, you should too." She softened her features. "Please, let us not argue, my sister."

"I am not arguing. Are you?"

She rolled her eyes. "Honestly, Celyse. Can we

simply be loving sisters, doing what is best for our family name? Can we do that?"

"What if what is best for the family name is not what is best for me?" I challenged, hoping to get through to her.

"*We* are the family name. They are one in the same. That is what you do not understand."

Maid Rell entered the room, and not a moment too soon. She clapped her hands. "The dressing chamber is ready."

Malena smiled with excitement and pulled at my hands. "Come, let us go see our dresses!"

Upon leaving my bedchamber, Malena noticed Jaid. "Why is Jaid here?" she asked as we made our way down the corridor. "And why is he following us?"

"Mother thinks I need a minder."

She smirked. "Well, I suppose you earned it."

Malena was not wrong about that, though I would never admit it.

The dressing chamber had been sprayed with oils, and every vase filled with fresh cuttings of rose and lavender. Four silk dresses were hung on dressing screens. Malena eyed them in turn, studying them with a critical eye. The dresses were green, blue, pink, and purple. The green and blue ones had dramatic full-sized skirts. The pink and purple ones featured an elegant sheath skirt with a small flare at the bottom.

"I think pink would be splendid on you for your first meeting with your betrothed," Malena said.

She looked at me to see if I approved, and I too

thought the pink was lovely. Not that I wanted to impress the son of the Sublands, but I did have a part that I needed to play. And play it I would. "The pink is fine."

Malena smiled with approval. "Most excellent. I will wear the green one." She kissed my forehead. "All will be well, my sister. I know it."

The maid servants got busy tending to Malena on one side of the room and me on the other. They combed my hair, braiding two thin strands at the front of my face. They painted my lips, eyes, and cheeks, then helped me slip on the dress. When I looked at myself in the full-length mirror, a blush rose to my cheeks. The neckline plunged way deeper than I had expected, and the dress hugged my body tightly. My mind drifted to Julio. I wished I was putting on the dress for him. What would he think of it?

"You look stunning," Malena declared, looking me over approvingly.

"As do you, my sister," I said.

She curtsied. "Thank you. I do love green on me." She eyed herself one last time in the mirror before saying, "I am going on ahead of you so that you may have a grand entrance. I will see you soon."

She left and the maid servants followed, leaving me to walk alone. But then I remembered I would not be by myself, as I was sure Jaid was outside the dressing chamber.

Drawing in a deep breath, I exited my room. Sure enough, there he stood. Feet wide apart, arms crossed, bow and quiver at his back. His stare met mine for a few seconds, then fixed on a spot just beyond me. I noticed an onyx knife slung at his belt, like the knife I used to wear against my thigh from time to time. I did not think I had seen him wearing the weapon earlier.

I pointed at it. "Why are you wearing that?"

"I keep it on me when I am assigned to monitor at a close distance. It is effective for hand-to-hand combat."

"Oh." My thoughts went to Rook Cailean. "You think the Sublander coming here tonight means me ill?"

Jaid shifted slightly. "I do not know what he means."

It was an honest answer, and one that matched my sentiments exactly. For once, I was glad to have my childhood friend minding me.

"I will be going to the receiving room now," I announced. I moved closer to him. "I would appreciate an extra watchful eye this evening."

"I have always kept an extra watchful eye on you, my lady." He took a long pause then said in a lower tone. "And I always will."

His words brought forward a surge of memories mixed with emotions of a simpler time when we were young and without cares. Now, we had too many cares.

"Thank you, Jaid."

Keeping one step behind me, Jaid followed me down the corridor, down the steps, and to the receiving room. He fell back as I stalled for a moment, eying the scene. Mother and Father were sitting in their regular oversized, plush white chairs. To their right sat Malena and next to her was my empty seat.

Across from them sat the Sublander.

With my head held high and my shoulders back, I pushed my fear aside and entered the room. The Sublander was the first to catch sight of me and rose to his feet swiftly. Dressed in all black, he had thick dark hair pulled back in a singular long braid. Unlike most fae, who were tall and lean, he was tall yet broad with muscular arms and strong legs. His eyes were deep brown, and they studied me with animalistic intensity.

"Lady Celyse." His voice was low and deep, and he bowed before me. "I am Rook Cailean of the Sublands. It is my great privilege to make your acquaintance and to have your hand."

"I am honored as well," I said with a nod, holding my stare at the ground for a few seconds as I concealed my surprise at Rook's unconventional appearance. I took my seat next to Malena.

"Rook," Mother said, leading the conversation as she always did. "How fared your journey to Strong Haven?"

He angled his body to her. "The journey took one day and a night by carriage, with quick speed and favorable conditions."

"That is good to hear," Father responded. "There is nothing worse than travel in adverse conditions. Once, when we were traveling to Sand Bluff, the heavens sent down droves of rain. It was most tedious maneuvering the carriage through the deluge, and it added days to our journey."

"That is most unfortunate," Rook replied.

"It was indeed. Luckily, the High Queen and my daughters were here at the palace and were spared the unpleasantness."

"Most fortunate," Rook said.

"And how are things in the Sublands?" Mother asked in her usual tone of superiority.

"They are well, High Queen. My mother and father have strengthened unity and stability in the region, and wealth and trade have been in abundance."

"What do you trade?" I asked, taking interest in the topic, wondering what the dry region could possibly have that any other region would favor.

"We mine and trade precious gems and stones."

I blinked. Leto said my mother and father were using the shimmers to take humans for mining. Was this happening in the Sublands? Were Rook Cailean and his family part of their operation? Now I understood Mother's desire for me to wed one of their sons. Father too, and it made me sick. They were using me as a pawn to advance their atrocities.

Father expanded. "The Sublands are known for their caves and layered rock. Their once fledgling mining enterprise has recently become quite fruitful."

I forced myself not to scowl. "How lucky for the Sublands."

Rook narrowed his gaze on me. "There is no such

thing as luck when it comes to the Sublands. We toil and bleed for what we have."

I wanted to shoot something clever back at him about luck, but was not quick enough. The meal servants took away the opportunity, entering the room with a bell signaling time for supper. Mother rose to her feet, then Father, Malena, and me. Rook was last.

Mother extended her long skinny fingers to Father. Father took them, and together they led the way outside to a large wooden table set up with cheeses, nuts, vegetables, breads, and dipping sauces. Malena hooked my arm with hers and squeezed. Her expression conveyed her approval of Rook, but she had no idea what I knew. And I could never tell her. She would never turn against Mother or Father, especially Mother.

The supper went on like any other supper. Mother and Father did most of the chatting with our guest, Malena chimed in, and I added where appropriate. But as the minutes turned into hours, something else about Rook began to niggle at me. I studied him when he was not looking, trying to put my finger on it, until it occurred to me—he was not taking much interest in me.

With Jorn, before he tried to compel me, it was clear he was attracted to me. Same thing with Barent. But with Rook, it was as if I was not even at the table. Malena too, for that matter. He gave his words to Mother and Father only. And then I noticed something else. He was studying the grounds. Not overtly, but in a clandestine way. He would take a few bites, then eye the shrubbery and trees. Between drinks, his gaze would drift to different angles of the palace. He paid attention to the wood of the table and the glass of the supperware. He even took careful note of the maid servants.

Rook Cailean was up to something.

When everyone finished with their meal and the conversation began to dull, Rook finally gave me his attention. "May I have the honor of an after-supper stroll?"

The last time I was asked that question, I was attacked. Would the same thing happen with Rook? I had to believe that if it did, Jaid would act.

"You may," I answered.

We left the table and started on the gravel path. Floating orbs dotted the pathway, illuminating our steps, and a soft, cool breeze rustled the trees. We wound our way through the garden in silence. I thought of the knife Ferna had held to my throat in the bakery, and the knife Jaid wore at his belt. I wished I was wearing mine at my thigh and made a decision to put it on as soon as I got back to my room.

"Who is trailing us?" Rook asked after a while.

My pace slowed as I considered my response. Jaid was undoubtedly close by, but close enough for Rook to hear? Not even I detected his sound. "One of the palace guards."

"The same one that killed Jorn Lind?" he asked.

I stopped and raised a brow, wondering if I should

twist my answer and shroud the truth, but then I thought it did not matter. Jorn deserved what he got.

"Yes, the same one."

"I see," Rook said as we continued walking.

Deciding to be bold, I added, "If you should threaten me in any way, you will meet the same fate."

"I expect no less," he answered.

He laced his fingers behind his back, not even bothering to touch me or get near me. Which I was glad for, but also slightly offended by. Perhaps he secretly wanted to wed Malena and only ended up with me because she wanted Alexander Kane. Not that it mattered. He was going to be quite surprised to find me absent on our wedding day.

"There are quite the murmurings floating around Faevenly regarding Jorn Lind and his family," he said as he admired the moon and the stars, as if we were having a casual and cordial conversation. "And the shimmers."

Stifling a gulp, I said nothing, keeping my eyes on the moon too, playing whatever game he came here to play. "Is that so?" I asked.

"It is so."

I started formulating my exit plan, thinking of the best excuse to take my leave, when suddenly he stopped. He turned to me. "I do not want to wed you."

My eyes grew wide. I was not expecting those words at all, and I had no idea how to respond.

"I also do not want to wed Malena."

With my mind churning, I took two steps back, not

even sure why I was increasing the distance between us but feeling like I needed to. "What do you want, then?"

He stepped closer. "I want to kill your mother."

An icy blast of surprise shot through my body, sending tingles all over me. I wondered if this was a test of my mother's and Rook was in on it. I needed to continue playing the part of a dutiful daughter. At least for now. "I could have your head for that."

"You could, but you will not." His towering frame lowered a bit and he moved even closer to me, as if telling me a secret. "I know this because you want the same thing. I see it in the way you carry yourself around her, your tone when addressing her, the way you leer at her when you think no one is looking. Word has spread of how she mistreats you, and now I have seen it for myself. You hate her. I am certain you want her dead too."

So, he was paying attention to me after all—keen attention. My hands trembled. My heart raced. I backed away from him, unsure of how to respond, then raised my hand slightly behind my back and flicked my fingers, the gesture Malena and I had been taught to make when we needed a guard.

In a flash, Jaid swooped in and stood by my side. He placed his hand on the small of my back. "My lady?"

"Rook of the Sublands has expressed his desire to take his leave. Can you please see him out?"

Jaid bowed. "Of course, my lady."

Jaid gestured for Rook to proceed ahead of him. Before he did, the malicious fae from the Sublands kept his dark stare on me. He gave me a deep nod. "Thank you for the enchanting evening, my betrothed. I will call on you in the morn. We wed in three days, after all."

Hatred for Rook filled me, and suspicion and distrust. But also, a fear that he knew my innermost thoughts. Was I that transparent with my feelings for my mother? And if I was, how was *he* able to see it and not my father and sister? And *did* I want her dead?

No matter how much I hated her, and she hated me, she was still my mother. I could not kill her or allow her to be killed.

Could I?

Turning on my heels, I stomped my way back to my room. When I got there, Malena was waiting for me, smiling eagerly.

"You must tell me everything!" she exclaimed. "What was Rook like? What did he say on your walk? And did you give him your first kiss?"

I paced about the room, unsure of how much to say to her, settling on the most basic truths. "He was wretched and sullen, and his company on our walk was abhorrent. And I most certainly did not give him my first kiss."

"Oh, Celyse. You are too hard to please," she said with a laugh.

"Well, if I am too hard to please, then you are too easy to please."

She laughed again. "Maybe I am."

She then started chatting about Alexander Kane and how dreamy he was and how wonderful his family was. She droned on and on about him until finally she ran out of words and retired to her bedchamber.

I paced my room, wringing my hands together, my mind running wild with everything about Rook—his appearance, his brashness, the way he had been able to see things about me and my mother.

Who in thunderation did he think he was?

I forced my hands to unclasp. I steadied my breathing. I would not let Rook get the better of me.

When I finally went to bed, I did not want to think about him at all. I hugged my pillow tightly, turning all my thoughts to Julio, wishing he was with me. I prayed to the sun, the moon, and the stars I would get another note, because I did not know how long I could last like this.

18

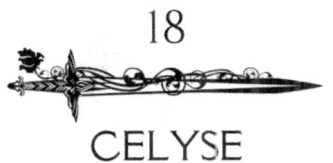

CELYSE

I woke up feeling as if I had not slept a wink, because I had not. My mind was plagued with Rook's disclosure that he was using me to kill my mother. And I had no idea what I was supposed to do with that information.

"Nothing," I muttered to myself. "I do nothing and escape. It is the only way. And if she is killed, then so be it."

Since my shimmer was left in the human realm, I would need to find another lost or misplaced one, which was unlikely. That left the shimmers at Torch Lake as my only option. Even though the sentinels were doubled, and the wolfbeasts were on the grounds, I would have to brave the lake myself. With their intricate underground tunnel system, I thought Adva and her brother could help me find a path there. I needed to find them.

But first, I needed my knife.

After dressing for the day, I started searching for my black onyx blade. I checked the desk, my wardrobe, my vanity. I even checked under my mattress. Where had it gone? I had not worn it in a

while, but I was sure I had left it in my desk. Had
someone been in my bedchamber? I thought Jaid
might know.

I emerged from my room and found him on alert. I
wondered if he ever slept or went to the washroom.

"Jaid, I require your presence in my bedchamber," I
ordered.

He swallowed, trying to conceal his surprise. "Yes,
my lady."

He entered my chamber but stayed near the door,
staring straight ahead instead of looking at me. I
glanced at the knife at his belt and the one strapped to
his thigh.

"Can I trust you with a request?" I asked.

He swept his gaze over to me as he held up his
hand. "Speak no further. I am obliged to the High
Queen and cannot entertain any contrary requests."
Then he added in a low tone, "But if I am compelled,
then whatever is requested of me would not put me at
odds with my directive."

He was asking me to compel him? And if that was
the case, then did that mean he was not completely
aligned with my mother? Perhaps I could count on his
friendship after all. I stood before him.

I stared into his violet eyes. I summoned all my
strength and will into my words, and when I felt a heat
rising inside of me, I said, "Hear me. **You will give me
your knife and tell no one that I compelled you to
give it to me, that you gave it to me, or that I have it.**"

He stood frozen for a few seconds, then leaned

over. He unfastened the band around his thigh that held his knife and handed the set over to me.

With a nod, I took it. "Thank you, Jaid. You may go back outside to the corridor."

He blinked a few times, then said, "Yes, my lady."

Alone again, I hiked up the skirt of my dress and strapped the band around my upper thigh. The leather was soft and comfortable, the knife warm and not too bulky. I had missed wearing a knife. I patted it, feeling confident that if anyone should threaten me, and if Jaid could not come to my aid in time, I would be fine. I needed to be able to take care of myself, and I was ready.

Leaving my bedchamber with Jaid at my heels, I made my way to the garden for breakfast. Like before, I meandered my way through the shrubs and vines, wondering if another gnome would have a note for me, but none appeared. Eventually, pangs of hunger cut my search short, and I wound my way to the breakfast table.

"There she is," my father announced. He was sitting with Mother and Malena at a table filled with our usual morning spread.

As I sat down, a meal servant appeared and filled my glass with mint berry juice. With a glance I could see it was not Adva. I did a quick scan of the other meal servants and attendants but did not find her amongst them. Where was she?

With Adva nowhere in sight, my attention went back to Mother. She avoided direct eye contact with me, but I could tell she was watching me from the corner of her eye. Like a vulture.

She took her napkin from her lap and dotted the corners of her mouth. "The wedding plans are underway," she announced. "Maid Rell is seeing to the dress, flowers, food, and drink. The provinces have all been notified and are sending their dignitaries posthaste."

I put my bread down, losing my appetite as I pictured Jorn with an arrow through his head. "What of Cuesta?"

"Ah, yes," Father said. "Cuesta. We received a falcon from them this morning."

"Father, you did not say," Malena chimed in, looked displeased that she had not been told. I could see why. She was the heir apparent after all.

"I wanted to wait for Celyse to join us," Father explained. "Now that she is here, I can tell you both that the Linds send their deepest regrets and contrition over the acts of their son, Jorn. They have vowed no further harm."

I resisted the urge to shake my head because the communication did not sound right at all. "Father, their son was killed and they offered *their* regrets?"

Mother's lip curled. "Their position came on the heels of a visit from Draven. He helped them see the folly in their son's actions."

"Draven the witch?" I asked with a gulp.

Malena and I exchanged glances. Draven was a powerful, mysterious, and fearsome witch. Rumored to be as old as the world itself, Draven answered to no one, but had formed a bond centuries ago with the Strongs, especially Mother. No one ever mentioned how the bond was formed, or even when, but whenever Mother or Father needed a witch, he appeared. His powers were said to rival all the gods of the sun and the moon and the stars, and none who defied him ever lived to tell.

"There will be no retaliation from the Linds then?" Malena asked.

"None," Mother answered. "I assure you; Draven's methods were thorough. The vow offered by House Lind is reliable."

"What did he do to them?" Malena asked, looking curious and somewhat delighted. "I hope something terrible."

"Draven's devices are his and his alone," Mother explained. Then she added, almost as an afterthought, "But I can promise it was most definitely terrible."

A shiver worked its way through me, but I kept it hidden. I needed to act as normal as possible, lest I draw any further ire from mother. But the mere mention of Draven had me on edge.

The conversation drifted to other wedding details, but I hardly joined in. Other than a few forced smiles and some less than enthusiastic nodding, I let Mother and Malena drive the discussion. At the conclusion of our meal, Mother and Father left to attend to Strong Haven business, and I decided to make my way to the cookhouse to look for Adva and her brother. With Jaid not far behind me, I took the long way through the garden so I could clear my mind and search for another note bearing gnome.

"Where are you off to?" Malena asked, coming up to me.

I had not planned on her company and paused a moment while I formulated a response. "I thought I would take in a stroll before my visit with Rook." My response was not a lie. I was indeed strolling, and at some point, Rook would be calling.

"May I walk with you, then?"

"Of course."

She leaned her head against mine as we continued walking together, arm in arm. I was never able to be mad at her for taking mother's affection. It was not her fault she came into the world before me and had a duty to fulfill as firstborn. I should not blame her for her timing. Indeed, I should thank her. I had no desire to rule Strong Haven or be the eventual High Queen of Faevenly. Instead, I longed to be in the human realm.

As eager as I was to leave, I thought I would miss my sister. I nestled my head against hers, enjoying her presence, soothed by the smell of her floral oils, surrounded by springtime blossoms and chirpings of new life. In a perfect world, she would rule Faevenly, and I would live in the human realm, and we would visit, and be with whomever we wished, and share stories of our lives.

But the world was not perfect.

"What is on your mind, my sister?" she asked.

Taking in a deep breath, I wished to tell her my

heart, but I could not. Instead, I settled on a simple declaration. "The imperfect world."

She squeezed my arm. "Do not be so dramatic! I prefer we speak of other things, like how grand your wedding will be, and mine later in the year. And even though we will be far apart, we will remain as close as ever. We will visit regularly and lean on each other for support and advice. Our children will be the best of friends, and one day I will rule all of Faevenly."

"Yes, that would be lovely," I sighed.

She stopped and pulled me in front of her. "Is that a sigh of contentment, or a sigh of sadness?"

"Both, I guess," I admitted, not wanting to expand on my feelings. There was no point. She could do nothing to help me.

"Are you not pleased with Rook?"

I scoffed. "Pleased? Is that a legitimate question? He is a Sublander and a monster."

She glanced down and twirled a lock of silver hair. "I must admit, I did not expect him to be so striking."

My mouth fell open. "Malena! Do you find him pleasing? He is vile!"

She dropped her hand quickly. "No! I most assuredly do not find him pleasing! He is your betrothed. Your wedding is nigh. I am in love with Alexander. But sister, he is not as bad as I had envisioned. Perhaps a union with him will be bearable. Do you not think so?"

"No! I most certainly do not think so!" No one compared to Julio. But I could not say that to her.

She took my hands and squeezed. "Well, maybe, at least, you can settle into him."

I shivered. "Never. Not if all the stars were falling would I ever settle for a fae like him." I shrugged off the hatred festering inside of me, not wanting to think of Rook and his wicked ways. I was not going to wed him anyway.

"Can we speak of something else, please?" I asked.

"Of course. I did not mean to irk you so."

We resumed our walk, chatting about things like flowers and dresses, two of Malena's favorite topics. After a while, and with a warm hug, she returned to the palace, finally leaving me to meander by myself.

I continued to the garden fountains and sat on a concrete bench. The steady trickling of the water as it sprayed into the air and splashed back down was the perfect accompaniment for my wandering mind. Malena had taken a fancy to Rook, and I was stunned. But Mother would have never approved of a union between them. The Sublands was too inferior of a place for Malena to end up, and she was only sending me there to get rid of me. I was more than happy to ruin her plan by leaving Faevenly.

But what of Rook wanting to kill her? I had not figured out what to do with that information, if anything.

Getting up from my place, I spotted a small green figure skitter across the path. A gnome. I scanned my surroundings. Not seeing anyone, including Jaid, I hurried over to the spot and saw another rolled up piece of paper. I snatched it up and held it close to me, then unfolded it.

Celyse. We are coming. Do not get married.

Julio

My heart soared. He was coming for me! But I thought I needed to find Adva anyway. I still might need her help. With a spring in my step, I slipped the note in my bodice and was headed for the cookhouse when I turned and nearly collided with Rook.

"Rook!" I exclaimed, taken aback. "I did not see you there."

"Of course not. Your gaze was fixed on a parchment that is now nestled in your bosom. You should take better care when you are attempting clandestine activities."

I drew in a sharp breath. "You are the one engaging in such activities," I accused, turning attention away from myself.

"Perhaps we both are," he smirked. "But truly, it makes no matter. Not to me, anyway. I am not your enemy. I assure you." He held out his hand. "May I accompany you?"

Hiding a silent gulp, I wrestled between pushing his hand away and accepting it.

"Come on, take it," he encouraged. "You know you want to."

"You are quite presumptuous."

"I cannot argue with that, Princess."

The need to know more from him won over my disdain, and I slipped my thin hand into his thick one.

It was rough and calloused, much like his personality. As we walked, he studied every tree, every bush, the path ahead of us, and even the skies above.

"What are you looking for?" I asked him.

"I am only studying your land. Not looking for anything."

Following his gaze, I tried to see things from his perspective. Strong Haven was lush with greenery and wildlife, while his home was barren with desert and rock. Perhaps he did not favor his land, though I could not help but think he belonged in the desert and rock.

"Do you want to know why I am going to kill your mother?" He asked so suddenly.

I snapped my hand back and halted in place, unsure of how to respond. I wanted to get as far away from him as possible, but a large part of me wanted to hear what he had to say. I raised my chin. "Explain."

The Sublander moved in. He kept his menacing stare on me. "After the Great Shimmer War, Strong Haven divided the land into provinces but kept the Sublands carved out and isolated. Many think it was our choice, but it was not. We wanted to be a part of the Council of Five, but we were not deemed worthy because of our role."

"Role?" I asked. "I know the history, but as far as the actions of the Sublands in the Great Shimmer War, I thought you had no role."

He laughed. "Oh, we had a role. A role that is hidden from the history tellings."

"What was your role then?" I asked, my mind spinning.

"We stood by the humans, protected them, fought with them, died with them."

I stifled the gasp that threatened to come out of me, my mind reeling. "You did?"

"We did. And we were punished because of it. Denied being named a province, forced to live without the backing of the precious almighty Strong Haven. Which suited us fine in the long run. Our rejection made us stronger. And then we found this."

He pulled a clear blue rock out of his pocket. It resembled the lightest part of the ocean. "This is called aquoise. This rock, shaved and mixed with the right herbs, enhances the innate powers of the user, but you need a lot of it to produce the effect, and the effect is finite."

This was it. This was the rock Leto had talked about. It had to be. I thought of the innate abilities of the fae and what a fae could do if those abilities were doubled or even tripled. With a rock like that, a fae could be invincible.

He put the rock back in his pocket. "We told Strong Haven about our findings, hoping to gain favor and a seat on the council, but they silenced us because they wanted the aquoise for themselves. So, we did their will, mined the rock for them, and they provided us with other things we needed—food, clothing, materials, favors."

My mind struggled to understand the nuances of

what he was telling me, because I felt like there was so much more he was not saying. "If you trade this rock, this aquoise, then how have I not heard of it?"

"We trade many rocks, but not aquoise. Aquoise belongs to the High King and High Queen. But excavating it is a deadly endeavor. It is so deep into the dirt it costs lives to free just one small piece."

"Lives?" I asked, horrified, but now knowing everything Leto had said was true. "So, my mother and father are indeed taking humans and using them to mine these rocks, using the shimmers unbeknownst to the other provinces."

"You know?" he asked.

"I have only recently heard," I muttered.

He stopped and studied my face as he fisted his hands at his sides. "Many humans have been taken and continue to be taken to get your precious High King and High Queen what they want. Good honest humans. And there is no stopping them. That is why I am going to kill the High Queen." He was out of breath, so worked up with fiery emotion that it took him a minute to calm down.

"And my father? Are you killing him too?"

"No, but I will if I have to. Your father does your mother's will. He has been under her compulsion for centuries."

I gasped. "That cannot be."

"It can be, and it is. Have you not noticed how he abides by her rule? He does not think without her first telling him what to think. He does not have any sort of independent thought in his brain. She controls all of him."

My mind recognized the truth of his words, but I refused to say so.

Rook went on. "Taking humans for slave labor was the High Queen's idea, and she is the one who will pay. The Sublands demand freedom and so do the humans."

I pictured my father, mindlessly following my mother's directives. I also pictured Julio, and even Manny. The idea of them being taken and forced into slave labor and killed turned my stomach.

"Why do you even care about humans?" I demanded. "Who are they to you?"

He swept his stare back on me. "Because I am human."

My mouth dropped and my mind reeled and I stepped back. "It is not possible," I muttered.

"Oh, it is. I am a human living as a fae and none of you are the wiser. As a child, I watched my people get taken and forced into the mines only to be brought out in body bags. Over the years, as I grew, I devised a plan. The fae that had control over the Sublands, the Caileans, had no love for Strong Haven and much sympathy for humans. They listened to my ideas, took me in as their son, groomed me for this very moment when I would stand beside the princess of Strong Haven before the High Queen and High King, surrounded by our allies at a wedding, and kill the

singular person responsible for decades of anguish—
the High Queen."

My body shook to the core and I was too stunned to
say anything. But I did not need to. He was more than
eager to go on.

"Do you want to know why you are going to help
me?" he asked.

My hand went to where my knife was, making sure
it was still there, wondering if I should draw it out
because everything about Rook horrified me—his wild
eyes, his flared nostrils, the veins that bulged from his
neck with each word that came out of him. Yet my
need to know more outweighed my fear.

Taking my silence as acquiescence, he brought his
face close to mine. "You are going to help me because
you are half human."

I placed my hand on my chest, thunderstruck, and
stumbled back.

"My lady," Jaid said, swooping in beside me and
placing his hand under my elbow. He stared Rook
down. "Is this Sublander causing you distress?"

For once, I was grateful for Jaid's watchful eye. I
backed further away from Rook, desperately needing
to get away from him. "Thank you, Jaid. I, uh." I
pinched the bridge of my nose as I struggled for what
to say. "I was just leaving."

With a swish of my skirt and my stomach in knots,
I walked away as fast as I could. Was Rook telling me
the truth? About himself, my mother and father, and
me? Was I truly half human? I was a twin, as was

Malena—did that mean Malena was half human too? If so, how could Mother have done that to Father? Bedded a human? She hated humans more than anyone. There was also the fact that fae were deadly to humans.

So many questions swirled through my mind, like a destructive tornado, tearing apart the familiar landscape that had been built over the years. Everything inside of me doubted Rook.

But I also believed him.

19

JULIO

As the day turned into night, I thought Leto must've unleashed a hundred or more arrows at me. They zipped over my head, grazed my neck, and nicked my ears and shoulders. And each time, I was unable to bring forth any kind of *curandero* mojo to defend myself. No aura, no spark, no powers. With a gashed forehead from the car crash, a bruised hand from punching the kitchen cabinet, and now tiny cuts all over from my shoulders up, I was sure I looked like a disaster survivor.

And I felt like one.

"I can't take it!" Manny called out, stepping between me and Leto with his arms outstretched. "This has crossed the line from being kinda cool to really not cool."

Manny was right. And the truth was, I was a little scared of being accidentally killed in my backyard, even if I was determined to do whatever it took to save Celyse. I wouldn't be able to help her if I was dead.

Leto lowered his weapon. "Manny speaks wisely. You need a break, Julio. And so do I."

With his quiver in hand, he walked around the

backyard retrieving his arrows. When everything was gathered up, he came over to me. "Whatever power lives inside of you is too smart for our trickery. It knows I will not strike you. You need a real threat."

While staring down Leto's arrows, I had the same thought. That I needed to actually be at risk for my aura to activate. "You think I'll be able to make it work if I'm in real trouble?"

He nodded. "I think so."

"Well, that's good enough for me. When do we leave?" I asked, eager to get Celyse.

He studied my face. "Go in and clean up. You are a literal bloody mess. After that we can talk about our departure."

I brought my hand to my neck and felt sticky cuts all over. They were small and not too deep, but annoying. A shower and a fresh bandage on my forehead would do me good, along with another shot of Leto's disgusting concoction. The one he had given me in the morning was starting to wear off.

"Fine," I gave in. "If we're finished out here, then I'm going to take a quick shower. Do you mind making me another drink?"

"I do not mind at all." Leto looked at Manny. "You want one too?"

Manny shook his head. "Another delicious shot of grossness? Nah. I'm good."

I left Leto and Manny and made my way to my room. Finally alone, I shut the door and sat on my bed, thinking of everything that had happened so far.

Nothing had gone our way—nothing. And I had a nagging feeling that wouldn't change.

My mom's ringtone cut my thoughts short. I pulled out my phone and answered with the most normal voice I could muster. "Hey, Mom."

"*Mijo*, how's it going? You haven't called me today."

"I know, *lo siento*. I've been out back, playing soccer with Manny. Guess I lost track of time."

"That's okay." She waited a second before continuing. "How are things at home? I can't help feeling like something is not quite right, but I can't put my finger on it."

I decided to mix the truth with a lie, hoping my mom could help me somehow. I really needed her wisdom. "Well, if you must know, there's this girl. Someone I've known for a few months. I really care about her and she's in trouble."

"Trouble? What kind?"

"She has these really awful parents. They're not very good to her and she wants to run away. And I want to help her."

"Oh, I see. Maybe I'm sensing your worry for her."

"Probably, because I can't stop thinking about her."

She paused for a bit. "If she is in danger, she needs to remove herself from the situation. Can she go to a trusted family member?"

"That's the thing—she doesn't have anyone to go to."

"Well, your friends are always welcome at our house. That includes this girl. I trust you will do whatever you can to help her. You have very good instincts, *Mijo*."

There was no way for me to ask her about auras or anything else that had to do with our abilities. She'd know something was up and come home. And right now, I needed her to stay where she was. "Thanks, Mom. You're the best."

"You're welcome, *Mijo*." She drew in deep breath, almost like a sigh. "One more thing."

"Yeah?"

"I'm feeling like I need to tell you it's okay to be who you are." She let her words sink in before adding, "That the power inside of you is amazing and can do great things. Does that make sense?"

"Actually, yes," I answered, feeling a little hopeful. "It does. Thanks, Mom."

"You are welcome, *Mijo*. I must go now, but call me tomorrow."

"I will."

After the conversation with my mom, I entered the shower with a renewed sense of purpose. Mom was right. I *did* have good instincts and I *could* do great things. I had to trust that if I could help Celyse back at the car crash, I could do it again.

Feeling rejuvenated, I finished my shower, got dressed, and went to the living room. Manny was freshly showered too and watching TV, but Leto was gone. "Where is he now?"

Manny shrugged. "Said he had to do a few things and that he'd be back." He pointed to a glass with yellow liquid on the coffee table. "Your special order is ready."

"Yum." I faked a smile, took the glass, and tossed the drink down. I shuddered while it worked its way through me, then let out a cough. "I think that may be worse the second time around."

"Hopefully, it'll help you out, because you look scary, dude. If your mom sees you like that all cut up and looking like death warmed over, she's gonna freak."

I eased myself onto the chair next to him. "I'll deal with that when the time comes. What about you? Was your dad there when you went home to shower? Did he see your lip?"

"He was home, but he didn't see it because he was sleeping. He's been working double shifts at the warehouse and naps whenever he can."

"I guess that's just as well."

"Yeah."

I took my phone out of my pocket to check the time. Eight o' clock. I placed it back, then started drumming my fingers on my knees. "Where is he?"

"He'll be here," Manny offered. "He hasn't even been gone that long. We should probably eat some dinner anyway."

A tingle struck my neck and worked down my body in a whoosh. I sat rigid and gripped my knees.

Manny snapped his attention to me. "You're getting a witchy vibe, aren't you?"

"Yeah," I said in a hushed voice, the tingle growing

in intensity. I slowly rose to my feet, glancing about the room, when Abigail darted through the wall.

"You have to go!" she urged with wide eyes. "Now!"

A blast from outside shook the house. Then another. "I think it's too late for that," I whispered to the girl.

"Too late for what?" Manny asked, fear plastered all over his face.

"To go," I answered. I grabbed his arm, moving away from the front door.

Abigail turned her attention to the front of the house. "I'll try to do what I can."

The ghost girl dashed back outside. Manny followed my line of sight, looking at the spot. "Is there a ghost here?"

"There was. She's outside now, trying to help."

"Help what?"

A crash sounded from the rear of the house. Leto, Ferna, and Parlan charged in. Ferna and Parlan had their bows up, arrows at the ready. They bolted in front of me and Manny, facing the door.

Another blast rocked the house. It was the same witch from when Leto's house burned down. I could feel it in my gut. "It's the witch from before," I said.

"Oh, no!" Manny called out. "The witch that started the fire?"

"The very one," Leto confirmed. He grabbed his bags. He slung one over his shoulder, then unzipped the other.

An old man and an old woman filtered into the

house. I knew them well. They died in a car crash on my street more than ten years ago, and their spirits roamed the neighborhood. Sometimes they'd come over and chat with my mom, but they never really bothered me.

"*Ellos vienen,*" the old, weathered woman said, her ghostly eyes filled with terror.

"They're coming!" I called out, translating her warning. "So, whatever you're doing, Leto, hurry!"

Leto drew a small, shimmery orb out of his bag. He stretched it out with his hands as my front door blasted away as if hit by a grenade. Ferna and Parlan held their position through the smoky debris, firing their arrows, zipping them one after another while Leto manipulated the shimmer until it formed a rectangle the size of a floor mirror. He grabbed me and Manny by the arms and shoved us toward the glow.

"Go!" Leto yelled.

He didn't have to ask me twice. With my hands on Manny's back, I pushed him through and followed behind him. We tumbled out onto a field and landed face first into dirt and grass. I whipped around to see Leto slip through after us, then Ferna and Parlan. Beyond them I spotted the black-robed witch still outside my house but moving in fast. He held a ball of fire in his hands and hurled it at us.

"Get down!" I yelled.

The red blast sailed through the shimmer. Leto and Ferna dodged it easily, but Parlan took a direct hit to the chest. The force lifted him and flung him away, knocking him to the ground with a thud.

"Freakin' close it!" Manny yelled.

Leto and Ferna grabbed the edges of the shimmer, minimizing it with a swoop. When it got as small as a baseball, Ferna let go and Leto smashed it to smithereens.

I watched the glowing bits float up into the night, thinking my home had just been destroyed, my mom was going to freak, and there was no way back.

Manny and I were stuck in Faevenly.

20

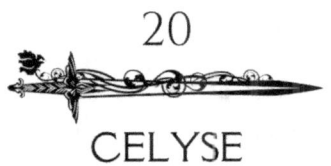

CELYSE

I spent the rest of the day by myself in my bedchamber, telling everyone I was not feeling well, but really, I needed to be by myself so I could think.

Rook was human, and claimed I was half human. But how could that be when I was a twin? And who could I ask? I could not ask Mother or Father, as they were implicated in Rook's allegations. Besides, if I went to Mother, she would most assuredly kill Rook and probably me too.

The maid servants bustled in with a tray of healing herbs and a bucket of hot water. I sat up in bed, not feeling like having steam in my face and herbs on my chest. I waved them away. "I am much better and do not need those things."

"Yes, my lady," they said, shuffling out of my room.

And then I thought of Maid Rell. As my minder and an integral part of my life since forever, she might know the truth. I sprang out of bed.

"Wait!" I called out. "Fetch Maid Rell, immediately."

"Yes, my lady," the trio said, shuffling out of my room.

I circled my room, anxious to see Maid Rell and get answers. Did I want to be half human? My thoughts went to Julio and my heart soared with the hope that maybe I could really and truly be with him. But what would it mean for me to be part of a race that was a mortal enemy to the fae?

Fae condemned mixed bloodlines.

Needing to calm myself, I opened my window and perched myself on my windowsill. I closed my eyes, letting the cool breeze work its way around my face and through my hair. The aroma of flowers and herbs wafting over me calmed my nerves.

A swift knock sounded on my door, and Maid Rell entered. Spotting me by the window, she rushed over and closed the window with a thud. "Your cold will only get worse, my lady! Now come, get back in bed."

I wrapped my hand around her thick wrist and whispered, "I am not ill, Maid Rell."

She frowned, then touched my forehead. She relaxed her scowl and caressed my face. "My dear, I know you do not want to wed. And I know your hasty marriage is not your doing."

A tear fell from my eye. "I most certainly do not want to wed. Not to a Sublander or anyone else from Faevenly. I am in love with..." I stopped, afraid of what her response would be to my confession.

"You may speak openly with me, my dear," she encouraged.

With a swallow, I went on. "I am in love with a human. One I met through a lost shimmer I found months ago."

Her eyes widened a bit before taking back their normal shape. She took my hands and pulled me over to sit with her on the edge of my bed. "My dear, a fancy is only that. A fancy. You must abide by your duty, no matter how hard it may be."

"No, Maid Rell," I said, shaking my head. "I am not going to marry Rook. I have a plan. Or the makings of a plan."

I did not know exactly how I was going to get out of marrying Rook, other than Julio and the others were coming, I had a knife at my thigh, and Rook did not want to marry me but only wanted to kill my mother. I gazed at the sympathetic face of my minder.

"I ask you to keep such things to yourself, my Lady," Maid Rell pleaded. "I would not forgive myself if I knew something and was forced to divulge the information."

"We are in agreement, there," I said. "And in truth, I did not ask you here to discuss wedding matters, but something else entirely."

"What is it, then?"

I drew in a deep breath, then blew it out. "Am I half human?"

Maid Rell's lips parted with surprise. Her eyes darted about the room, as if making sure no one else was around. Satisfied we were alone, she scooted closer to me.

"My dear, I am going to tell you the story of your birth, though I have been ordered to never do so. But you have asked, and the story has weighed heavy on me all these years. You should finally know the truth. Orders be damned."

I gulped. "If you are sure, I am most eager to know."

Maid Rell steadied her breathing, then began in a low voice. "The story begins with me explaining about your mother, the High Queen. My mother was your mother's minder, and so I have known your mother since we were little. We grew up together, played together, laughed together, and even cried together. She was a dutiful and proud girl, much like Malena, and she was my very best friend. She aspired to be the greatest queen that ever was and marry the most powerful king ever. And she did. She loved your father so very much, and he loved her. But over the years, she began to love power and position more."

She paused for a few moments, her eyes appearing lost in memory.

"Your father had great patience with her, but it began to wane over the years. As she traveled the provinces securing the position of Strong Haven and amassing loyalty and favors, your father found himself alone, wandering the grounds of Strong Haven, getting lost in the trees, seeking solace with nature."

"Like me," I whispered.

"Yes, my dear. Exactly like you. And like you, he came across a shimmer and became enamored with a human. So much so, he enlisted Draven the witch's help to be with her."

I sucked in a breath. "He did?"

Maid Rell stroked my hand. "He did. Draven made him a potion to counteract the deadly effect of fae on humans. And so they had relations and she became with child at the same time the High Queen became with child."

My entire body froze as Maid Rell's words sunk in.

"The High Queen learned of this woman and her unborn child and ordered an execution, but your father forbade it. This young woman was brought to the palace and kept hidden while she and the High Queen carried to term. And when you were born from your human mother, Malena was born from the High Queen, on the exact same day, mere hours apart. With Malena being born first."

Maid Rell stopped and waited for me to say something, but I had no words. I was stunned.

She held my hands firmly in hers. "At your father's insistence, he and the High Queen decided to hold you and your sister out as twins, saying Malena came first from the Queen. The words of trickery were easy since she did indeed come first from the Queen. No words were spoken of when you came, or from whom.

"The palace sent out notices to all the provinces of the good news that daughters were born at Strong Haven. It was easy to let others assume you were born of the same mother, as you and Malena looked so much alike. As you grew older, the only difference was your slightly stunted ears and your streak of black. A streak you share with your mother."

My hands went to my ears. I always wondered why they were not as pointed as everyone else's; now I knew. I stroked my hair. "I do not have an uncle with a dark streak?"

"A fae uncle? No, but again, it was an easy trickery of words as you mostly certainly do have an uncle in the human realm with a streak like that. Your mother told me."

The room fell quiet as we sat in silence for a few long seconds. Finally, I asked, "What happened to my mother?"

Maid Rell's eyes watered over. She tightened her hold on my hands. "The High Queen had your mother executed after you were born."

My heart snapped, and a sea of tears surged out of me. I leaned into Maid Rell and let my sorrow spill out as she held me in her arms, crying with me. After every tear was spent, I pulled away.

Maid Rell stroked my face. "I am so sorry, my dear love. So very sorry."

"Me too," I whispered as I rubbed my eyes. "But I want to be alone now."

"Very well." She was getting up to leave when I thought of something.

"Maid Rell, what was my mother's name?"

"Sarah. Her name was Sarah. She was your father's true love. And she was most lovely."

WITH MAID RELL GONE, I WANDERED BACK TO MY windowsill and pressed my forehead against the cool glass, the reality of who I was working its way through me —I was part human and part fae. Filled with a mystical darkness, but also a caring and loving heart. Finally, I understood why my mother—or rather, the High Queen —hated me. I was not her child but that of a human with whom my father had fallen in love. I understood that feeling because I had fallen in love with a human too.

My spirit called to the human realm, to Julio—to his warm smile, the way he looked at me, the tenderness when he touched me, the fierce protectiveness he had for me. He was the most amazing and wondrous creature I had ever met. My heart also loved my poor father who had been compelled for so long. I loved Malena too because she was my half-sister and innocent in all things. But the High Queen? I hated her. She was nothing to me. She had killed my mother.

And I wanted her dead.

With my gaze on the skies, I watched the darkness slowly take over the light, the moon and the stars illuminating as my mind replayed my conversation with Maid Rell over and over. I was fae blooded and human blooded.

And Rook knew.

I had stormed away from him when he told me the truth, but with our supposed wedding in less than twenty-four hours, I needed to see my would-be husband.

Our conversation was not complete.

With a renewed sense of purpose, I gathered my emotions and prepared myself mentally for another talk with Rook. I exited my room and found Jaid in his usual spot. I breezed past him and hurried downstairs and outside while he followed. With darkness falling, the orbs that lined the garden and walkways shone bright, dotting the path through the grounds and to the guest housing that sat on the edge of the property.

After a brisk two-mile walk, the stone cottage came into view. Without a word, Jaid fell back while I stood at the door, catching my breath before I knocked, my mind formulating what I would say.

"Lady Celyse," Rook called from behind me.

With a start, I turned to see Rook on the path, returning to the cottage. "Rook," I said with a nod, moving away from the door to allow him access. "I am here for a visit."

"I see that." He opened the door and held it ajar for me. "Please, come in."

I swept past the brooding human, went into the living room, and took a seat on a chunky wooden chair. The lights were dimmed, and a fire crackled in the fireplace. The smell of woodsy spice permeated the room.

Rook sat across from me. He studied me with his usual intensity. "I am supposing you are here because you have found my account of your lineage to be true."

Folding my hands on my lap I said, "I am, and I have."

He kept silent, waiting for me to continue. But now that I was with him, I did not even know what to say or where to begin.

My thoughts were wild. Finally, I settled on the most basic thing I wanted to know. "How did you know I was half human?"

Rook leaned forward. "Before your mother became with child and moved into the palace, she lived in the Sublands."

"The Sublands?" I asked with surprise. Maid Rell had left that part out.

"Yes, the Sublands. Your father kept her there in secret while his seed grew within her. With no other province interested in us, it served as the perfect hiding place."

"I see," I mumbled. "Did you know her then? My mother?"

"I did not. She lived in solitude, shrouded in privacy with only a singular attendant. The only time I saw her was when your father came for her to move her into the palace. I was but a boy and did not understand the implications of it all, until later."

With a gulp, I glanced down, thinking of how awful it must have been for my mother to be hidden away and then brought to the palace for birthing only to meet her demise soon after. I felt sick to my stomach and hated the High Queen even more.

"Is there anything else?" Rook asked.

My eyes met his and I studied his features—prominent dark eyebrows, piercing brown eyes, thick midnight hair with just a glimmer of pointed ears showing through. I considered the shape.

"I did not know humans have pointed ears."

He brushed his hair back and leaned forward so I could see his entire ear. The outermost edging of the helix had a thin scar that traveled from the middle up to the point.

I drew in a breath. "You carved them that way."

"Some human ears can be slightly pointed. Mine were not. I had to slice them to complete my ruse." He dropped his hair and sat back. "The thickness of my hair conceals the evidence."

I wanted to touch my own ears that were not as pointed as most fae's but stopped myself. He must have sensed my thoughts.

"Your ears are a hybrid it seems. Distinctively and naturally pointed, but not overly. It is probably what spared your life. The Queen would have murdered you herself if you had been born with rounded human shaped ears."

A shudder worked its way through me because he was right. If my ears had looked more human, I would not be alive.

"Is there anything else, Princess?"

I brought my gaze back to his, my disdain for him dissipating now that I knew we both had human blood. "Only one thing. I want the High Queen dead."

He nodded. "So, you *will* help me."

"I will not help you. But I will not stop you," I corrected.

He shifted in his seat, considering my position. "That is acceptable."

"Good." I stood, ready to leave, when it occurred to me that I had not asked him how he would do the deed. I eased myself back down on the chair. "You mentioned earlier in the garden that you would strike at the wedding with your allies. Who are they and how will you strike?"

"The less you know, the better. That way, if I fail, you can say you did not know my plan."

Fail? It never occurred to me that he would fail, he seemed so sure of himself. But he had a good point. The High Queen was cunning and powerful, and the Strong Haven guards formidable. Rook had a mighty foe to face.

"Very well," I said with a nod. I rose to my feet. "I will see you tomorrow then."

"Yes, tomorrow."

Glad to be outside, I let out a breath I had been holding deep inside me. Then I spotted Jaid and relaxed some. Having him around made me feel safe, even if he was reporting my every move to the High Queen. I wondered how he would react when he found out everything I had learned about myself and my father and the High Queen.

What would he think?

I approached him. "Are you getting tired of being my minder yet?"

Without waiting for him to reply, I started walking home, because his answer did not matter. We all had our roles to play now. And his and mine were opposed. Yet still, I longed for the company of my childhood friend.

Wanting to escape my lot in life for a little while and pretend everything was normal, I asked over my shoulder, "Do you remember that first time you showed me the secret path to Torch Lake so I could look at the shimmers?"

Jaid stayed behind me. "I do."

I turned to face him, remembering how young we were that very first time and how nervous he was to show me the path. Now the High Queen had him in her clutches, and I hated it.

"That was such a simpler time, was it not, Jaid? We were both so different. You were so focused on ambition while I had not a care in the world." My voice drifted. "Now, I have too many cares."

He hesitated before saying, "It was, and we were."

"Sometimes I think I would like to go back to that time of innocence. But I know there is no way."

Jaid maintained his silence, and I could not blame him. He belonged to the High Queen now. Sparing him from my forlorn chatter, I continued along the path as I walked back to my bedchamber.

Before I opened the door to my room, I turned to Jaid and studied his face. Should I warn him about what was going to happen to the Queen? I most certainly did not want him hurt, but I could not risk jeopardizing Rook's plan. Plus, if I knew Jaid, he could handle himself. Yet still, I wanted to say something.

"Jaid, everything is going to change tomorrow."

His eyes searched mine, but he only gave me a solemn nod before resuming his position in the corridor.

Inside my room, I leaned against the door, thinking I was ready for change but also scared. I had no idea how tomorrow would unfold, but I knew one thing for certain.

My life was about to be altered forever.

21

JULIO

Shock swept over me as I watched the particles of the portal to my house fade into the dark, drifting up into the night sky like fireflies burning into extinction.

"What the hell just happened?" Manny asked, his mouth open as he stared at the flecks of shimmer floating away. "Are we like, stuck here?"

"I think so," I mumbled, trying to wrap my brain around Leto smashing the shimmery portal to bits.

Manny grabbed his hair and pulled. "No, no, no."

Parlan let out a moan, clutching his chest as he walked over to us.

"Parlan!" Ferna called out, dropping her bow and arrow, and rushing over to him. "Are you okay?"

He rubbed his chest and moaned. "I am okay; it is only a flesh wound."

"Well, I'm not okay," Manny blurted out. "We were almost killed!" He spun around, looking in all directions. "Are we even safe right now?"

"Yes, we are safe," Leto answered. He secured his bags over his shoulders. "But we need to move."

With my breathing finally steadied, I held out my

hand to slow Leto. "Hang on a sec. My house was just destroyed!"

The tall, slender fae set his things down. "What do you want, Julio? Consolation of some sort? A hug? This is no time for human emotion. The Queen's witch did not follow us through, but he knows we are here, and he will come after us. So set aside your hurt feelings and fragility and pull yourself together."

My blood boiled over. "Hurt feelings? Fragility? Listen here asshole, those emotions you criticize make humans better than fae by a long shot. We have feelings because we give a damn. That's what makes us who we are!"

He stamped over to me and got up in my face. "It will also make you dead."

Ferna sidled between us, pushing us apart with a shove. "Enough! Nobody wants to die. I think we can all agree on that. So stop this!"

I turned away from Leto, trying to keep my cool, and realized Ferna was right. Nobody wanted to die. "Fine. Where are we going?"

"To High Meadow. My home," Leto answered in a huff. "If we walk all night, we will be there by dawn."

He took off with his bags on his shoulders, tramping through the long blades of grass. Ferna and Parlan followed, and Manny and I brought up the rear.

Manny moved in close, then whispered, "I'm with you, one hundred percent, and I want to help Celyse and the whole human race and all that, but we're in way over our heads."

Remorse filled me for having involved Manny in my mess. I vowed that no matter what, even if it meant my own life, I'd get him home. "I know, and I'm really sorry. I never meant to drag you into this."

"I know you didn't." He waited a few seconds before continuing. "But if we can find a way home, we need to take it."

I slowed down a bit, not thinking we'd find a way home, but wanting to calm Manny. "Yeah, absolutely."

For the next several hours, we walked and walked and walked. Every now and again, we'd come across a stream and stop for a drink. But mostly, we trudged along. When day broke and the skies started to lighten, the vast beauty of High Meadow came into view.

If there was a color greener than green, it would be the hue of the lush landscape before me. Waves of grassy fields rolled as far as the eye could see. Flowers clustered together in brilliant patches of red, purple, and pink. Oversized orange and yellow butterflies the size of birds flitted about, jumping from flower to flower, and in the distance a herd of sheep roamed freely. At least, I thought they were sheep.

"This is amazing," I said. "Everything is so beautiful and vibrant."

"It is," Ferna agreed solemnly, taking in a deep breath. "I have missed it so."

It never occurred to me to ask Ferna and Parlan, or even Leto, how long they'd been in the human realm and why they left the fae realm. I figured it was their business and I didn't need to pry. But scanning the landscape, with a soft cool breeze in my face and the clean floral smell in the air, I wondered why anyone would leave. Now I knew why it was called Faevenly.

"My home is over that hill," Leto pointed straight ahead.

"Thank you, Jesus," Manny blew out. "We're almost there."

Just like back on Lake Travis in Austin, Leto's native home sat nestled amidst bushes and trees. In fact, if you weren't looking for the quaint stone cottage, you'd miss it.

"Home sweet home," Leto announced.

When we walked in, we found the curtains closed and the furniture covered with sheets. Leto got busy tidying up, pulling back the curtains and opening the windows.

"Can I help with anything?" I asked.

"No. But you can have a seat and rest. You too, Manny. You both must be exhausted."

Manny was happy to comply, collapsing on an oversized chair. His eyelids were heavy, and dark circles encased his puffy eyes. "Can I nap right here?" he asked, resting his head on a throw pillow. "Because I don't think I can move another muscle."

"Of course," Leto answered. He eyed the other chair then looked at me. "Go on. Get some shuteye while you can. I need you well rested."

"You and the others don't need to rest?" I asked.

"No, we do not."

"Is that a fae thing?" Manny asked.

"Yes, it is. Now rest, please."

My anger and fear and anxiety about what had happened to my house had supercharged me and helped me get through an entire night of walking. But now, I was dead. As much as I didn't want to sleep, my body demanded it.

I slumped down into the chair. "Don't let us sleep too long."

Leto tossed each of us blankets. "I will not."

A VOICE WHISPERED AND A HAND SHOOK MY SHOULDER, pulling me out of a deep sleep. "Julio, time to get up."

I pried open my eyes and saw Ferna. Manny was still snuggled in his chair. "How long were we asleep?" I asked, feeling as if I had just closed my eyes.

"Nearly two hours."

I rubbed my face. "Two hours?"

"Yes, two hours. We have some stew prepared. Wake Manny and meet us in the kitchen."

The windows in the room were open, the sheer curtains fluttering in the cool breeze. The savory aroma of vegetable soup wafted over to me, reminding me of my mom's *caldo*. A pang of sorrow struck me deep. I hoped she wasn't too worried about me. But who was I kidding? Our house had been destroyed and I was missing. I was sure she'd already talked to the cops and consulted with every ghost she knew. I thought of the couple who had flitted into my house right before that witch unleashed his explosion. I wondered what they saw and what they told my mom.

"I must be dreaming that I'm at your house," Manny mumbled with his eyes still closed. "Because I swear, I can smell Mama A's *caldo*."

I rubbed my eyes. "Nope, we're still at Leto's. But there's stew."

"Stew? So I'm not dreaming?"

"Not dreaming."

He shifted, but kept his eyes closed, "I could eat."

For as long as I'd known Manny, nothing got in the way of his appetite. I sat up all the way and stared at him. "Is there ever a time that you can't eat?"

"Come on, now."

We sat together in silence a few long seconds before peeling our tired bodies off our chairs and heading toward the aroma. If the stew smelled delicious from the living room, it was even more heavenly in the kitchen. My mouth watered and my stomach growled as I spotted a wood-burning oven that reminded me of something you'd see in a pizza restaurant. Inside was an oversized reddish pot.

"Have a seat." Leto motioned to two empty stools at a long wooden table across from where Ferna and Parlan were sitting. He retrieved a stone stick and brought out the pot. He placed it on a trivet on the table and served up two bowls. He handed them to us.

"Thanks, Leto," I said.

"Yeah, thanks," Manny echoed.

I wondered where they got all the food. I didn't see a pantry or anything.

"If you haven't been here in a while, how were you able to whip up this meal?" I asked Leto, eyeing the chunky carrots, celery, and potatoes.

"Everything we need to eat is right outside. All we need to do is go out and get it."

"Really?" Manny asked.

"Yes, really," Leto answered.

Farm to table had never been so fresh. Or tasty. With a couple of bites in me, I wanted to get right to business, because the sooner we saved Celyse and did the shimmer thing, the sooner Manny and I could get home.

"Now that we're here, we get Celyse, right?" I asked. "And then do the thing where we get rid of the shimmers?"

Ferna and Parlan flashed each other curious looks, then looked to Leto.

"Yes," Leto said. "We will go get her."

I took another bite of stew, chewing the vegetables slowly, savoring the flavors while wondering what was up with the looks from Ferna and Parlan to Leto.

I swallowed my bite and pushed my bowl away. "What gives?"

Leto finished a bite of his own. He swallowed. "There has been a new development."

I let out an incredulous laugh. "Of course there has. I mean, why not?"

Leto folded his hands together on the table, his

violet eyes indicating that whatever he had to say was going to suck. "When we get Celyse, we will be getting her from her wedding."

My spoon fell out of my hand and thudded on the wooden table. "What?"

Manny gulped. "Wedding?"

Leto sat back from the table. "Yes, wedding. We have received word that Celyse has been arranged to a Sublander. The wedding is today."

My heart sank while my stomach plunged. "She's getting married? Today?"

"Word from our source in Strong Haven is she does not want to wed," Ferna explained. "And that this Sublander has devious intentions. If we leave right now, we can make it to Strong Haven before the ceremony."

"We have gathered five Enbarr steeds to take us there," Parlan added.

I sat up with a start. "Let's go. Now."

Leto rose to his feet. "We will. But first, you and Manny need to change clothes and weapon up."

Manny eyes grew wide, and the hint of a smile tugged at his lip. "We get weapons?"

I tossed him a look. "We just found out Celyse is getting married, and you're excited about weapons?"

"I wouldn't say I'm excited. I'm only, you know," he shrugged, "trying to look at the bright side of things."

After we gulped down the stew and cleaned up our dishes, Leto led Manny and me to a back room. On one side was a bed and a wardrobe. On the other side was a table with a wash bowl and a pitcher.

Leto motioned to the wardrobe. "You will find trousers and tunics in there. I trust you will find something suitable." He pointed at a door I hadn't noticed. "In there is a washroom. Meet me in the front room when you are finished."

When Leto left, Manny closed in and started whispering. "You know, I was initially pumped about the whole weapon-up thing, but now I'm freaked." He started chewing his thumb. "Are you getting a vibe?" He moved in even closer. "Anything witchy? Any tingling?"

I rubbed the back of my neck. "I've actually been waiting for a tingling warning myself, but so far, nothing."

He relaxed some. "Okay, whew. That's a good sign. Right?"

"Well, it's not a bad sign."

We took turns in the washroom, then ended up back at the oversized, wooden, wardrobe. A quick inspection of our options revealed dark green pants, thick belts, and long-sleeved black shirts. Luckily, there was a set of clothes that fit me perfectly, and a set that fit Manny too.

Dressed and ready, we joined the others. They too had changed from jeans and T-shirts to the same fae attire as us. They had their hair pulled back in braids with their pointed ears showing through. Quivers and bows were slung at their backs, they wore thick belts with knives attached, and spears hung from their sides.

Manny glanced at me. "We really are storming the castle."

"The palace," Ferna corrected. "We are storming the palace."

"But not exactly storming," Parlan added. "We are going in stealth mode dressed as guards. The storming will happen once we are in place."

"Exactly," Leto said. "Now listen up." He unzipped one of his duffel bags. Glowy orbs filled the insides. "I've got shimmers to help us get back to the human realm when we are finished. So, this bag is important." He zipped it back up, then unzipped the other bag to reveal arrows and knives. "As you can see, our quivers are filled, so these are our reserves." He took out one of the black bladed knives. "Fae cannot wield iron. The metal is deadly to us. So we use these black onyx daggers. But if you reach through to the bottom of the bag, you will find a smaller bag and inside that, iron knives. I want you two to wield those."

He handed me the bag. Sifting through, I found the smaller bag, and inside were the iron knives. The handles were thick and rigid, the blades long and pointy. An intricate vine pattern was etched along the sides. I took one and handed the other to Manny.

"Do you know how to wield those?" Parlan asked.

"Uh, no," I said.

"It is not hard," he explained. "Get close and ram it

in. If you can, go for a major artery, like the jugular. While fae are immortal, we can still be killed."

Manny and I slipped our knives into the sheaths at our belts. Leto took the duffle bags and led the way outside to five magnificent white horses with full flowing manes.

"These are Enbarr," Leto explained. "They traverse both land and sea and are faster than the wind. They will get us to Strong Haven swiftly. Do you ride?"

"We've ridden horses a few times," I answered for Manny and myself. "At camp when we were little."

"Good," Leto said. "This will be no different."

He secured the bags to the saddle of the largest beast, then mounted with ease. Ferna, and Parlan mounted their horses next. I struggled some, and Manny a little more, but we were able to manage.

Leto's horse danced around in a circle. "I will take the lead," he instructed. "Julio and Manny will take the middle. Ferna and Parlan will bring up the rear. If anyone needs to stop, give a whistle."

The Enbarr raised their heads and nickered with excitement, prancing and shaking their heads. And when Leto took off, the rest followed. Holding on for dear life as the landscape whizzed by me, I touched my shirt where my cross hung and prayed we would get to Celyse in time.

We had to.

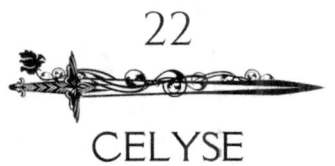

22

CELYSE

Staring out my window from my bed, bundled in my covers, I watched as streaks of pink filtered across the sky. The sight made me think of the morning of my birthday. It was not that long ago, and yet it seemed like another lifetime. Malena had awoken me, and Maid Rell and the maid servants had swept in, getting us ready for our first day of courtship season, a day I had dreaded and Malena had looked forward to.

Now, I would be getting ready for a fake wedding.

I let out a heavy sigh, telling myself everything would work out as my mind started strategizing. I could not count on Julio or the others to make it in time to help me. And even though I knew nothing of Rook, other than what he had told me, I had no other choice but to trust him. I would let him have his killing.

The High Queen deserved it.

Patting the onyx knife I wore under my night-dress, I thought of the wedding formalities that preceded the binding. Although I had already been promised to Rook, there was the matter of the traditional asking where Rook would request my hand. This would be done privately, with my father, the High Queen, and myself. After the asking, my father and the High Queen would announce to the guests that the asking had been accepted. Then Rook and I would enter the Great Hall together for the binding ritual.

Rook had said he would have allies amongst the guests. I did not know who they were or when they would make their move. And although I had told Rook I would not help, I had to be prepared to jump in if needed. I had spent plenty of time practicing weaponry, so I knew I could handle myself. But how could I access my knife if it was snuggled against my thigh underneath my wedding dress?

My gaze drifted across the room until I spotted my white, satin, tissue pouch. It was small and unobtrusive. Queens and ladies carried them often, and I thought it would do perfectly.

I unhooked my knife from my thigh, then went over to my desk where my tissue pouch was. Taking it, I removed a few sheets of tissue, slipped in the knife, and replaced the top tissues so that the knife nestled in the middle. I would carry that with me during the ceremony and none would be the wiser.

A hard knock sounded on my door, followed by two claps from Maid Rell as she swept into my bedchamber. Three maid servants trailed behind her.

"It is your wedding day!" she announced. "Time to prepare!"

My stomach plunged and twisted into a knot. There was no going back now.

Maid Rell clapped again. "The washroom will not be coming to you, you know," she said, shepherding me away to do my morning refreshing.

Once outside my bedchamber, I halted in the corridor, glad to escape the hustle and bustle that had suddenly descended on my room. Then I noticed there was no sign of Jaid. Maybe he did sleep and use the washroom after all. As my childhood friend, I hoped no harm would come to him today.

After my morning routine, I made my way back to the dressing chamber and found it overflowing with activity. Two maidservants prepared the face powders and paints, two others were readying the supplies for nails, and Maid Rell stood with an assortment of brushes and combs.

The ordeal of preparing was sure to last all day, and I wondered when Malena would show up. An affair of this size featuring this much primping was her dream. Even though it was not her wedding day, she would be standing by my side. I knew full well she would want to look her best. Especially with Alexander Kane in attendance. He had not yet asked for her hand, but I could only assume it would happen soon.

I sat in front of Maid Rell, preparing for her to tackle my long tresses, when a knock took my attention. Two more maid servants entered the room carrying a magnificent golden-hued dress of silk and crystals that shimmered when the light hit it, showcasing its opulent iridescence like a monochromatic kaleidoscope.

A collective "ooh" sounded in the room. Malena followed the dress bearers, wearing all smiles. "Is it not breathtaking?"

"It most certainly is," I uttered, marveling at the gown. Sad for it to go to such waste.

Another maid servant entered the room, carrying a simpler yet still elegant gown in the same hued fabric. Malena clapped her hands with delight. "There's mine!"

A profound sadness struck me, because I knew Malena would hate me after what was going to happen to her mother, and then hate me even more when she found out I was half human. She loathed humans. But then again, maybe she would surprise me. I was half fae and we did share a father after all. Maybe that would be enough for her to still love me.

With Malena busying herself on the other side of the room, the maid servants got back to working on me. Over the next several hours, there was hair brushing and braiding, followed by nail filing, buffing, and coloring.

The last order of business was the face. An artist specializing in ceremonial occasions had arrived in the morning. Her name was Flourish. She was a pixie with short-cropped purple hair, green skin, and the most magnificent shiny purple wings. Leaves of red and gold strategically covered her body but left more of her exposed.

She flew into the room with a sweet smile on her face, showcasing rows of tiny white teeth. "I am most honored to be serving you today, Princess," she said in a soft and melodious high-pitched voice.

"The honor is mine," I said with a bow of my head.

Her eyes twinkled and her lashes fluttered. "You are too kind. Now," she said, flitting in front of my face, "let me create something spectacular for you."

She applied hues of gold and copper on my eyelids, taking care to accentuate the natural shape of my eyes with upward shadowing. Then she lined my eyes with soft brush strokes, finishing with a lengthening balm on the lashes. After examining her work carefully, she moved on to applying a pink paste to my cheeks. With the color in place, she dotted a light shimmery liquid above my cheekbones, down the bridge of my nose, on the inner corners of my eyes, and above the peaks of my lips. She blended everything carefully with the pads of her tiny fingers. Lastly, she painted a dark red stain on my lips.

She hovered before me and held her tiny hands together at her chest. "You are most radiant, Princess Celyse. Take a look."

When I turned to face the mirror Maid Rell was holding, my mouth nearly fell open. I had never been so perfectly painted. "Flourish, thank you so much. I am...stunned."

She giggled. "Good. Then my work here is done." With a bow and twirl, she flew out the window, leaving a trail of sparkling dust in her wake.

Malena pattered over to me, and smiled wide. "So perfect."

"Now the dresses," Maid Rell said, pulling us back on task.

Malena returned to her area and slipped hers on with ease, but mine was so ornate it required more work.

"We will lay it on the floor, and you will step into the opening," Maid Rell instructed.

I moved into position and Maid Rell lifted the dress. She held the bodice together as the maidservants fastened the crystal buttons in the back. When they finished, I studied myself in the mirror. The dress rivaled any I had ever seen. Long and flowy, the fabric sparkled with every movement. I had never thought I had much cleavage, but with the plunging neckline and the snug bodice, I realized I had plenty.

"Is it too much?" I asked, blushing at how much I was revealing, placing my hand over my provocatively displayed bosom.

"Absolutely not," Malena scoffed, pulling my hand down. "Your body is beautiful, and you should show it off."

Maid Rell held out a tray of oils. "All that is left is for you to pick your fragrance."

Scanning the selections, I took a whiff of each, settling on an aroma filled with rose, lavender, lily, jasmine, and sandalwood. I dabbed the oil behind my ears and on my wrists.

"I knew you would pick that one," Malena smiled.

She plucked one from the tray. "I will use this one. It is so—"

"—romantic," we said at the same time with a laugh.

As I stared at Malena delighting in the application of her oils, the reality that this would be my last moment of joy with her set in.

I took her hands and held them. "I love you, my sister. No matter what. Please do not forget that."

"And I you." She hugged me, then said, "I will see you in the Great Hall."

As she left, the petite maid servants began tidying up the room while Maid Rell carried a solemn look on her face. "Are you ready, my dear?"

Ready for the monster who executed my mother and treated me with disdain my entire life to be killed? Ready to free myself from a life of trickery and deceit? Ready to be with Julio in the human realm?

It was always going to be him.

"Yes," I said resolutely, picking up my tissue pouch. "I am ready."

I walked across my bedchamber, letting the maid servants spread out the magnificent train behind me. Then, with my head held high and my shoulders back, I stepped out of my room.

I was disappointed to not see Jaid, but figured it was just as well. He did not need to escort me any longer. I continued down the corridor, made my way down the stairs, and headed for the receiving room where Rook would officially ask for my hand. With each step, my heart beat a little faster, my palms grew a little slicker. And when I faced the entrance to the room, it was not the change in decor from the usual blue and silver to gold and silver that stunned me, it was the surprise guest.

The High Queen and my father were dressed in their finest silver with threads of white silk and ornate lace, their heads adorned with their ceremonial crowns of crystals and pearls. Behind the High Queen stood Draven the witch.

My breathing hitched. A shudder raced through my body.

Clad in all black with his hood on and his face shrouded in shadow, he stood with his legs wide and his arms behind his back. He cast an ominous vibration in the room. The High Queen must have suspected something was up, either with me or with Rook, because Draven rarely showed up at palace events.

I glided in, concealing my shock at seeing him. Father rose to his feet as I got closer, his eyes soft and sentimental. "My dear beautiful daughter, you are more radiant than all the stars in the heavens."

"Thank you, my father," I said with a smile.

I took my seat, clutching my tissue pouch on my lap, thinking there was no way Rook could move against the High Queen with Draven around. He would end Rook on the spot. Me too, for that matter. I wondered what Rook would do.

A trio of harps strummed in the corner while we

waited. I took slow, deep breaths, and it was not too long before Rook appeared. He wore black silk trousers and a long-sleeved tunic made of the same fabric as my dress with a long dark coat over. His thick hair was elegantly combed and worn loose down his back. He strode in with full confidence and approached the High Queen and my father as if Draven was not even in the room.

He nodded low to me, then nodded low to the High Queen before getting down on both knees before my father. "High King of Strong Haven," he said in his deep, booming voice. "I, Rook Cailean of the Sublands, humbly ask for the hand of your daughter, Celyse."

Father stared him down, then said in a voice to match, "You may have it."

Rook rose to his feet. He took his place beside my chair, hand on my shoulder, while Father and the High Queen rose from their seats. Hand in hand, they walked out of the room, heading toward the Great Hall where the binding would take place before the dignitaries and guests of Faevenly.

With them gone, an eerie silence filled the room, like an uncomfortable foreboding. It was thick, heavy, and threatening. Draven remained motionless behind the High Queen's chair. His darkness filled my peripheral vision, emanating like a black cloud.

Rook broke the smothering silence. "Are you ready to proceed, my Princess?"

I clutched my tissue pouch, squeezing it tight. "I am ready."

Rising to my feet, I straightened my back and raised my chin, assuming full princess mode. I had no idea what the High Queen was up to, but as far as anyone knew, I was still a daughter of Strong Haven.

Rook held out his hand for me, but before I took it, I swept around to face Draven. He held his stance with his hood draped low. I had never seen his face and wondered what he looked like.

"You are no guest of mine, Draven the witch," I declared with conviction. "You would do well to stay away from me."

Without giving him a chance to respond, I turned back around and took Rook's hand. Together, and with my head held high, we walked down the long corridor of the main wing of the palace. Soft twinkling lights floated overhead like majestic stars. The most magnificent floral arrangements of roses, orchids, and tulips lined the walkways. The melodic tunes of harps and flutes filled the air.

We rounded the corner and the Great Hall sprang into view. Greenery with ribbons and lace lined the entrance. Beyond that gathered a sizeable crowd of Faevenly dignitaries, and the far end of the room glowed with candlelight and floating orbs.

My heart raced while my thoughts ran wild. Could Rook make good on what he said he could do? Who were his allies? Where was Julio and the others?

But the overriding thought that surpassed all others was what in thunderation were the High Queen and Draven planning?

23

JULIO

At first, I thought it would be cool to ride a horse faster than the wind, but I soon found out it was not cool. Not at all. The air blasted my face as we dashed across Faevenly, forcing my eyes closed. Every once in a while, I attempted cracking them open so I could see where we were, but everything was a blur. So I kept them shut and held on as we bulleted our way from Leto's home in High Meadow to Celyse's palace in Strong Haven.

We traveled north, across flat and hilly terrain. We even crossed a few bodies of water, not that I could really see them. After a while, the air turned cool and crisp. A few hours and one stop later, the Enbarr slowed their pace. I blinked to adjust my blurry vision until my sight cleared.

We were trotting through an area of trees. Some of them were tall and skinny. Others were short and thick, like Christmas trees. Leto brought his Enbarr to a full stop, and the others followed suit.

"Are we here?" I asked.

Leto dismounted. "We are close. We go the rest of the way on foot. My source will be meeting us ahead."

I hopped off my ride, and so did everyone else. I started moving around, stretching out my stiff legs and back. "That kinda sucked."

"What do you mean, kinda? That all the way sucked. My ass is killing me," Manny moaned, nearly dropping to the ground.

"Humans," Ferna said to Parlan with a shake of her head.

With my circulation flowing better, I faced Leto. "Can we trust your source?"

He adjusted his quiver and bow, as well as his knives and spear. "We can. I have known him a long time. He is one of the palace guards and will help us blend in with the guard detail."

"What about the duffel bags?" I asked.

"We leave them," Leto said. "The Enbarr will bring them to us if we need them."

I considered the beasts, then said with a shrug, "if you say so."

Leto had finished putting his weapons in place, then pointed at me and Manny. "Hoods up. You two do not exactly blend in."

Manny and I pulled our hoods up and over our heads, then followed Leto in a single file using the same order as our ride. Leto in front, Manny and me in the middle, and Ferna and Parlan in the rear.

As we trudged along, a hazy blur came into view, then took the shape of a man. He rushed over to me. "You are a human?" he asked with shock and bewilderment. "What are you doing here? It isn't safe!"

I hadn't counted on seeing a ghost in Faevenly, and seeing the tall red-headed man dressed in brown pants and a brown shirt surprised me.

"I'm here to rescue a friend," I explained.

Leto stopped. He surveyed the space around me. "Is there a spirit here?"

I pointed to the man. "Yeah, right there. He's human and he's telling me it isn't safe here."

"He is not wrong," Leto agreed as he kept walking. "Many humans died on these grounds during the Great Shimmer War. His warning is valid. You may see more spirits, so be prepared."

The ghost man walked away, joining a few other ghosts, mostly men, wearing the same clothing. They watched me with curiosity and concern. I looked away and focused on where I was going, trying not to let the man's warning get to me.

Not more than twenty yards out, Leto raised his hand and crouched low. Everyone followed. Stretching my senses to see if I could hear anything, I detected a low-pitched whistle. Leto stood, and a figure came into a view. He was tall and slender with long silver hair, dressed exactly like us with the same weapons as Leto and the others. As he came closer, I noticed the same violet eyes as Leto.

"Traeliorn," the fae said with a smile.

"Jaid," Leto smiled back.

As they embraced, I recognized the fae right away. He took Celyse from Leto's cottage. Manny nudged me, recognizing him too.

"Hey!" I called out. "You took Celyse!"

Jaid separated from Leto. "I did. I was under orders and being watched through the shimmer. I had to comply."

"Julio, Manny, this is Jaid," Leto said. "He is my brother. He is a trusted guard to the High Queen but loyal to our cause."

Jaid nodded at us. "I am honored to meet you both."

"Uh, you too," I said, raising a brow at Leto, wondering why he hadn't told me his brother was a palace spy.

"You did not need to know until now," Leto explained without me even asking.

Jaid hugged Ferna and Parlan. After a short greeting, he explained the situation. "The palace is prepared for the wedding, and the guests are arriving. My teams are ready. The ones who stand with me know you will be with me. The ones loyal to the High Queen have no idea what is afoot. But before we go, there are two things you need to know."

"What?" Leto asked.

"Firstly, the one taking Celyse's hand is Rook Cailean, a Sublander. Word has reached us that his only aim is to kill the queen."

"A Sublander? Who wants to kill the High Queen? Interesting," Leto said, rubbing his chin.

"Hey, that's great," I added, thrilled that something was going our way. "He's on our side then, right?"

"He is, but his motives are unclear," Jaid answered.

"What is the second thing?" Leto asked.

Jaid crossed his arms. "Draven the witch is here."

"The witch that attacked us?" I asked.

"Yes, him," Leto answered. Looking unfazed he said to Jaid, "We barely escaped him when we crossed over from the human realm. But never fear, we have our own witch."

Jaid's brows stitched together. "We do?"

"Where?" Manny muttered, looking around.

"Right here." Leto jerked his chin in my direction. "Julio."

"This human?" Jaid asked, looking surprised. He faced me and gave me the once-over. "You are a witch?"

"Uh..." I rubbed the back of my neck. "I can do a few things, I guess."

"You can do plenty," Leto cut in. "But now that we know Rook is planning something, all we need to do is let the Sublander make a move, and then we jump in and grab Celyse. If Draven should interfere, Julio will take care of him."

I held up my hand. "Hold on a second. Can I remind you that I have no idea how to do whatever it is I can do with my aura?"

"You need to have a little more faith in yourself," Leto said. "Now come on; we are wasting valuable time."

Jaid and Leto led the way, and the rest of us followed. My hand drifted to my shirt, touching the fabric where my cross hung. I thought of how my mom had always said for me to trust myself. Now

Leto was saying the same thing. But did I? I didn't know.

We trooped through the thick grass, winding our way through the trees and brush, the grounds transforming from natural and wild to manicured and cultivated. Dense vines and overgrown foliage gave way to orderly clusters of purple roses, pink hydrangeas, white azaleas, and a slew of other flowers I had never seen before. I thought my mother would love it here.

"Wow, look," Manny uttered, patting my arm and pointing up.

An ivory and gold structure peeked through the trees. With each step forward, the trees thinned out, revealing a massive palace. Three stories high with spires that dotted the roof and windows that lined the walls, the palace rivaled anything I'd ever seen before.

"How big is that thing?" I asked as my eyes scanned the enormity.

"Big enough to house several hundred rooms," Jaid answered. "It is the biggest palace in all of Faevenly."

"I knew she was a princess, but I didn't know she was a *princess*," Manny muttered, awestruck at the sight.

"I didn't either," I said.

Fae guards were stationed around the gardens, their numbers bigger as we got closer to the palace. Even the ghosts around me grew in number. I wished they would go away; they were starting to unnerve me.

We approached a side entrance, and Jaid started

issuing orders. "Once we are inside, I will lead you to the Great Hall. I will position you to the side of the dais closest to where Celyse will be standing. Keep your heads down and your hoods up. All of you so that you all look the same. Do not address anyone."

One by one, we followed Jaid through the door and down a corridor. The sounds of harps and flutes filled the air. The aroma of herbs and flowers wafted about. Greenery and twinkle lights floated along the corridor, and the marble floor beneath our boots sparkled with what looked like flecks of pure gold. A murmuring of voices grew louder with each step as we walked into a huge ballroom decked out with the most amazing lights, candles, and smells. We hugged the perimeter of the room, staying out of the way, and edged our way to the front to an area surrounded by greenery, candles, and floating lights.

"Line up here," Jaid said in a low voice. "I will be across from you."

A tingle gathered at the back of my neck, like a small tickle. Was something about to happen? I raised my eyes a little and scanned the room. The most striking fae men and women were chatting and laughing, dressed in opulent clothes that shone as if weaved from real gold and silver. Some of them even wore crowns. Luckily, none of them paid any attention to me or the others.

Without warning, the room silenced. The lights dimmed. The fae guests parted, leaving a walkway in the middle of the room. I gulped and glanced at Manny. He peeked back, looking terrified.

This was it. This was happening.

24

JULIO

The harp and the flute changed their tune from a light and airy melody to a richly ceremonial one. Everyone turned to face the entrance. A tall commanding man with long loose silver hair and a tall regal woman with silver hair pulled up in the front but loose in the back strolled into the room. The king and queen of Faevenly. Celyse's parents.

They were dressed in sparkling silver and white—the king in an elaborate suit with a long coat and the queen in a sparkly sheath dress that flared out into a long train. Tall crowns made of brilliant crystals and pearls with thin white intertwining branches adorned their heads. They made their way close to where we were standing and sat in two high back, silver-cushioned chairs opposite our position. They kept their focus on the rear of the room where they had come from.

Next, a girl who looked like Celyse, minus the black streak in her hair, glided down the aisle. She held herself straight and tall, as if *she* were the queen. This must be Celyse's sister, Malena. When she reached the dais, she stood in front of where we were lined up and turned to face the crowd.

The music stopped. The crowd turned back around to face the entrance. A chorus of bells rang out, loud and triumphant. When they finished, a harp and a flute, joined by a violin, played a soft regal tune. Seconds later, Celyse stepped into the room.

My heart stopped beating and my stomach flipped. She wore a glittery gold dress that hugged her upper body in the most amazing way with a full and elaborate skirt at the bottom. Her hair was pulled up, with loose strands framing her beautiful face. She looked like a goddess, and an explosion of feelings raced through me—love, longing, protectiveness. She glanced in my direction for a second, and I wondered if her heart felt mine, it was so loud.

My gaze zeroed in on the tall and muscular dark-haired fae next to her. Jaid had said his name was Rook. Even though I knew how Celyse felt about me, and Jaid had said Rook was there for the queen, sharp jealousy struck me anyway.

Hands together and raised to shoulder level, Celyse and Rook took slow steps to the front of the room. When they got in position, they turned to face the guests. From where I stood, I could see Celyse from the side. She looked so elegant and so strong, and everything inside of me itched to go to her. But I couldn't. Not yet.

The music lulled to a soft strumming of harps. I was waiting for Rook to make his move when a low murmuring cascaded through the room as the guests faced the entrance again.

Carefully raising my head, I saw Draven the witch. He had entered the room dressed in his usual all black, his hood pulled down low and shadowing his face.

Manny sucked in an audible gasp, then glanced at me.

We knew Draven would be there. Jaid had told us, but seeing the sinister witch coming our way chilled my blood. I knew what he was capable of.

"¿*Mijo*? Is that you?"

Huh? I looked around and spotted the opaque form of a man coming my way. His image grew sharp and clear as he glided over. He had tan skin, dark hair, and a slim build, and I'd know him anywhere. I'd seen his pictures.

"Dad?" I mouthed.

"Julio! It's you!" He rushed over to me, his arms whooshing around me like a cool breeze.

Ripples of shock traveled through my body as I faced the man that for eighteen years I thought had abandoned me and my mom. But he hadn't. He was here in Faevenly, as a ghost.

"My boy. My beautiful boy," he stared at me, his eyes glistening with emotions. But then he eyed the king and queen. "*Mijo*, listen to me. You must run. These people are evil. They took me and countless others, forced us into labor. Many of us were killed." His hands passed through my shoulders, as if he wanted to grip them and shake me. He brought his face close to mine. "Please, *Mijo*! You must get out of here!"

I shook my head slowly and widened my eyes, trying to tell him I couldn't go. That I had to stay. I motioned my eyes toward Celyse, hoping he'd catch on that I was here for her.

Manny elbowed me and shot me a raised eyebrow, knowing something was up. Before I could give him any indication of what was going on, the High Queen rose to her feet. She made a grand gesture with her arms.

"My honored guests, today's binding of Princess Celyse with Rook Cailean of the Sublands will be performed by Draven. The High King and I are honored to have his service."

Draven moved toward the dais. His cloak rippled behind him. He stopped in front of Celyse and Rook. He pulled back his hood, revealing smooth jet-black hair braided at the sides while the rest flowed down his back. His skin was porcelain white, and his eyes sparkled like diamonds.

Celyse's face stormed over. Rook's fingers twitched. I kept my hands loose at my sides, ready to unsheathe my knife.

"Now!" Rook hollered, charging for the queen.

"Get the witch!" Leto shouted.

Weapons clanged. Arrows whizzed. The room erupted in fighting. Rook and a group of weapon-bearing guests charged the queen and king. Malena moved to block Rook, but with a flash of her little purse, Celyse drew an onyx knife and brought it to her sister's throat.

"Not so fast," Celyse threatened.

"Sister!" Shock flashed across Malena's face, followed by anger. "Release me!"

Arrows flew by them from all corners. I rushed toward Celyse, my iron knife raised. Manny, Leto, and the others charged with me.

"Wall!" Jaid ordered, as he and his team zipped in front of Celyse, standing shoulder to shoulder.

Draven flung off his cloak and brandished a slender, black spear. He licked his lips as a wicked grin covered his face. In a blur, he spun as if performing a deadly dance, jabbing and slicing as he picked off Jaid's line one by one while at the same time deflecting each arrow that came his way.

I reached Celyse as a fae with a spear lunged at her. I swiped at the fae's legs, and he toppled over. Celyse whipped around and hurled her knife, lodging it straight into the fae's neck. Free from Celyse's weapon, Malena broke away and dashed off, but one of Jaid's guards caught her.

"Julio!" Celyse called out.

"Celyse!"

Another fae jabbed his spear our way. Celyse dodged it while Manny jumped and kicked it away. With the spear knocked loose, Ferna charged, whacking with her weapon, slicing the fae's head right off his body.

"Look out!" my dad cried.

I did a backbend as a spear swiped the air right where my head had been. Recovering in a flash, I kicked out my leg, sending my fae attacker tumbling. I raised my knife, ready to plunge it in him, when a voice cut through the din.

"**Hear me!**"

My attention snapped to Draven as my body froze. My knife fell out of my hand. My will was not my own anymore. There was only Draven and his command.

The witch threw his hands out, hurling a blast of red throughout the room. It was his aura. It sizzled in the air like an electric fog, then trickled down on everyone. Heat coursed through my insides, scorching my throat and burning my nose. But it wasn't just me who couldn't move.

Everyone was immobilized.

Draven snaked his way around the bodies on the floor and the bodies on their feet, his glare zeroed in on Celyse. He moved close to her with calculated steps. When he got within inches of her face, he reached out and placed a long, thin finger on her forehead, then dragged it down to her chin.

"You have been a very bad princess," he taunted. "And you must be punished."

"Julio," my dad rushed out, bringing his face close to mine. "I know his name. His full name. The witch. I know it."

What? I studied my dad, trying to understand the significance of knowing Draven's full name, when

Leto's lessons while I dodged his arrows flooded my mind.

If you give a fae your name, you give away your power. If a fae causes you to not know your name, you lose all sense of yourself. If a fae's name is hidden and you know what it is, you can use it against the fae.

His name! My dad knew his full name! But I couldn't move. That's when I knew what I needed to do. I needed to call on my aura before Draven killed Celyse and the rest of us.

Pushing all other thoughts aside, I went deep into my mind. I pictured my body with a blue glow emanating all around me. I could see the hue in the memory of me as a boy in the tub, at the car crash, and at Leto's house. I thought of what it meant to be an Avila and a Rodriguez.

"Hurry," my dad urged. "Use your gifts."

I directed my thoughts to my color, imagining it bursting out of me like a solar blast, bigger and brighter than the red from Draven.

"He has his hands around the princess's throat!" my dad cried.

A hum filled my ears and heat like a warm summer sun kissed my skin.

"You got it, *Mijo*. His name is—"

A blast of blue shot out of me as I broke from Draven's hold and hollered the name my dad put in my head.

"Draven Midlothian!"

Draven froze while everyone released. I stumbled

forward, then raced over to Celyse. Draven's hands had locked around her neck.

"Off," she squeaked, trying to pry them off her.

I gripped Draven's wrists and pulled, but couldn't budge him. Manny rushed in and grabbed Draven's fingers, pulling with a grunt and using his entire body weight as leverage. Finally, the witch's grip opened.

Celyse gulped for air, rubbing her neck. She gazed at me with wonder. "You did it."

"I did," I mumbled out loud.

"You did, *Mijo*," my father said with pride.

Rook had the queen hooked in a chokehold while Leto, Ferna, and Parlan aimed their arrows at the king and Malena. Jaid's guards surrounded a large group of guests.

"Guards!" the king hollered.

"Unhand me!" the queen bellowed.

"The guards do not answer to you anymore," Jaid said. He moved to the queen and tore a piece of fabric from her dress. He ripped it into pieces, shoving one in her mouth and the others in the king's and Malena's.

I stared at Draven's motionless form, hardly believing what I had done.

Celyse took my hand and threaded her fingers through mine. Leto, Jaid, Manny, Ferna, and Parlan came to my side. Together, we circled the witch, all of us stunned, halfway expecting him to move, but he didn't.

"What do we do now?" I asked, unsure of our next

move because none of us had really planned to get this far.

Celyse squeezed my hand before letting go. She held her head high and moved close to Draven's face.

"Now you get rid of him," she said to me.

I faced the deadly witch. I stared into his magical looking crystal-clear, menacing eyes. With the room silent and still, I looked down at my hands. I focused on my aura, the tingle still rippling through me. I let my instincts take over completely.

"Draven Midlothian." My voice came out sure and steady. "Be gone from this place forever."

A wind gathered around me, sweeping through the room. It was breezy at first, then grew in speed and strength. It swooshed and swirled around the witch like a tornado, spinning and twirling with flashes of blue sparks until eventually it slowed down and evaporated like a fog, revealing emptiness where the witch had stood.

"I told you we had our witch," Leto said to Jaid.

"You did indeed," Jaid replied.

Manny punched my arm. "That's right."

Jaid surveyed the room, as if making sure Draven was really gone. He brought his attention to Celyse and his eyes expanded. "The princess is bleeding."

Celyse looked down. A small stain dotted her gold fabric dress, near her stomach. She touched the spot. "I did not even feel it."

I spun around to check her back and saw a splotch of red oozing in all directions. My heart caught in my throat as she sank to her knees. I held her to me, afraid to touch her back.

I frantically scanned the room. "Is there a doctor here? Or a healer? Anyone!"

Leto knelt beside me. "The Green Falls," he urged.

"That's right! The healing waters!" But then I thought of Manny. I turned to face him.

"Go! I'll be fine!"

Leto pressed his lips together and whistled. "I've called for an Enbarr. Quick, let us get her outside."

"I do not think I can walk," Celyse whispered, her face starting to lose color.

"I've got you," I said. "Don't worry."

Jaid pulled out his knife and cut the train from Celyse's dress while I scooped her up and cradled her in my arms. She buried her head into the crook of my neck, whimpering as I followed Jaid and Leto to the nearest door where an Enbarr waited. Looking up at the large horse, I had no idea how I'd get us both mounted, when the beast lowered itself to the ground.

"I'll hold the princess while you mount," Jaid instructed.

I placed Celyse in his arms, then climbed onto the horse. Once I was on, Jaid helped her slide in front of me. The Enbarr carefully rose to full height, as if it knew Celyse was injured.

Back at Leto's, when Celyse and I were talking about the falls, she said only those deemed worthy could find them. I hoped she and I fell into that category.

I patted the beast's neck. "Please, take us to the Green Falls. As fast as possible."

With a snort and a whinny, the Enbarr sped off, slicing through the air with precision and speed. I closed my eyes and held Celyse to me, praying we'd make it there in time.

I couldn't lose her. Not now.

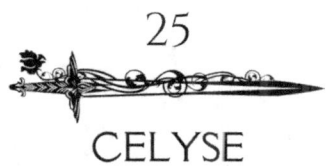

25

CELYSE

J ulio had come for me. He had banished Draven. But now I was dying. Holding on to him as we sped across the land on an Enbarr, I forced myself not to think of my father, the High Queen, my sister, or even Rook. I had to trust that with the number of fae standing against the High Queen, she would find herself ousted. Or possibly even dead. I only hoped my father and Malena would be okay.

"Hold on, Celyse," Julio whispered.

With the pain coursing through my body, I could not answer. I squeezed him instead, letting him know I had heard him and was doing everything I could to stay with him.

After racing and climbing and jumping and swimming, the Enbarr slowed until it came to a stop. It lowered to the ground. Julio slid off, then helped me into his arms.

"We made it, babe. The Green Falls. Not much farther," he said, walking with haste.

The sound of rushing water filled the air and a soft wind rustled the leaves, carrying with it the crisp clean scent of a fresh stream mixed with lemon and mint. I could not lift my head or even open my eyes to look around, but I knew we were close.

Julio grunted, pushing forward as fast as he could without jostling me. But I could not hold on to life anymore. Indescribable weakness swept over me and my head lolled back.

"No, no, no," he pleaded. He held me to him and picked up his pace. "Please don't leave me, Celyse. Please. We're almost there."

I summoned all my strength, everything I had left in me, and told myself to hold on, no matter what. For him, for me, for the future I longed to experience. I was not ready to journey to the Passing Place.

The rushing sound of water grew louder, and Julio's pace slowed. "There's a pool of water and a waterfall. I'm going to wade in with you in my arms."

He strode into the water with a splash, then ambled forward until the cool liquid rose to my neck. He stopped and held me even tighter. I knew I was submerged in the water. I could hear the lapping all around me, but I could not feel it against my body.

"Babe, please." His voice choked over. "Hold on."

I cracked my eyes open and saw Julio looking down on me with love and concern etched on his beautiful face while tears welled up in his eyes. The glow from the setting sun cast a radiance about him, illuminating him like a precious treasure.

He let out a sigh of relief and a small smile met his lips. "You're still with me." He stroked the hair away from my face, then trailed his fingers across my forehead and down my cheek.

Working my throat, I managed a swallow and mumbled, "Yes."

"Can you feel your legs?"

"No," I breathed.

He stroked the back of my head, continuing to hold me close. "It probably needs more time."

Before I could even reply, my feet started tingling. Slowly at first, the prickly sensation worked its way up my calves and then my thighs, until it gathered in my stomach in a pleasing swirl.

"Something is happening," I whispered.

"Try moving your toes," he said as he reached down and slipped off my shoes.

I closed me eyes and concentrated on my toes, willing them to move, when they twitched.

"You did it," he said with a hopeful tone. "You moved them."

Staying perfectly still, I let the tingle work through me for a while before opening my eyes fully, finally feeling the coolness of the green water around me.

"Hey," he soothed.

"Hey," I whispered back. He kissed the top of my head. "Can you move your legs?"

I flexed my calves, wiggling my toes and stretching out my feet. "Yes," I said, continuing my movement. "I think I might be able to stand too."

"Okay, let's give it a try. Grab on to me if you need to."

He eased his arm out from underneath me. I let my legs float for a few seconds before I straightened them out and touched my feet to the bottom of the pond. My weight was easy to carry, and most of the pain in my body had dissipated.

I smiled. "I am standing."

He smiled back. "Let me check your back."

I turned around. He placed his hands on me, pressing the spot where I had been stabbed. "I don't feel any wound or anything. Does it hurt?"

"It feels a little achy, but otherwise I am well," I said, facing him again.

He exhaled and hugged me tight. "I thought I had lost you. Really and truly lost you."

I hugged him back, nestling into him and holding on fiercely. "I thought so too."

We stayed lock in our embrace, neither one of us wanting to let go. He slowly pulled back and stared into my eyes. "I want to kiss you so bad it hurts, but I know we can't. Leto told me about the fae human deadly kiss thing."

The fact that I was half human sprang to mind, along with the hope that I could truly be with him. "Maybe we can. I have discovered that I am half human."

"What?" His face brightened with curiosity. "You're half human?"

"It is true," I rested my hands on his strong chest. "I found out yesterday."

He licked his lips. "Do you think that means I can kiss you and not die?"

A fluttering of excitement swirled inside of me, and every part of me yearned for him. "Yes, I think you can."

He stared into my eyes with passion and love, and I melted under his gaze. "Well," he said, stroking my hair from my face. "If there's any place to try a deadly kiss, I think in the middle of healing waters would be it."

"I think you are right," I breathed.

He closed the gap between us. He brushed his lips against mine tenderly, then drew back. We waited a few seconds and when nothing happened, our lips met again. This time he didn't hold back. And neither did I.

Our mouths parted, and our tongues connected completely and intimately. We kissed slow and deep, embracing each other with fierce longing. Everything about him sent my head into the clouds—his softness, his taste, his smell. I wanted all of him, and wanted him to have all of me, and we kissed again and again and again.

With so much passion and heat building inside of me, I did not want to stop, but knew we had to. We separated slowly and stared at each other as we caught our breath.

Julio pressed his forehead against mine. "Wow."

"All the wow," I said, kissing him again, finally knowing what it meant to have one's head in the clouds. If we were not holding each other, I would have floated away. But then the harsh reality of what we had left at Strong Haven grounded me. There would be much to do after the overtaking of the High Queen. I was still a daughter of Strong Haven, after all.

"We must return to the palace," I said.

Hands intertwined, we sloshed out of the water and made our way back to the Enbarr. The steed lowered when it saw us. Julio placed my slippers back on my feet then helped me climb on. He mounted next and snuggled in behind me.

I patted the magnificent creature on the neck. "Back to Strong Haven Palace."

The Enbarr whinnied and took off. I held on to the Enbarr's mane and Julio held on to me as we raced across Faevenly.

When we arrived back at the palace, we were met by Maid Rell. She rushed over to us with a dire expression on her face. "My lady, my lord," she urged in a frantic whisper. "Come with me into the woods. Hurry."

The woods? Exchanging a worried glance with Julio, we dismounted the Enbarr. After a quick thank you to the steed, we clasped hands and followed Maid Rell through the trees. Although the sky had started to darken, there was still enough remnants of light to allow us to see Maid Rell as she chugged her away around the bark and brush.

"Slow down, Maid Rell," I said, scared to see her carrying on in such a manner, and wondering what had happened.

She stopped and struggled to catch her breath, her gaze darting around. Julio's brows were stitched as he glanced about too.

"What is the matter?" I asked her as fear grew inside me. "Why are we running?"

"Oh, my lady," she said with shaky hands. "The High Queen had her name taken by Rook. She lies in a state of undeath. But the High Queen has loyalists still, and they struck back, killing Rook."

I gasped, her words rocking me to my core. "And my father?"

"The truth of your lineage was exposed. He has been stripped of his crown and banished to the Sublands, along with those who stood against Strong Haven—the human boy, the trio of fae that came from the human realm, even Jaid and his troops."

With my mind reeling, I imagined the melee that must have happened in the Great Hall after I was stabbed and carried away. I felt sick.

"Who banished them?" I asked.

Maid Rell's lip quivered and tears spilled from her eyes. "Malena did. She has assumed the crown with the aid of Alexander Kane and his family. She is awaiting your return so she may exact punishment on you." She gulped. "You and this human. She is holding you both responsible for everything. I slipped away and came out here so I could warn you." A choking sob took her over, and she struggled to regain herself. "I fear she may order you both executed."

My body shook, my heart broke, and my throat

clogged with tears. I stared at the spires that dotted the roof of my home, a place that now did not belong to me. I had no idea what to do, but Maid Rell had a plan.

She pulled a small shimmer out of her pocket. "You have to run away, my dear. And stay away." She eyed me, and then Julio. "The both of you."

"I-I-I..." Words failed me as my mind struggled with a response. I wanted nothing more than to run away forever with Julio, but it was not only us anymore. There was father, Jaid, Manny, Leto, and Ferna and Parlan. They had all helped me. I could not desert them.

"I'm not leaving Manny," Julio insisted.

"Agreed," I replied, squeezing his hand.

A howl pierced the air, and I detected the sound of enormous paws thudding against the dirt and grass. "The wolfbeasts," I muttered.

If Malena was sending them for me, did that mean they were now loyal to her only? Would they still be bound to me? I did not know, and I did not want to find out. The thought of being ripped to shreds in a flurry of fangs and claws terrified me.

I studied Julio's face, my mind processing everything quickly. "We have to go. It is the only way. We can come back later."

Julio's eyes widened, and I could tell he was grappling with my suggestion. He looked down, defeated, but understood the wisdom of my words. "Okay," he gave in. "We leave so we can get away from the wolfbeasts and Malena, then we regroup and come back for Manny and the others. Leto told me there are other fae living in Austin. We'll need to find them."

I nodded, then took the shimmer from Maid Rell's grasp and began manipulating it as the sound of the wolfbeasts neared.

"Hurry, my dear," Maid Rell pleaded. "Hurry."

With the shimmer stretched out, I said to Julio, "You go first. I will follow so I can collapse it behind me quickly."

He flashed me a hesitant look, pressed his lips against mine, then stepped through. I turned to say a fast goodbye to Maid Rell when an arrow whizzed past me and pierced her head with a thump. Her mouth parted and she let out a gasp as she crumpled to the floor. A hand grabbed me from behind and shoved me to the ground, my face slamming against the dirt.

Stunned, I reached for my cheek, then rolled over and saw Malena standing over me with a group of guards by her side. She lurched for the shimmer Julio had slipped through, collapsed it, and smashed it to bits. She glared at me with dark anger.

"How could you do this, Celyse? How!" She screamed so loud her voice echoed all around. The wolfbeasts circled around her protectively. "Because of you, mother is undead! Our fae bloodline is tarnished!" She pointed at Maid Rell's dead body not far from mine. "And look! You made me order the kill of my favorite maid servant!"

A tear slid onto my check and I wiped it away. I had no love lost for the High Queen, but I did for Maid

Rell. She had treated me like a daughter, and I loved her like one. Peering at her lifeless form, endless sorrow gathered inside of me.

"She was much more than a maid servant, Malena. But you would not know."

Her lip curled. "I would not know?" she huffed. "Well, let me tell you what I *do* know. You are half human. Inferior in every way. What father did to me, and mother, and this house, is unforgivable!"

I rose to my feet. "Father only fell in love with a human because your mother is a monster!"

Malena raised her hand and struck me. "Mother and I are not the monsters," she seethed. "You humans are."

If not for her guards and the wolfbeasts, I would have struck her back. Instead, I moved in and said, "I may be half human, Malena, but I am still your sister. I share blood with you."

She composed herself and straightened her posture. "Oh, I know who you are. That is why I am sparing your life." She snapped her fingers, and two guards grabbed my arms. "You are henceforth banished to the Sublands. The name Strong will be stripped from you forever. You will live the remainder of your days in the barren wasteland under lock and key for what you have done to me and my house."

I blinked. The idea of being banished meant never seeing Julio again. Those who had helped me were probably doomed too.

"Malena," I whispered, my heart crushing into a

million pieces. "Please, let me and the others go to the human realm. We will never come back here. I promise."

She kept her cold gaze on me. "You want me to let you and your allies leave Faevenly for a life of happiness in the human realm after what you have done?" She laughed. "I do not think so. You deserve no happiness."

"Malena," I choked out.

She narrowed her eyes at me. "You have done this. Not me." She raised her brow and commanded the guards, "Take her."

The guards pushed me forward, leading me to a carriage. Without a single possession, and all alone, I climbed in. With the wheels creaking forward and the tears spilling from my eyes, I gazed out the window, at the dark night that had fallen, and watched Strong Haven Palace roll by. I had always wanted to escape the duties and obligations of my station, but I did not want it to happen like this. Lives were lost, including Rook, Maid Rell, and others during the skirmish in the Great Hall. Those who had stood by me had been banished.

And Julio was gone.

I glanced down at my torn and damp wedding dress. The iridescence sparkled on its own, casting a soft light around me. I wished I could go back in time and do everything differently, but it was too late for that. What was done could not be undone. I wrapped my arms around myself, glancing out at the magnificent trees I had roamed through countless times.

Would they miss me?

With a heavy sigh, I wiped my tears with my hands and rested my head against the carriage when a breeze wafted through the window, carrying with it a small white feather. It drifted back and forth before landing beside me on the velvet seat. I gasped, recognizing the quill. It was the white feather that had led me to Julio's shimmer, or one just like it. I scooped it up and held it to my chest, fresh hope soaring inside of me.

If I had found Julio once, I could do it again. I would save my allies and eliminate anyone that might stand in my way.

I would find him again. No matter what.

My story was far from over.

CONCLUSION OF BOOK ONE

She broke the rules to find him.
What comes next could destroy everything.

Continue the story in *Fae Fractured*.
Start Book 2 now.

THE FAE BLOODLINES SERIES

Fae Away, book 1

Fae Fractured, book 2

Fae Hunted, book 3

Fae Rising, book 4

For a full listing of Rose's books, visit her website at
www.RoseGarciaBooks.com/GARCIAVERSE

Subscribe to Rose's newsletter at
www.RoseGarciaBooks.com/newsletter

Fae Bloodlines Series

A ROYAL ROMANTIC FANTASY SERIES
FEATURING HISPANIC CHARACTERS,
POWERFUL FAMILIES, DYNAMIC
FRIENDSHIPS, AND FORBIDDEN
ROMANCE

WWW.ROSEGARCIABOOKS.COM

ACKNOWLEDGMENTS

There's nothing more exciting, and more terrifying, than starting a new project. Doubly so in the middle of a pandemic! For years I was immersed in the Final Life Series, and I loved every minute of it! And then, during the peak of Covid, I decided to plunge into something new—fae fantasy. It was not an easy transition for me. The world was in a state of flux, my family life, like the lives of so many others, was turned upside down. I felt as if my creativity was tapped. And yet, I forged through and I have so many people to thank!

First and foremost, I have to give thanks to God for keeping me and my family healthy. I don't mention religion much because I consider it to be a very personal thing, but faith is a big part of my life.

I have to thank my family for helping me hash out all the great and not so great ideas I had for Fae Away. My family is my rock, and they are the best sounding board, even when they don't want to be a sounding board, lol.

To my writer besties, the Queens of the Quill. Y'all have kept me sane! And productive! And moving forward! Even when I didn't want to! I honestly cannot imagine muddling through this past year without y'all in my corner.

To my reader group, The Rose Bud Society! Rose Buds, y'all are the wind beneath my wings! Thank you so much for hanging with me on the FB page and posting silly memes and GIF's, answering polls, playing games, and, most importantly, reading and loving my books! A huge shoutout to my ARC reviewers: Jessica, Jen, Kelly, Gloria, Diana, Dee, Gracie, Heather, Nikita, Crystal, Steph, Darien, Jeannette, Barbara, Jaci, Sarah, Li, and Nicole. (I hope I didn't forget anyone, and I'm sorry if I did!)

A special shoutout to the Rose Buds that helped me come up with the name for Traeliorn Letormis: Darien, Sarah, Gloria, Jaci, Jessica, Li, and Barbara. I had so much fun tossing names around with y'all!

I can go on and on with thanking people, but I'm sure you don't have all day or night to read these acknowledgments. So let me just say, for those who've cheered me on and supported me, you know who you are, and I know who you are!

ABOUT THE AUTHOR

 **Rose Garcia** is a *USA Today* bestselling author and screenwriter. She is known for crafting heart-stopping fantasy stories where belief is power, love defies all, and hope burns brightest.

Magic is real in her world —and the only thing more dangerous than a broken heart... is a hopeful one.

A lawyer turned writer, Rose weaves stories of complicated romance, powerful families, deep-rooted friendships, and ancestral magic drawn from her Mexican American heritage. Her flawed yet optimistic heroes are driven by bold hearts, forced to confront tangled destinies and make impossible choices.

When she's not writing, you can find her designing escape rooms for her husband, obsessing over fantasy books and shows, traveling, or hanging out with her overly needy and precious rescue dogs.

Rose lives in Houston, Texas, and believes tacos are a core food group—because well, they are!

For more on Rose, visit www.rosegarciabooks.com.

A final request: please review her books and spread the word about her stories. She would be most appreciative!

Join Rose's Facebook Fan Group!
www.facebook.com/groups/TheRoseBudSociety

Subscribe to Rose's Newsletter!
www.rosegarciabooks.com/newsletter